Ace Books by Christina Henry

BLACK WINGS
BLACK NIGHT

BLACK NIGHT

CHRISTINA HENRY

ACE BOOKS, NEW YORK

THE BERKLEY PUBLISHING GROUP
Published by the Penguin Group
Penguin Group (USA) Inc.
375 Hudson Street, New York, New York 10014, USA
Penguin Group (Canada), 90 Eglinton Avenue East, Suite 700, Toronto, Ontario M4P 2Y3, Canada
(a division of Pearson Penguin Canada Inc.)
Penguin Books Ltd., 80 Strand, London WC2R 0RL, England
Penguin Group Ireland, 25 St. Stephen's Green, Dublin 2, Ireland (a division of Penguin Books Ltd.)
Penguin Group (Australia), 250 Camberwell Road, Camberwell, Victoria 3124, Australia
(a division of Pearson Australia Group Pty. Ltd.)
Penguin Books India Pvt. Ltd., 11 Community Centre, Panchsheel Park, New Delhi—110 017, India
Penguin Group (NZ), 67 Apollo Drive, Rosedale, Auckland 0632, New Zealand
(a division of Pearson New Zealand Ltd.)
Penguin Books (South Africa) (Pty.) Ltd., 24 Sturdee Avenue, Rosebank, Johannesburg 2196,
South Africa

Penguin Books Ltd., Registered Offices: 80 Strand, London WC2R 0RL, England

BLACK NIGHT

An Ace Book / published by arrangement with the author

PRINTING HISTORY
Ace mass-market edition / August 2011

Copyright © 2011 by Tina Raffaele.
Cover art by Kris Keller.
Interior text design by Tiffany Estreicher.

ISBN: 978-1-937007-06-5

ACE
Ace Books are published by The Berkley Publishing Group,
a division of Penguin Group (USA) Inc.,
375 Hudson Street, New York, New York 10014.
ACE and the "A" design are trademarks of Penguin Group (USA) Inc.

PRINTED IN THE UNITED STATES OF AMERICA

10 9 8 7 6 5 4 3 2 1

For Mom and Dad, with much love

ACKNOWLEDGMENTS

Much gratitude is due to Danielle Stockley, editor extraordinaire, who not only helped make *Black Night* a better book but patiently answered all my crazy questions. I could not do this without you, Danielle!

Lots of thanks to my publicist, Rosanne Romanello, for her dedication and hard work on behalf of the world of *Black Wings*.

Thanks to Kris Keller for his amazing cover art.

A very big thank-you to Nancy Holzner for her generous support and guidance. You rock, Nancy!

A special shout-out to Dimo, Cynthia and the rest of the crew at Einstein's on Southport, who kept me in bagels and coffee while I wrote this book.

Many thanks to Sarah Kaiser, my "study buddy," who

listened to all my crazy ideas and thought they sounded great even if they made no sense.

Finally, I could not do this without the love and support of my husband, Chris, and son, Henry. I am so grateful for both of you every day.

1

I STOOD IN THE ALLEY BETWEEN DAMEN AND WOLCOTT in the recently trendy neighborhood of Wicker Park. There was a parking lot filled with cars directly across the alley from my position. It was bordered on the other three sides by four-story apartment buildings. Behind the wall that I leaned on, the clubs, bars and restaurants of Division Street did a brisk trade in liquor and lust for the upscale singles who had purchased all the new condos in the area. The cold November night was no deterrent to business. After all, if you lived in Chicago, then you understood that there are only two seasons—winter and construction. If you let a little cold slow you down, then you should probably move somewhere else.

I shifted a little, flexing my toes inside my boots in a vain effort to keep them warm. When I had died and been reborn a month ago, my human heart had been replaced by an angel's heartstone. As a result, I was usually a little warmer than ordinary human beings, since angels' hearts are made of the sun. But a half angel's body is still no match for the Windy City.

My gargoyle, Beezle, poked his head out of the lapel of my wool peacoat. He's the color of stone, about the size of an overweight guinea pig, and he's got little wings, the better to flap around my head and annoy me with.

Before we had left the house he had trimmed a child-sized scarf for his own use. He had a small strip of rainbow-colored wool wrapped around each horn and a longer piece wound several times around his lower face. The edge of his beak poked through the material. He mumbled something through the cloth and I glared at him.

"I can't understand you when your mouth is buried like that," I said.

Beezle narrowed his cat eyes at me and commenced unwinding his muffler. He huffed melodramatically before speaking. "I said, have you got anything to eat?"

"How can you possibly be hungry? You ate a whole bowl of popcorn before we left the house."

"But I am. And I'm cold. And I want a doughnut," he whined.

"Stop wriggling. We're supposed to be undercover here. In point of fact, you're not supposed to be here at all. You're supposed to be at home, being a *home guardian*, like all the other gargoyles."

"Do you think I would trust your life to *him*?" Beezle snapped.

"*He* can hear you, gargoyle," Gabriel said dryly.

My tenant and bodyguard, Gabriel, had been so quiet I'd almost forgotten he was there. Almost. He's a little difficult to overlook—six foot plus, dark hair, dark eyes, the face of an angel. I mean that literally. Gabriel was half-angel.

Have I mentioned that I am in love with him and he with me, and that our love is doomed, in a really melodramatic we-will-both-be-killed-if-we-ever-act-on-our-feelings sort of way?

I'm a half angel, too. My father is Azazel, a fallen angel and a chief of the Grigori, a right-hand man of Lucifer himself. I'd discovered this tidbit only recently, having spent most of my life believing my father to be an ordinary deadbeat (or possibly dead) human dad.

Beezle had been a little unreasonable about my safety ever since I'd had my human heart torn out by a nephilim— long story—and now refused to let me leave the house without him. You'd think the fact that I'd managed to come back from the dead would count in my favor.

Azazel's orders stated that Gabriel was not supposed to leave my side when I was out of the house. I had spent the last month with a beautiful bodyguard at my elbow and an overweight gargoyle hanging off me like a baby orangutan. It was making my job a little difficult—very difficult, in fact. It's not easy being unobtrusive with those two around.

When I'm not Azazel's daughter and Beezle's doughnut enabler, I'm an Agent of death. It's not as glamorous as it sounds. Every week I get a list of names, places and times. I go to the appointed place at the appointed time, pick up the soul and bring it to the Door. At the Door the soul chooses whether to pass on to whatever is behind the Door (don't ask me; I'm not allowed to know) or to stay and haunt the earth forever.

Most of the time my job is as straightforward as it sounds. I'm kind of like a UPS delivery guy. I don't know what's in the boxes and I don't care. It's just my job to deliver them on time and to the correct location. I also have to file paperwork—lots and lots of paperwork, and the forms are annoying and redundant. Being an Agent of death isn't such a great gig, really, but it's an inherited job (I got mine when my mom died) and one that doesn't go away until you take the trip to the Door yourself.

So there I was, a week before Thanksgiving, shivering in thirty-degree weather and thinking longingly of my crocheted blankets and a cup of hot chocolate, waiting to pick up a soul who was scheduled to die at 1:27 A.M. somewhere in this alley.

Beezle carefully rewrapped his scarf around his chubby neck. It draped over his wings in the back.

"I hope that this isn't one of those disgusting alley murders," he said conversationally. "The last one put me off my feed."

"Is that even possible?" Gabriel murmured for my ears only, and I smiled. Then I straightened a little, pushing away from the wall. Gabriel came to attention beside me. "What is it?"

"I don't think you have to worry about hacked-up body parts this time, Beezle," I said.

"Why not?"

"Because I can see the vampire." I nodded at the innocuous-looking man making his way across the parking lot.

He looked like any moderately successful single guy out on a Saturday night. His hair was blond and stylishly cut, his clothes were good without being flashy, and his face was sort of ordinary-handsome. You wouldn't know he was a vampire, which is good for their kind. The most successful hunters are the ones with the best camouflage.

He crossed out of the lot and into the alley, his footsteps

slowing as he approached us. We were tucked unobtrusively in a little four-foot depression in the building, one of those architectural oddities that seem to have no explanation. The building went straight across and then it dipped in, like someone had planned to put a closet there, and then resumed its normal course. It was just enough to keep us from being seen by anyone who passed by.

The vampire stopped dead, a few feet away. I saw his nostrils flare.

"I know you're there, Agent," he said.

I stepped out of the depression and into the light of the one yellow streetlamp that hung over the parking lot. Gabriel followed and stood behind my shoulder. I said nothing. The vampire's eyes widened a little when he saw Gabriel.

He smirked. "You must be the famous Madeline Black, the only Agent with a guard dog."

If the vampire thought he could make a little sport for himself by getting a rise out of Gabriel, he had another think coming. Gabriel is the type that burns slow—so slow, I wonder sometimes if he's got a pulse.

"What is your business, vampire?" I asked.

"If you are here, then you know my business," he said. He raised an eyebrow at me. "You will not interfere?"

"You know I am bound against it," I said, and there was a little shivering of magic as I said it, as if the source of my power was affirming the truth of that statement.

That was one of the suck things about being an Agent. I saw a lot of death, and most of those deaths would break my heart if I let them. Stupid accidents, horrific murders, deaths of children and young mothers and college kids before their time. But it was not for me to judge which lives should be saved. If their name was on my list, then their death was fated and I was bound not to interfere. I'd learned early on to adopt a circle-of-life attitude for my own sanity. It didn't mean that I liked it.

The vampire sidled a little closer to me, and I could almost feel Gabriel's hackles rise. He loves me, he can't have me, but he does not like other men coming near me. If Gabriel had his way, there would be a thirty-six-inch man-free radius around me at all times.

"I have heard stories of your beauty," the vampire purred. His nostrils flared again. "I see that they are not exaggerated."

I crossed my arms. My beauty is *so* not legendary. "Do I look like I just fell off the turnip truck? Get lost. I'm not the helpless victim you're looking for."

I saw a glint of fang as he stepped closer. He seemed hypnotized by some scent. "But the blood of angels . . . I have always wanted . . . and you are Lucifer's own . . ."

I opened my palm in front of me, extended my will, and a little ball of blue flame about the size of a baseball hovered above my hand. "I understand that fire is unpleasant for vampires."

The vampire hissed and backed away several feet. He shook his head, seeming to come out of a trance. For a moment I thought he would try again, but then he appeared to think better of it.

"Perhaps you are right," he said, regaining his composure. "There must be easy prey awaiting me if you are here."

I closed my fist and the ball of nightfire disappeared, leaving behind a lingering trace of sulfur. I flicked my fingers at the vampire. "Move along, then."

He gave me a sarcastic bow and continued past us. Gabriel stared stonily at the vampire's back as he went by. A few feet past us, the vampire stopped. I couldn't see his face but I was sure he was scenting the air. I felt the thrum of magic that told me a soul was approaching that was marked for death. A moment later a too-skinny blonde came tottering into the alley on four-inch heels.

I sighed and slipped back into the shadows. I didn't need to see what happened next. I just had to be there to pick up the pieces, like always.

About an hour later I was flying home. Gabriel met me in the air about half a mile away from the Door. For reasons that we don't understand, Gabriel can't come within a certain radius of the Door. This tends to make him annoyed, since he is charged with keeping me safe at all times. However, other non-Agents seem to be bound by the same restriction. None of my enemies have been able to cross the invisible line that keeps Gabriel from the Door. I know because I have seen some of them try.

We were about ten minutes from home when I saw it. A flash of green light somewhere on the city streets below, a pulse so large I was surprised that it didn't wake up everyone in a four-block radius. Then the shock wave hit us.

Gabriel and I were thrown upward by a wave of energy that emanated from the pulse. I decided to relax instead of struggling against it, but as the magical energy inside the shock wave reached me, I cried out. There was malice in that magic, a sense of wrongness that chilled my heart.

The wave passed through me, but I was frozen by fear. I had felt something like this before, when Ramuell the nephilim had been released from his prison to hunt and kill. It was a sense that the natural order had been upended, that death stalked without plan or mercy.

But Ramuell was dead. I had killed him myself. How could this be happening again?

I thought all of this in an instant, but an instant of immobility in the air can kill you. I heard Gabriel's anguished voice calling my name. I shook my head, realized that I was free-falling, my face turned toward the sky. I tried to flap my wings, to turn over and right myself, but my wings had disappeared. They do that, so that I can look like a normal human most of the time. They only appear when I need them for a magical reason, like when I'm carrying out my Agent duties.

But the shock wave had temporarily knocked out my magic, like an electrical surge will cause a fuse to blow. I tried to stay calm, to concentrate on the power inside me, but I was gathering speed. I could see Gabriel's face, white and strained, as he arrowed toward me in the air, but I was falling too fast. He wasn't going to make it. I closed my eyes.

And then I was plucked from the air by a pair of strong arms, and I heard a grunt as my speed was arrested. I opened my eyes to see a pair of bright green ones flashing at me through wire-rimmed glasses.

"Next time you might want to try a parachute," J.B. said as he fluttered us slowly to the ground.

I opened my mouth to speak, to thank him, and was horrified to feel tears pricking my eyes.

"Hey," J.B. said, and cuddled me closer. "Hey, it's okay."

I decided it was easier to cry it out than try to talk through suppressed tears. I buried my face in his T-shirt. He said nothing, only held me there until I lifted my face and sniffled.

"Better?" he asked.

I nodded.

"You can put her down now," Gabriel said, and his voice had a note of steel.

I looked in the direction of his voice and saw him

standing a few feet away, arms locked against his sides as if he were keeping himself from pummeling J.B.

J.B's arms tightened around me. "Finders keepers. I didn't see you keeping her from turning into scrambled eggs."

Gabriel stepped forward. I could see stars blazing in his dark eyes, always a sign of trouble. Like I said, Gabriel is a slow burn. But when he explodes you'd better get the hell out of the way.

"Put her down, human. You're squashing my ear," a muffled voice said from inside my coat.

"Beezle!" I gasped. "I forgot he was in there."

J.B. reluctantly released me, his hands lingering just a moment too long at my back. I would be flattered except that I knew at least part of the reason he did it was to piss off Gabriel.

A month ago J.B. was my boss, and we didn't get along. At all. But J.B. had helped Gabriel and me get through a demon attack on the Agency, and in the process we'd developed a kind of friendship. The attack had taken out a lot of the upper management and J.B. had been promoted by virtue of being one of the few supervisors left standing. Demon encounters plus the promotion seemed to have removed the stick that had formerly been lodged up his ass. He was a lot nicer these days.

He'd also shocked me by asking me out on a date. I'd refused, but he'd taken my refusal with surprising grace. It's not that I wasn't attracted to J.B.—I was; anything human would be—it was just that my confusing relationship with Gabriel seemed to preclude the possibility of having a confusing relationship with J.B.

Beezle poked his head out, looking distinctly disgruntled. "What in the name of the four hells happened? What's J.B. doing here? Why aren't we at home?"

"You didn't feel that electro-pulse thingy?" I asked. "You didn't feel us falling out of the sky?"

"I was napping," Beezle said.

"Napping," J.B. said in disbelief.

"You can just keep that disrespectful tone out of your voice, Jacob Benjamin. I'm an old gargoyle. And what is that horrible smell?"

Now that Beezle mentioned it, I did notice a distinctly malodorous scent lingering in the alley. And something else. A trace of cinnamon.

"Something angelic was here," I said.

"How do you know?" J.B. asked.

"Whenever something of an angelic bloodline uses its powers, I always smell cinnamon."

I started to move cautiously in Gabriel's direction. It seemed the smell was coming from just beyond him. J.B. followed.

"And there was something else, when the pulse happened. Did you feel it?" I looked questioningly at Gabriel, who was still giving J.B. the hairy eyeball. I saw him take a deep breath and refocus his attention on me.

"Yes. A sense of evil. It felt like . . ."

". . . Ramuell," we said at the same time.

I felt J.B. start next to me. "Ramuell? That nephilim that you killed?"

Gabriel nodded. "I do not know how it could be. Another nephilim could not have broken free from the Forbidden Lands. Lucifer persuaded all of the fallen to give some of their power to redouble the creatures' bindings. It would take more than the power of a single angel or demon to free one of them. Even I could not do it now, despite my bloodline."

"And it can't be Ramuell. He's dead."

"Are you sure?" J.B. asked.

I thought of Ramuell burning, molecule by molecule, dissolving before my eyes until the last of his essence was gone and the souls that were bound within him were released.

"I'm sure," I replied grimly.

We crept carefully through the alley. I wasn't sure where we were—Chicago looks pretty much the same when all you see are Dumpsters and the back sides of brick buildings. We had been flying over the north side but the fall had disoriented me.

"Where were you coming from, J.B.?" I whispered as we crept closer to the source of the smell. The odor had to be amazingly powerful to cut through the cold air.

"Drop-off, same as you," he replied.

"I thought that a regional supervisor would get to delegate the scut work," I teased.

J.B. shrugged. "The new midwestern supervisor wants us to do fieldwork. He wants us to stay in touch with our roots or something. Anyway, I saw you flying back and was trying to catch up when that . . . thing happened. How come you fell out of the sky? What happened to your wings?"

"I don't know," I said slowly. "It was like that pulse kind of short-circuited my magic, and when that happened my wings disappeared."

"That is dangerous," said Gabriel. "If your enemies were to learn that such a thing could disable your abilities, even temporarily . . ."

He trailed off. I didn't need him to elaborate. My enemies, which are many and mostly inherited from conflicts that Lucifer and my father, Azazel, created, would turn me into Korean barbecue in the blink of an eye if they thought I had a weakness. I'd recently discovered I was descended from Lucifer through my mother's line, and I was not enjoying having another potentially fatal familial relationship.

"Let's not worry about that right now," I said brightly, trying not to think of my half brother, Antares, and his personal vendetta against me. Antares would be more than delighted to short-circuit my powers.

The alley came to a T-junction just as we passed out of the light of a streetlamp. It was pitch-black in both directions, the only light coming from the streets beyond. I wondered what happened to the rest of the streetlights.

The smell was nearly overwhelming now. It was something rotted and metallic, and there was a distinct scent of burned fur. Underneath it all was a trace of scorched cinnamon and sulfur—the smell that I associated with Ramuell.

I opened my palm and tried to create the same blue ball of flame that had scared away the vampire earlier. All that came out were a few blue sparks.

"I guess I'm still broken," I said, and tried not to panic. I had no idea if the effects of the pulse were permanent. "Gabriel, can you?"

A moment later the alley was illuminated by nightfire. Gabriel is a more skilled practitioner than I, and so was able to send the ball of flame ahead of him instead of holding it in his hand. The light danced along down the right turn of the T-junction until I gasped. Gabriel raised the light up higher and turned up the illumination with a murmured word. J.B. covered his mouth beside me and made a retching noise.

It was difficult to make sense of what my eyes were seeing. There was blood—lots of blood, more blood than I thought could possibly be inside one human. And there were parts that were recognizable as human—a tibia, an ulna, a femur—all skinned but with small bits of flesh clinging to the bone. There was a torso that looked as though it had been through a shredder, and some scraps of cloth that might have been a flannel shirt.

But there was no head. And there was a hand that looked almost completely human save the fact that it was covered in fur.

"It's a werewolf," I said, trying not to gag.

"What could have done that to a werewolf?" Beezle asked.

"Another wolf?" J.B. said, speaking through his hand.

I shook my head. "There's not usually that much disparity in wolf strength. Sure, the alpha and his lieutenants will be stronger than the other wolves, but not so much that one wolf could tear apart another like this. And where is the head?"

"More importantly, where is the Agent? This death wasn't in my paperwork for the week," J.B. said.

The implications were clear. If the death was not on file, then it was not meant to be. It was a death outside the natural order. And the last time there had been a death outside the natural order was when Ramuell had cut a swath through the innocent of this city.

"It can't be," I said as Gabriel stared at me. "It *can't*. I killed him. If there's one thing I'm sure of, it's that I killed Ramuell. Lucifer's been dangling it over my head ever since."

"Then it must be another nephilim," Gabriel said slowly.

"You just said that couldn't happen," J.B. said.

"Do you have another explanation, Agent?"

"No, but I'm not the one calling Maddy a liar."

Gabriel narrowed his eyes. "I did not call Madeline a liar."

"You implied it," J.B. fired back.

"You'd better do something before this turns into a scene from a high school romcom," Beezle muttered.

I stepped forward, intending to get between them and push them apart—they were practically nose to nose—when I heard somebody groaning. I froze, trying to determine the location of the noise, but I couldn't pick it out over the sound of bickering.

"Shut up," I snapped, and both of them turned to stare at me. "Somebody else is here."

I heard the groaning again, very faint, farther along the alley and closer to the street. I started forward and Gabriel gripped my arm.

"Wait. It may be a trap," Gabriel said. "Stay behind me."

"Because I'm small and helpless?" I asked, annoyed.

"Because your powers do not seem to be functioning normally right now," he answered reasonably.

I supposed I couldn't argue with that even if it did make me feel useless.

J.B. took up a position behind me and we proceeded slowly toward the sound, picking our way carefully through the remains of the werewolf. I felt things squishing beneath my boots and tried not to think about what I was doing. My body thrummed with tension. What was waiting for us? Another of this creature's victims, or the creature itself?

Gabriel directed the ball of nightfire toward the sound. There were white feathers splashed with red scattered around just past the gore from the werewolf. A bloodied hand came into view, then an arm, then a gigantic pair of white wings covering a body lying prone on the ground. A golden-haired head was just visible.

"It's an angel," I said.

"Or something that looks like one," Gabriel agreed. "Gargoyle?"

Beezle squinted, his clawed hands gripping the lapel of

my coat, and I knew that he was looking through the layers of reality to find the creature's essence.

"It's an angel." Beezle nudged me with a sharp little elbow. "See, I'm handy to have around."

"Sometimes," I agreed.

Gabriel signaled to me to stay behind and J.B. put his hand on my shoulder to make sure that I understood. I shrugged off his touch, resenting their high-handedness. I wasn't stupid. I knew that I wasn't up to tangling with anything supernatural at the moment.

My bodyguard approached the body carefully, knelt beside the angel and rolled the creature to its back. The angel's face was splattered with blood and there was a large and ugly gash across his bare chest.

Gabriel beckoned the ball of nightfire closer to him. "It's Baraqiel."

"What's he doing here?" asked Beezle, surprise evident in his voice.

"Who's Baraqiel?" J.B. and I asked together.

"Lucifer's personal messenger," Beezle said.

I wondered what Lucifer was up to now. Why was his personal messenger lying wounded in an alley only a few feet away from the mangled corpse of a werewolf? Had Baraqiel just been in the wrong place at the wrong time, or was he the werewolf's killer?

Gabriel laid his hands on the wound and the alley grew brighter as the light of the sun came from his palms. The air filled with the scent of apple pie baking—a smell that was unique to Gabriel.

Baraqiel gasped for air and his eyes flew open as Gabriel lifted his hands away from the angel's chest. The wound was healed.

"Gabriel?" he asked, his gaze confused and frantic. "Where am I? Where is he?"

"Where is who?" I asked.

Baraqiel shook his head and sat up, staring at me. His eyes were a startling silver blue that looked almost clear. I shivered. The effect of pale eyes against his blood-covered face was ghastly. He pushed up from the ground and wobbled as he attempted to stand.

Gabriel rose beside him and placed a steadying hand on Baraqiel's shoulder. "Be at peace. You need to rest. You are still weak."

Baraqiel shook his head, still staring at me. "There is no time. You are Azazel's daughter?"

"Yes," I said.

"You must go. Samiel is coming for you."

A cave in an ash-burned land. A flash of green eyes, alight with hatred and madness.

"Samiel," I breathed.

"Who's he, now?" J.B. asked, obviously bewildered.

The child of an angel and a nephilim. A being who would have every reason to seek vengeance against me. My voice was barely more than a whisper. "Ramuell's son."

2

"OH," J.B. SAID.

"Yeah, oh," I replied. "You think he's pissed at me for melting his daddy?"

"Did Samiel do this to the werewolf?" Gabriel asked.

Baraqiel shook his head, surveying the carnage. "I do not know what caused this."

"What are you doing here, then?" I asked.

"I was to deliver a message to you from Lord Lucifer. I heard the cries of the wolf and came to investigate. Before I reached this place, I was attacked by Samiel."

"Wait a second," I said. "I'm confused. How did you recognize Samiel? Nobody even knew of his existence until a month ago. I was under the impression that nobody had seen him but me, and then only for a moment."

Was it my imagination, or did something crafty flicker across Baraqiel's face?

"Samiel named himself when he attacked. I also have been informed of his existence by Lord Lucifer, who has been anticipating an attempt on your life."

I narrowed my eyes. "Really. You'd think he could have informed me of that little piece of news."

Baraqiel bowed his head. "It is not for me to know the ways of Lord Lucifer."

"Nor me, apparently," I said dryly.

To say that Lucifer kept things close to the chest was an understatement. I'd deliberately concealed the knowledge of Samiel's existence from Lucifer in order to protect Gabriel. Gabriel's life was pretty much always in jeopardy because of his parentage. Ramuell was Gabriel's father also, a fact that should have been his death sentence at birth. I hadn't wanted to draw any attention to Samiel lest the eyes of the Grigori fell on Gabriel, too. How had Lucifer found out?

"I hate to interrupt," said Beezle loudly, "but I don't think that this is a place we should be hanging around. It would probably look suspicious to the human authorities."

"You're right," I said reluctantly.

I didn't like the idea of leaving the wolf's remains like this. I knew that the police would have no idea what could have been done to the wolf, or even what they were looking at. The average human didn't know anything about vampires, or werewolves, or angels and demons. And if, in the course of investigating this murder, the police did stumble upon something supernatural, it was highly unlikely that said supernatural thing would just quietly answer questions and then send the nice officers on their way.

At the same time, it wasn't as though I had any clue as to the perpetrator's identity. Baraqiel claimed that Samiel had not killed the wolf, but he hadn't actually seen the wolf's attacker. And something about the power signature from the pulse had reminded me of Ramuell, which meant only Samiel could be the source. Could the pulse have been created when he attacked Baraqiel?

I wanted to stay and check around the crime scene a little more, see if I could ferret anything out. I don't claim to be any kind of great investigator, but there was something not right here.

"The gargoyle is correct. I believe I hear the sounds of sirens," Gabriel said.

He extinguished the ball of nightfire, plunging the alley into darkness.

"Gabriel, I need to have a private word with you, from Lord Lucifer," Baraqiel said. His pale eyes glowed in the faint light that trickled into the alley.

I could feel Gabriel's reluctance. "I am charged with staying with Madeline. Can this not wait until we have safely returned her home?"

"My lord was most insistent that these words be for your ears alone," Baraqiel said.

"It's okay, Gabriel," I said. "Maybe you can check around the area for some more clues."

Gabriel shook his head. "I must stay with you. Azazel has entrusted me with your safety."

"I think I can manage to watch her for a few minutes," J.B. said, and he scooped me up and took to the sky before Gabriel could protest. He grinned down at me as we zipped upward, cleared the roofs and headed toward my house.

I felt a little flutter in the vicinity of my heart. J.B. could charm when he was so inclined. "You do know that you're asking for it, right?"

He shrugged. "I've dealt with your Rottweiler before."

"He's supposed to keep me safe. He's been ordered to do

so by my father and by Lucifer. He takes that responsibility seriously."

"If you think that's all he's interested in, I've got a Skyway to sell you," J.B. said.

I worried in silence about my powers as we flew home. I'd really only just started to get a handle on them in the last month or so. Before I'd discovered that I was a fallen angel's daughter I hadn't even realized that I had powers beyond that of an Agent. Then I'd gained all those talents plus more—a little boost from Lucifer's lost lover Evangeline, my many-greats grandmother, who had possessed me briefly during the Ramuell incident.

Once I'd cleared Evangeline out of my system, I'd discovered I wasn't quite as powerful as I'd thought. Evangeline had given me some pretty nifty—albeit totally destructive—abilities that had disappeared when she had. I was learning what I could do, very slowly. I could sense that there was untapped magic inside me but I wasn't yet capable of drawing it out.

We approached my house in the deepest part of the night, that time about an hour before the sun rises. I live in a run-down brick two-flat in the west Lakeview neighborhood. I had inherited the house from my mother when she died. The red paint on the front porch was peeling, the chimney was crumbling, and the heating system was in desperate need of an update. I was always broke or on the verge of it, so it seemed that repairs were something that were deferred to a day when food wasn't a priority, or possibly that magical day when I won the lottery.

I was thinking idly about dinner as we descended in silence toward the house. We landed in the backyard and J.B. set me on my feet with a grin. That was when the blast hit him.

There was a bolt of blue lightning accompanied by the smell of ozone and sage. J.B. cried out and flew across the yard. I turned to face my attacker but before I could think, before I could breathe, his arms were around me.

Claws bit cruelly into my flesh as I was drawn close. I looked up into the red face of a half demon that I knew well.

"Hello, Antares," I said, and resisted the urge to cry out as his claws drew blood.

"Hello, little sister," he hissed.

Antares looks like a medieval priest's idea of a demon. He's got huge, curving black horns, oversized bat wings, curling ebony claws, slitted pupils, skin the color of raw meat and many pointy teeth. He's also my father's second-born child, the issue of Azazel's affair with a witch-demon.

Azazel is the most powerful of the fallen save the Morningstar himself, and the witch-demon was a practitioner of exceptional ability. Despite all of this, Antares had been born oddly powerless. This made him resentful of everything, particularly me, whose head he wanted on a spit.

He saw me as the usurper to his inheritance—Azazel's throne. I would have happily gift wrapped the throne and all the bullshit that went with it, but Azazel had named me his heir and I hadn't yet determined how to wriggle out of it.

"Actually, you're my little brother. I'm Azazel's first-born, you know," I said casually. The scent of sulfur filled my nostrils and I fought down nausea.

As I'd expected, that set him off. His lack of status in Azazel's court was a major sore spot, especially since Azazel had put out a death warrant on Antares for trying to kill me. Normally Grigori were forbidden from harming members of one another's courts, but Antares had killed a lot of innocents in his attack on the Agency, and even Lucifer couldn't ignore that infraction.

"First born and first to die!" he hissed, his saliva splattering all over my face. My skin burned where it touched.

"If you say so," I said, feigning boredom.

I'd never let Antares know, but I actually was afraid of him. He'd almost killed me once, and that kind of thing tends to leave psychological marks. Antares had no magic of his own, but he was fox-crafty and able to wield magical objects that had been created by his powerful mother.

I didn't want to look around for fear of drawing Antares's attention to J.B., and I was sure that Gabriel would be arriving any second now. He would never voluntarily leave me with J.B. for so long.

"Don't expect your guard dog anytime soon," Antares crooned in my ear. "My men had orders to take your companions as soon as I had you."

I trembled involuntarily as his mouth touched my ear. The physical proximity to Antares was making me sick. I fought to control myself. I might be powerless at the moment, but I still had brains, and Antares was laughably easy to manipulate.

"Your men?" I asked, a faint note of contempt in my voice. "You mean that cowardly little blob demon and his friend who looks like a pile of walking snot?"

"Be careful, sister. Those demons that you hold in such contempt will be your masters soon enough."

I tried not to imagine what he was talking about and failed. It is not pleasant to contemplate a future in which you will be raped and tortured by demons. I hoped that Antares could see none of this on my face, and kept my voice even.

"I doubt that very much. Those two ran off as soon as Gabriel looked at them sternly, remember?" I said, referring to the time when Antares had tried taking J.B. hostage in order to draw me out. "He's probably tying them in knots as we speak."

Doubt flickered across Antares's face for a moment. He tightened his embrace. We would look like lovers but for the blood running from my skin at his touch. I felt a wriggling around the vicinity of my ribs and I froze, remembering Beezle. He'd probably fallen asleep in my pocket again and was now trying to get out.

Stay down, Beezle, I thought desperately. Antares had put Beezle in a gargoyle version of a coma once, and Beezle had taken it personally. I didn't want him trying anything stupid in the name of revenge.

I put my hands on Antares's chest and did my best to look threatening. It's hard to look like a badass when you are very petite but I gave it my best.

"You'd better let me go or I'll blast you from here to Gary, Indiana," I said. The wriggling in my pocket grew more frantic and I could hear Beezle's muffled, indignant cries.

Antares smiled, and his smile chilled me to the bone. "No, you will not do that, little sister. I understand that your powers have left you."

How could he know that already? I wondered. *Unless . . .*

"Have you been following me?" I said, and my voice dripped with contempt. "Like some mangy sneak-thief?"

Antares's grip tightened, and I realized I was growing faint from blood loss. I could feel it running in rivulets from my arms and back.

"This mangy sneak-thief managed to catch you and that foolish human unawares. You should show me more respect, sister. I know something that you do not."

"I find that extremely difficult to believe."

"I know what slaughtered the wolf. I know what hunts you. I know secrets that you cannot even begin to fathom."

I tried not to show it, but I was definitely interested. I wanted to know what had happened to that wolf.

"If you're talking about Samiel, you're not telling me anything new."

"There are things worse than a nephilim's child. Horrors that you cannot comprehend. But I know. I know of matters that the lords of the Grigori themselves do not know." The pupils of his eyes grew thinner in his excitement. "I will make you respect me before you die."

I am not afraid of death. You can't be afraid of death when you do my job. But I did not want to die screaming at the hands of a demon. And as I thought that, I felt something rise up inside of me, and I knew that my magic had only been sleeping awhile. Then I heard a gurgling yell.

Antares looked away from me for a moment, and I pushed that magic up, up to the tips of my fingers still planted on his chest. Electricity crackled where I touched.

He turned his face back to me. I smiled and said, "Boo."

Then I let loose the magic, and it surged through me and into Antares, blue fire that blasted him away from me. I heard him screaming in pain as he was launched several blocks away.

My wings having reappeared along with my powers, I fluttered up from the ground and looked around. Antares had disappeared. This was not unusual. It was a neat little magic trick that he had inherited from his mother. It generally followed a battle in which he had a lot of wound-licking to do.

Beezle popped out of my pocket and glared up at me. "You kept me in there on purpose."

"Absolutely. I didn't want Antares to turn you into gargoyle bits."

"I can handle that powerless fool," he said indignantly.

I stroked his head soothingly. "Yes, I'm very unreasonable. I just don't know what I would do without you."

Beezle tried not to look pleased and failed.

There was a groan from nearby, and I looked around the backyard. J.B. was lying facedown in my fallow vegetable garden. He had been wearing a puffy green ski jacket, and the back of the jacket had been scorched away by the bolt. The garment hung in blackened ribbons from his shoulders. I could see long shiny welts on his back where the magic had burned through his clothing.

I rushed to his side as he attempted to turn over. Beezle emerged from my pocket and flapped around us like a bossy mosquito.

"Don't turn him that way. You'll get dirt on the burns," he said.

"I think I can handle this without instruction," I said, annoyed.

Kneeling in the dirt, I helped J.B. to sit up. His face was scraped and bruised from the impact with the ground.

"Was there a tornado?" he asked, wincing in pain as I helped him to his feet.

"A tornado named Antares," I said grimly.

"Where are the others?"

"I don't know," I said, and tried not to worry about Gabriel. Surely he'd just been delayed at the crime scene with Baraqiel. Antares's henchmen were no match for a half nephilim, whatever my deluded brother might think.

J.B. leaned heavily on my shoulders and we hobbled toward my back porch. He negotiated the three wooden steps very slowly.

"I don't think we can get to the second floor like this," I said, my head spinning. The loss of blood and the shock of my earlier fall from the sky finally caught up with me. I sat down on the top step and J.B. collapsed beside me. We leaned on each other like two drunks, both of us panting from exertion.

"You need an elevator," J.B. said.

"She needs help from that useless devil, is what she needs," Beezle said, fluttering around my head anxiously. "He could heal her in a trice if only he were where he was supposed to be."

"You don't think that Antares's men really could have harmed him?" I asked.

Beezle scoffed. "Those two miscreants? Not a chance. And remember, Baraqiel was with him."

"Baraqiel was injured," I pointed out.

"And if it was so easy to handle Antares's men, where are Gabriel and Baraqiel?" J.B. asked.

Once worry was given free rein, I could conjure any number of scenarios in which Gabriel and Baraqiel could disappear. They had been attacked by Samiel. They had been attacked by Focalor, one of the Grigori who hated Azazel. They had been attacked by some other horror that I hadn't thought of yet.

Horrors that you cannot comprehend. That was what Antares had said. He was a braggart, and most of the time I was inclined to ignore what came out of his mouth. But there had been truth in his voice. He knew something about what had happened in that alley. He knew, and he was obviously planning to use that information to his advantage. In the meantime, Gabriel was missing, J.B. was horribly burned, and I was bleeding out on my back porch. And Beezle was driving me crazy by fluttering around and muttering imprecations about Gabriel.

"Beezle, why don't you make yourself useful and find some Band-Aids?" I said.

"And possibly some kind of burn cream," added J.B.

Beezle flew around the house to the window that was always open on the east side. As he went, I was sure I heard him say something about needing a doughnut.

"No doughnuts until I stop bleeding!" I shouted after him.

J.B. snorted a laugh, then grabbed his side. "It hurts to laugh."

I had enough sense to realize that J.B.'s injuries were worse than mine. He might be hemorrhaging internally or have a broken rib from when Antares blasted him across the yard. The burns on his back had to be causing him incredible pain. He needed medical attention, and I needed to get my bleeding self together and provide it.

I didn't have the knack of healing that Gabriel and many other angels seemed to possess. Or if I did, I couldn't yet access or control it.

But I could call an Agent Medi-Team. They were specially trained to deal with supernatural injuries that occurred on the job. If I had been thinking clearly, I would have called them already. I groped in my coat pocket for my cell phone and couldn't find it. I patted all of the pockets in frustration and realized that it had probably fallen out during my skydiving attempt.

"Do you have your cell phone?" I asked J.B. as he watched me curiously.

He looked kind of glazed, like he was drunk. I probably looked the same way. I felt myself getting more lightheaded as the minutes passed, and it occurred to me that Antares must have some kind of anticoagulant in his claws. I was still bleeding as heavily as before and the wounds showed no signs of clotting.

J.B. was slow to respond, so I started patting him all over, looking for the telltale bulge of the phone.

"Is this really the time?" J.B. asked as he leaned against the wall and closed his eyes while I searched. "You haven't even taken me to dinner yet."

I checked the inside and outside of his ruined jacket, and even the pockets of his jeans, but there was no phone.

"Might have fallen out when I was blasted. Or before that. Who knows?" J.B. murmured. He sounded like he was falling asleep.

That was bad. I knew enough about medicine to know that if he went to sleep now, he might never wake up.

"Beezle!" I shouted, heedless of the hour and my sleeping neighbors. "Beezle, come here now!"

I heard the scrape of a window against its frame, and looked up to see Beezle shooting out of the kitchen with a small first aid kit clutched in his claws.

"What's the fire?" he asked, tossing me the kit.

"Go and get the portable phone from the house. J.B.'s barely holding it together and I need to call a Medi-Team for him." I patted J.B.'s cheek and he grunted. "Don't go to sleep."

"I don't know if the portable phone will work out here," Beezle said doubtfully.

"Just get it, Beezle!" I snapped. "I don't have time to debate with you."

"This wouldn't be necessary if *he* were here to do his job," Beezle grumbled as he flew back toward the kitchen window.

I silently agreed with him. If Gabriel were here, he could have healed both me and J.B. without much effort. But unlike Beezle, I didn't read any sinister implications in Gabriel's absence. If he could be at my side, he would be. It was that simple. Never mind the bond between us; if Azazel found out that I came to harm because of Gabriel's absence, he would grind Gabriel into small and bloody pieces.

Beezle came zooming out again with the phone. I snatched it from his hands and dialed the Medi-Team number. But when I held the receiver to my ears I heard nothing but the crackle of static.

"Dammit," I muttered.

"I told you," Beezle said.

It was hard to think. Blood flowed from the wounds at my back and arms, slow but unceasing. I tried to stand but found that I was too weak, and my knees slipped in the blood pooling on the peeling wood of the porch. My face slammed into the railing and I saw stars.

"Maddy, don't try to move," Beezle said, his voice alarmed. "I'll get help."

"From where?" I asked, holding my hand to the side of my face. I thought I'd heard something crack when my cheek hit the wood.

"I'll get Azazel," he said.

I had to think for a minute about why that was bad. "If you get Azazel and he comes here and finds Gabriel missing, he will kill him."

"If I don't get Azazel now and you bleed to death in your own backyard, he will kill *me*."

"Don't get him. I'll figure out something." The last person I wanted to see at that moment was Daddy dearest.

The wind picked up, and I shivered inside my coat. Beezle was having trouble staying close, his wings buffeted by a breeze that was fast becoming a gale. I reached out and grabbed him, stuffing him inside my pocket before he blew away.

"What the . . . ?" I said, and crawled slowly toward J.B., who wasn't moving at all. I felt for a pulse and found one, but he did not stir at my touch.

The wind racketed around us. My hair came free of the

woolen hat I was wearing. I covered J.B.'s still body with my own, clinging to his shoulders.

A faint red light appeared just above my garden, and the light grew until it was a circle the size of a city Dumpster. Inside the circle, wind swirled and electricity pulsed.

Beezle poked his head out of my pocket.

"It's a portal," he shouted.

I knew that. I just didn't know who was in it, and if they were friend or foe. My magic crackled feebly across my fingertips. I was too weak to do anything.

A figure emerged from the portal, tall and blond and radiantly beautiful. He brushed some imaginary lint from his white-feathered wings. The portal closed behind him and the wind died down. The angel looked up, and the natural arrogance on his face turned to surprise.

I had been wrong. There *was* one person that I wanted to see less than my father.

"Hello, Nathaniel," I said to my fiancé.

3

NATHANIEL HURRIED TOWARD THE PORCH, TAKING IN the situation in an instant.

"Madeline, what has happened?" he said, as he pulled me away from J.B., put me in his lap and checked my wounds. "Where is your bodyguard?"

Nathaniel never referred to Gabriel by his name, which was just one of many things that I disliked about the man whom my father had engaged me to against my will.

"Antares," I said briefly. I felt dizzy, and Nathaniel wasn't helping by shaking me around.

"How did you incur these injuries?" he said, covering each with his hands one after another. I felt a familiar heat, like the light of the sun was burning through my veins.

This kind of healing used to be very painful for me, when I was still mostly human. Now that I had acknowledged my heritage and my heart had been replaced by an angel's heartstone, it was only slightly less painful. The half of me that would always be human knew that the sun was not supposed to run wild in your blood, nor was it supposed to heal you. The angelic half of me welcomed the heat and the burn like homecoming.

The blood ceased to flow, and I felt the skin knit together painfully. I didn't feel like getting up and dancing around yet, though. The kind of healing that Nathaniel did could close up injuries but it didn't help with recovery time.

"Thanks," I said, and tried not to sound resentful as I did. It wasn't Nathaniel's fault that my father had affianced us without my permission, or that I wanted someone else. It was his fault, however, that he was totally unlikable in every way.

"What about J.B.?" I asked, squirming off his lap and onto the porch.

Too much proximity to Nathaniel made me uncomfortable. He is beautiful, and it is hard not to be drawn to beauty. But he is also a giant jerk, and no amount of attractiveness can make up for that. I did not want to think about our wedding night.

"J.B.?" he said, his eyebrows raised. "This human that you were . . ."

He trailed off, staring at J.B.'s limp form.

"Gods above and below," he swore, and rushed to J.B.'s side. He lifted J.B.'s eyelids, checked his pulse, and then picked him up as if a six-foot-plus man weighed nothing. "What have you done with Amarantha's son?"

I looked at Beezle, who was perched like a crow on the railing of the porch. He looked surprised.

"Who is Amarantha, and what does she have to do with J.B.?" I asked, pulling myself to my feet. The world wobbled in many directions.

Nathaniel kicked open the door and flew up the back stairs to my apartment without answering me. I heard a crash as he knocked out the door upstairs as well.

"Those locks cost money, you know!" I shouted, annoyed by both his high-handedness and his abandonment of me. Did he think I could walk or fly in this state? "What crawled up his ass?"

"Amarantha is the queen of the local faerie court," Beezle said. "I didn't know J.B. was her son."

Beezle was like a phone book of things that go bump in the night. He knew every species, every subspecies, every hierarchy and every rule. He could run the gamut from werewolf law to the vampire courts to the reigns of demons. There was very little that Beezle did not know. I wondered how J.B. had managed to conceal his status from my gargoyle.

"Well, presumably Amarantha is someone with a lot of influence or else Nathaniel wouldn't have touched J.B. even if he were wearing gloves," I said, staggering toward my back door. "On the upside, this means that he is probably healing J.B. as we speak, and I don't have to threaten him to do it."

I grabbed the doorframe and leaned on it for a minute, which gave me a good look at the damage Nathaniel had done to the lock by kicking it. The door normally locked with a dead bolt. The bolt had torn through the wooden frame and was now totally useless, which left my abode uncomfortably open to the aforementioned things that go bump.

A threshold, even without a door, is enough to stop most supernatural beings of power. Vampires, werewolves, fallen angels, demons . . . none of them could cross a threshold without an invitation. Nathaniel had been (reluctantly) invited inside by me before, so he was able to cross the threshold without penalty.

But there were plenty of lesser magical beings for whom the rules were a little more fuzzy. They could construe an unlocked or open door as an invitation. I didn't fancy an infestation of gremlins eating all of Beezle's precious popcorn stash or an imp whispering nasty things to me while I slept. And repairs cost money, money that I didn't have. I usually generate some income by working as a freelance recipe developer, but since I'd been running around trying to keep up with my Agent duties and Azazel's demands, I hadn't had much time for that work lately. Although I supposed that since Nathaniel had done the kicking and the breaking I could get him to pay for the repairs.

I dragged myself up the back stairs, holding on to the railing as if it were a lifeline. Beezle fluttered around my head, cajoling me to keep moving forward when I wanted to stop and rest.

When I got to the top of the stairs, I saw that Nathaniel had repeated his destroying act on the upstairs door, which hung drunkenly from its hinges like a scene from a Bugs Bunny cartoon. I slumped on the landing, exhausted and annoyed.

"Come on, Maddy, get up," Beezle said, pulling ineffectually at my collar.

I waved him away. "Leave me alone. I'll get up and go inside when I'm ready."

"I want to find out what Nathaniel's doing to J.B.," Beezle said, tugging at me again.

"So go," I said, leaning my head against the wall and closing my eyes. I heard Beezle flap uncertainly for a moment, and then the sound of his wings receding as he went inside the apartment.

I want Gabriel, I thought. I couldn't help it. When he was away from me, I was like a planet without a sun. I wasn't supposed to love him, and maybe if I could have had a normal relationship with him, I could have gotten him out of my system. But the longing . . . the longing . . .

"Madeline, wake up."

Gabriel?

"Madeline, please. Madeline."

I'm dreaming you. I need you.

"Madeline."

Hands on my shoulders, on my face. Warmth like the light of the sun.

I opened my eyes. His face was so close to mine that I could see the stars deep in his black eyes, and as I watched I saw one of them burst and flare and fall away, and I knew that my eyes looked the same.

His breath was on my lips, a whisper away.

"Madeline, what has happened? Why are you sleeping on the stairs?"

His words reminded me of J.B. and Nathaniel only a few feet away inside the apartment. If I gave in to the impulse to kiss Gabriel and Nathaniel found us, Gabriel would be dead before you could say "Jack Robinson."

I shook my head to clear away the cobwebs, and shifted away from the wall. Slowly I realized that Baraqiel stood a few feet behind Gabriel, watching us with an avid gaze. There was a knowledge in his eyes that I did not like, and I wondered how much of my need for Gabriel had been revealed to the messenger.

"What happened to you guys?" I asked. "You were gone forever."

"Baraqiel suggested we observe the human investigation for a time to see if they discovered anything. I sensed the death of the wolf was important to you and thought you would be safe enough with Bennett for a short time. Apparently, I was mistaken. What happened?" he repeated.

I told him that Antares had attacked us as I shuffled into the kitchen and filled the teakettle with water. The muscles in Gabriel's face froze one by one.

"I should not have left you," he said, and his voice was filled with heat.

I shrugged, not wanting to get into this in front of a witness. Something about Baraqiel told me he was collecting everything he saw and filing it away for later use. I wondered what he would report to Lucifer.

I could hear a murmur of voices from the living room. I couldn't understand what was being said but Nathaniel's tone was absurdly deferential, almost as if he were talking to my father. I wondered again what it was about J.B. that made Nathaniel act this way.

"Madeline," Gabriel said, frowning. "What did Antares do?"

"Oh, the usual," I said lightly. "Threatened to pull my entrails through my nose. Clawed me up some. J.B. got set on fire."

"How did you escape? You were completely powerless," Baraqiel said. He still had a speculative look on his face, like he was trying to decide whether or not it would be worth it to blackmail me over Gabriel.

I shrugged. "My powers came back. For a little while, at least."

"And now?" Baraqiel persisted.

I narrowed my eyes at him. "Why are you so interested, anyway?" My tone of voice indicated that I was Azazel's daughter and he was just a messenger. Sometimes it is an advantage to be royalty in a highly hierarchical society.

His manner immediately became deferential. "I apologize, my lady. I am only concerned for your welfare."

I wasn't so certain about that. "Baraqiel, you never did tell us what you were doing when you were waylaid by Samiel."

He bowed so deeply I thought that he was going to fall over. "Again, my apologies, granddaughter of Lucifer. I was sent by the Lightbringer to deliver a message. I have been astonishingly remiss in that capacity."

I rolled my hand in his direction, indicating that he should continue.

Baraqiel reached underneath his right arm and pulled out a small piece of parchment that had been rolled and tied to his wing. He presented it to me on his outstretched hand in such a way that I could avoid touching him if I so chose. I wondered if most of Baraqiel's recipients disdained the touch of a lowly messenger, and my face burned when I thought of how I had spoken to him a moment earlier. I realize it's the lifetime goal of many little girls, but I don't really enjoy being a princess.

"Thank you," I said, taking the parchment from him and unrolling it. I could feel my face growing thunderous as I read Lucifer's message.

My grandfather is a totally manipulative bastard—big surprise—and it was obvious that he had been holding this task for me in his fist until he felt the time was right.

Trouble was, if I refused Lucifer, he would likely kill Gabriel—or rather, have the Grigori do it for him. And after that, he would probably kill Beezle. And then J.B. And so on, until he had taken everything from me and broken me to his will. That was why he was the first of the fallen, and the lord high devil himself. He knew that emotional pain is a far more powerful motivator than physical pain, and he also knew that I would do anything to keep those I loved safe.

"What is it?" Gabriel asked.

I thrust the parchment at him wordlessly and waited while he read it. His mouth was grim when he finished and handed it back to me.

"Lord Lucifer requires me to wait and bring a response," Baraqiel said. He inched away from me a little when I looked up at him.

"Don't," Gabriel said, his voice full of warning.

I swallowed the "tell Lord Lucifer he can stick this parchment up his ass" that was on my tongue and attempted to modulate my voice. "Tell Lord Lucifer that his granddaughter would be pleased to fulfill this duty for him."

Baraqiel raised his eyebrow slightly, but he nodded and said, "I must return to my lord immediately with your response."

"Don't you want to wash your face first?" I asked. Baraqiel was still covered in the blood that he had shed during his altercation with Samiel.

"I have already been gone too long," he said, and swept out of the kitchen and down the stairs. It was still full dark outside, which was a good thing, because I don't know what my neighbors would have made of an angel taking off from my backyard.

I looked at Gabriel, sighed, and then kicked one of the cabinet doors. It made a very satisfying thump.

"That was very childish," Gabriel said.

"Absolutely," I replied. "But it feels good."

I took another deep breath and inspected the damage. There was a crack in the cabinet door. Sometimes I forget that I am stronger now than I used to be.

"Let's find out what's going on with J.B.," I said, and led the way into the living room.

J.B. was propped on a pile of cushions on the sofa, and covered in a blanket. His face was bloodless, his eyes were tired and his hair stuck up in every direction. The ends even looked a little singed. Other than that, he appeared surprisingly hale for someone who had been knocked out.

Nathaniel had pulled a chair from the dining room and sat at his side. His fawning expression gave me the willies.

"How are you feeling?" I asked J.B.

"Like I got shot with magical lightning and crash-landed on hard ground," he said.

"Is there anything else I can do for you?" Nathaniel asked.

"No, thank you. You can finish your business with Maddy now," J.B. said. He looked a little disconcerted by Nathaniel's solicitous manner.

.I gave J.B. what-the-hell-is-up-with-him eyes and J.B. shrugged in response.

"Of course. And if there is anything else that I or the court of Azazel can do for you . . ." he said, standing.

"He'll let you know," I said, taking Nathaniel by the arm and tugging him away into the kitchen. I wanted Nathaniel to say whatever it was he had to say and leave so I could talk to J.B. and find out why my fiancé was tripping over himself in J.B.'s presence.

Gabriel stayed in the living room and I heard him talking quietly to J.B. Nathaniel reluctantly allowed himself to be led into the kitchen. Once we were there, I released him immediately. I really don't like to touch him more than I absolutely must. I leaned against the kitchen counter and crossed my arms.

"So what did you come for?" I said.

His lips compressed in a tight line at the belligerent tone of my voice. "You might show a small amount of gratitude, Madeline. Not only did I save your life; I saved the life of Amarantha's son."

Which is a lot more meaningful to you than to me, I thought, *since I have no freaking idea why Amarantha is so damn important to you.*

But I wasn't ungrateful to him for helping me, or for saving the life of my friend, no matter what the identity of J.B.'s mother.

"Thank you," I said, and tried not to sound surly. "You certainly arrived in a timely manner. Now, was there something that you wanted to speak with me about?"

He looked like he was considering further taking me to task for my lack of graciousness, but then apparently decided against it.

"Lord Azazel has asked me to accompany you to the faerie court," Nathaniel said.

I stared at him. "How do you know about that? I just received the message from Lucifer a few minutes ago."

Nathaniel shrugged. "Lucifer himself asked your father to allow me to escort you on your diplomatic mission."

Diplomatic mission. That was a nice way to put it. I was supposed to go to the faerie court and negotiate a new land and power treaty on behalf of the fallen. I knew nothing about the faeries or what Lucifer was after—I had been promised further details upon acceptance of my mission. What I did know was that the faerie court had as arcane and complex a caste system as the fallen, and that since I had a terrible habit of shoving my boot in my mouth, I was just as likely to fail as to succeed.

I didn't know why Lucifer was sticking my neck out like

this. He was sure to have some ulterior motive beyond a simple treaty. If he was only interested in what he stated, then he would have sent a more adept negotiator.

And it was beyond annoying that he had specifically ordered Nathaniel to come with me. Well, maybe it was time to try out my diplomatic skills.

"Listen, Nathaniel—I don't think it's necessary for you to join me. It will probably be boring, negotiating a treaty."

Nathaniel's pale blue eyes sparkled. "You have never experienced the wonders of the faerie court, Madeline. I assure you, the negotiations will be anything but boring."

Oookay. Time for a different tack.

"I'm sure my father has more important things for you to attend to in his court."

"What could be more important that accompanying my betrothed on a vital mission for our highest lord?"

I blew out a breath in frustration and decided diplomacy was overrated. "What will it take to get you to stay home?"

He narrowed his eyes at me. "There is nothing you can say or do to compel me to remain in Lord Azazel's court. I have suspected for some time, Madeline, that you are not taking our betrothal seriously. You must. You are bound to me by Azazel's word before the court."

"I do not and will not consider myself betrothed to you unless it is by my word, not Azazel's," I shot back.

Nathaniel loomed closer, crowding me, and I glared up at him. "Don't try to physically intimidate me. I'm not afraid of you."

He sneered. "Because your loyal dog is in the next room?"

"Because I know that I can blast you down those stairs and out of this building if I want to." And just as if I had called it, I felt my magic alight within me again, feral and hungry, fed by my anger and frustration.

A small part of me knew that I should rein it in, not reveal myself to Nathaniel in this manner. I had been very careful over the last month whenever we met, and had pretended not to shudder when he touched my arm or placed his lips on my cheek. I knew that any coldness on my part would be interpreted as nerves or shyness by my father and that he would explain my behavior to Nathaniel as such. I shouldn't be showing him now that I despised him.

"Don't push me," I said raggedly, trying to keep my magic and my temper under control. "I did not choose this."

"Nor did I," he replied angrily. "Do you think it is my wish to be engaged to a woman who clearly hates me?"

I looked up at him in surprise. There had been something in his voice, some hurt that I hadn't suspected. It flickered in his eyes for an instant before he covered it with anger.

"I don't hate you," I said, and the lie tasted bitter on my tongue. Anything less than the truth would encourage him. But I had to walk the line that Azazel had laid out for me until I could figure out a way to break free of the binding.

Nathaniel looked uncertain for a moment. Then he surprised me, leaned forward as if he intended to kiss my mouth. For a second I felt a strange, unwanted flare of desire. The thought was so foreign that I couldn't help my unconscious reaction, and stepped back until I felt my butt hit the counter. Irritation flared in his eyes.

"If you do not hate me, you are doing an excellent approximation of it."

"What does it matter to you?" I said, feeling slightly embarrassed. "You get to marry Lord Azazel's daughter, don't you?"

"Yes," he said tightly. "I do. I will arrive in three days to escort you to the court."

He swept into a mocking bow and then exited out the open back door. And that reminded me.

I followed him to the top of the stairs and shouted down. "You're going to pay for those doors you broke, buddy!"

"Yeah, good luck with that," Beezle snorted from behind me, and I turned around. He had flown in while my back was turned and was in the process of pulling a clawful of cookies from the cookie jar. I wondered how much of my conversation with Nathaniel he had listened to. "You could just use the money that Azazel gave you to fix them. Nathaniel was here on Azazel's business."

"I don't want to touch that money," I said.

Beezle shrugged and shoved chocolate mint cookies in his beak. "I don't see why not."

"You know why not. It's just a rope by any other name, and I will not be bound to Azazel's plans any more than I already am."

"You won't be bound to his plans by using that money to fix your doors."

"No, but I'll feel indebted to him. And he wants that. He wants me to accept what he offers so that he can manipulate me into place like a chess piece. Lucifer does, too."

"Yeah, well. REALLY good luck trying to extricate yourself from those two. They've been tying mortals in knots for ages untold."

"Yes," I said, rubbing my head. I felt a headache coming on. This day, like so many others of late, had exhausted me. I remembered with fondness a time when the most difficult part of my day was filling out forms in triplicate.

I wandered listlessly into the living room, thinking I could convince J.B. or Gabriel to spring for a pizza for all of us.

"So," J.B. said as soon as I entered the room. "I hear you've got a big mission coming up."

I glared at Gabriel. "What did you blab about that for?"

Gabriel looked surprised. "Because he is Amarantha's son."

"The court that I'm supposed to be going to."

"Yup," J.B. said.

"That's your mom."

"Yup."

"Do you think you might have mentioned sooner that you were a faerie prince?" I said, annoyed.

"Do you think you might have mentioned sooner that you were the daughter of one of the fallen?" he retorted.

"I didn't find out until . . . Never mind," I said, not wanting to get into a childish argument. "Whatever. So, you've got an in with the court. You can help me negotiate with your mom, then."

J.B. shrugged. "Maybe. Maybe not. I'm her heir, but she doesn't really like me."

"Wonderful," I said. "Is there any useful information you can give me?"

"Yeah. Don't go. The last emissary from the fallen was beheaded in front of the entire court."

I stared at J.B., who looked completely serious.

"You're not fucking with me, are you?"

He shook his head. "The negotiator sent by Lucifer so offended the queen—"

"Your mom," I interjected.

"—that she had him summarily executed in front of the assembled court. Upon review of the diplomat's actions, Lucifer agreed that offense had been given and that the queen's actions were correct. However, it's taken almost a year for the queen to accept the possibility of a new negotiation. My mother tends to hold grudges."

"I see. I'm so looking forward to this trip. Hey, wait a second," I said. "When I told you that I was Azazel's daughter, you acted like you knew nothing of the fallen."

"Which is exactly what I was supposed to do until I had discussed the matter with the queen."

"Why?"

Gabriel glanced at J.B. "Faerie courts are very tightly protected, even among supernatural beings. Faeries tend to be quite . . ."

". . . rigid and unreasonable," J.B. finished. "There is a certain order, a certain procedure, for everything."

"So that's why you're such an anal stick in the mud when you're at work," I said.

He ignored my jibe and continued. "Contact with other species is strictly limited by clearance from the queen. I came into contact with you at work, but that did not mean that I could reveal to you what I knew about the fallen without telling you my own identity."

"If your identity is such a big secret, then how come Nathaniel knew who you were?"

"I met with him during the negotiations to accept a new diplomat to the court. I am frequently my mother's errand boy," he said, and he didn't look too happy about it.

I supposed I could be annoyed at J.B. for not telling me about this sooner, but really, what right had I to the information? We were friends, but nothing more than that. Still, it made me look at him in a new light. He seemed just as constrained by his heritage as I.

"Are there any useful tips you can give me at all? I'd really like to make it through my first diplomatic mission without getting my head chopped off."

J.B. blew out a breath. "There are so many rules, so many potential breaches of etiquette . . ."

"I am not entirely sure that Madeline is the best person for this mission," Gabriel said.

"Sarcasm is not productive," I said.

"I am not being sarcastic. Lucifer surely has members of his own court that understand the complex rules of the faeries and could negotiate them better than you."

"That means there's some special reason why he wants me there," I said.

"What reason could that be?" J.B. asked.

"I don't know yet," I said grimly. "But I will find out, sooner or later."

"Let's hope that in the meantime you manage to keep your head," J.B. said.

Literally and figuratively, I thought. My temper always ran close to the surface. And when my emotions were high it became difficult for me to think clearly. For some reason, my magic seemed to feed off this and encourage it. A quick temper and unstable emotions—not to mention almost total lack of knowledge about the species in question— were not the best combination for a delicate diplomatic mission.

Lucifer was obviously up to something—besides yanking my chain, that is. He had some plan that I couldn't see yet. And while I was trying to figure out that plan, I had to make sure I didn't take an early trip to the Door.

J.B. seemed recovered enough to head home and rest, so Gabriel and I helped him into a cab and sent him on his way. As J.B.'s cab pulled away in the light of the rising sun, I remembered that I had another pickup—an early one.

"No rest for the weary," I said, sighing.

Gabriel glanced at me. "Or the wicked."

"Hey, I'm supposed to be one of the good guys," I said, a little offended.

"Try to remember that when you are about Lucifer's business."

I felt myself growing angry. "Do you think I chose this?"

"I know that you did not," he said patiently. "But Lord Lucifer has a way of making choices seem . . . gray."

I wanted to tell Gabriel that one of the reasons I was forced to do Lucifer's business in the first place was to keep him breathing, but I didn't. I knew enough about Gabriel to know that he wouldn't want me to do anything for his sake. And anyway, it was my choice, even if it sometimes seemed like my options had been taken away from the moment I had discovered I was Azazel's daughter.

"I think I can hold my own against Lucifer," I said. "I am aware of his reputation."

"Do not make any assumptions where Lord Lucifer is concerned," Gabriel warned. "He has forgotten more about human nature than you will ever know."

"That's the second time today I've been told that," I said. "Don't you have any faith in me?"

"I have plenty of faith in you, Madeline," Gabriel said. "I just know Lord Lucifer better than you do. He has been playing chess for centuries, and he knows how to win. And who to sacrifice."

I felt myself grow cold. Somehow, I hadn't considered that Lucifer might be sending me to the faerie court to get rid of me.

"I thought that I would be more valuable to him, being the last direct descendant of his union with Evangeline."

Gabriel stared broodingly after J.B.'s taxi. "I'm not sure that family ties are that meaningful to Lord Lucifer. I am his grandson, after all, and I only barely managed to escape the knife at my birth."

"But he was furious with me for killing Ramuell," I said

thoughtfully. "I think maybe his family is more important than you think. I don't think he would have let the Grigori kill you no matter what. I bet he just wanted to see how things would play out, and who would speak out against his grandson. I'm sure he's holding it against any Grigori that did so."

"I suppose it is possible," Gabriel said, still staring off into the middle distance somewhere.

"Hey," I said, taking his hand. I felt the familiar hum of electricity that always sparked between us at the slightest touch. "It doesn't matter what Lucifer wants or doesn't want. I want you, son of Ramuell or not."

His hand gripped mine tighter but he still did not turn his head in my direction. "Son of Ramuell is what I will always be, and that is why we cannot do this. I have told you over and over and you will not listen."

I pressed closer to him, made him look at me. His eyes were tormented.

"And I have told you over and over," I said, my face very close to his, "that I do not care what the rules say."

He gave me what I wanted, pressed his mouth against mine for an instant, and then pulled away. His face was full of need and regret.

"It is madness, Madeline, and I cannot do it. I will not be responsible for your death."

There wasn't a lot I could say to that. I watched him walk away from me, the way he seemed to over and over.

4

MY HAND HOVERED INSIDE THE BAKERY CASE. I WAITED a second or two, trying to decide which doughnut was the right one. The two doughnuts that remained were filled with some kind of cream and both had chocolate icing on top. I grabbed the one on the right.

"That's not the right kind," Beezle muttered from the inside pocket of my coat. "That kind has cream inside, not custard."

"How can you tell from there?" I hissed, putting the doughnut back.

"I can smell it," he replied, his voice muffled by the wool.

"Well, I can't tell the difference so you get what you get," I said.

"Just get the other one," he said. His short gray horns and yellow cat eyes peeked out from underneath the lapel of my black winter coat.

A harried-looking woman with two small boys in her grocery cart pushed past us to get at the baguettes.

"Look, Mommy, there's a rat in her pocket!" one of the boys shouted, pointing at me. Several other people shopping in the section turned to look.

The mother widened her eyes at Beezle, grabbed her French bread and tossed it in the cart. She "shushed" the little boy while moving away from me as quickly as possible.

I gave the other shoppers a sickly smile. "It's my guinea pig," I said, moving away from the doughnut case and shoving Beezle back in my pocket with my free hand.

I'd completed my pickup and decided to hit the Jewel for a few necessities. Of course, Beezle had a different notion of necessity than I did.

"What about my doughnut?" he whined.

"You only get doughnuts if you can stay incognito," I hissed.

"How is this not incognito? Am I inside your pocket or what?" Beezle grumped. "It's hot in here."

"Yesterday you were cold; now you're hot," I said.

"People are staring," Gabriel murmured next to me.

"Oh, gee, why would they stare?" I said. "It's not like I'm having an argument with my coat lapel or anything."

The corners of his mouth turned up as I tossed a couple of oranges in my basket.

"That is fruit, not a doughnut," Beezle muttered. "We don't want any of that healthy stuff."

"You know, it would probably be good for you to replace some junk food with fruit. You're getting pretty heavy in there."

"Gargoyles are supposed to be round," Beezle said, and his tone was clearly miffed. "We are home guardians."

"And I ask it again: then why the hell don't you stay at home instead of making me drag your heavy ass all over town?"

I was spared Beezle's reply because just then I felt a wave of energy pulse through the store, the same power signature that I'd experienced only a few hours earlier. Gabriel looked alarmed, and I felt Beezle stiffen inside my coat.

"The wolf-killer," I said, dropping my basket on the floor and heading toward the front of the store. "Where?"

Gabriel fell into stride beside me. "Nearby, but not too close. The pulse didn't disable you this time?"

I felt the familiar flicker of magic under the surface of my skin. "No. Either I'm getting used to it or ground zero was far enough away not to harm me."

"Or you were protected by the building," Beezle said, his voice still muffled. "Earlier you were in the sky, completely exposed."

I looked at Gabriel questioningly and he shrugged. "Your magic is a constant mystery to me, Madeline. It seems to operate differently from others I have known."

We exited the store and stood for a moment in the morning sunshine, trying to get our bearings. It was hard to find the source of a supernatural event that had already happened, but Gabriel had some skill in tracking power signatures. He looked around, then pointed north.

"This way," he said.

We crossed the parking lot and then Wellington. This was a busy area, with two strip malls right next to one another and a large development of condos across the street behind them.

"I can't believe this creature would do anything in an area this crowded," I said. "Someone must have seen it."

Gabriel didn't look at me. He was intent on following the traces of magic to their source. "Perhaps. Perhaps not. People tend to see only what they want to see."

The two strip malls faced Ashland, which was a main thoroughfare that ran north-south through the city. A few blocks away was the Lincoln-Belmont-Ashland intersection, a major convergence of traffic and businesses. In between were blocks stuffed with homes and apartments.

Gabriel tracked through the post office parking lot, across another street, and into an alley. We wandered for a few moments, turning left and right, and then I could smell it before I saw it. Burnt cinnamon, and raw meat.

"He's killed someone again," I breathed.

We turned to the right at a T-junction and saw the bloody remains scattered all over the alley, just like the last time.

I heard bone crunch underneath my boot and looked down to see the shredded remains of a furred paw.

"Another wolf," I said, breathing shallowly. "Why is Samiel killing wolves?"

"How do we know it's Samiel?" Beezle said, sticking his head out of my pocket.

"Are you trying to say that Ramuell might have another unknown child running around somewhere?" I said, as I picked my way carefully among the remains. Gabriel moved silently through the alley, checking as I did for a clue, something that would tell me why these wolves were being targeted.

"It might have nothing to do with Ramuell at all," Beezle said insistently. "Someone could just be trying to point you in that direction."

"But why?" I said. "How could anyone know that I would just happen to be nearby two murder sites? Don't you think it's a little presumptuous to assume this is all for my benefit? And besides, if this death was planned, a part of the natural order, where is the Agent? Where is the soul?"

"Could have come and gone already," Beezle said stubbornly.

"Well, it's easily checked," I said, thinking I would do just that the next time I was in the office. I crouched down by what appeared to be a pair of jeans covered in blood. There were some pieces of broken plastic embedded in the cloth that might have been bits of a credit card or ID. "But the wolf murders still don't make sense. I thought the werewolf packs in this area mostly stayed out of the city."

"And so we do, unless business requires us to be here," growled a voice from nearby. "Whoever has done this will pay, Agent."

I looked up to the T-junction and came to my feet. Gabriel was at my side in an instant, his hand on my shoulder.

Two of the biggest men I had ever seen stood just past the T-junction. They both easily cleared six feet, and the one on the right wore only a plain white T-shirt and denim vest over jeans, despite the chill. Everywhere I looked muscles bulged through the cloth. His pale face was covered in a red beard liberally streaked with white, and eerie blue gray eyes watched me with suspicion. I could see the faint traces of long scars that puckered the skin underneath his beard.

The man next to him was African American, just as tall and strong looking, but with a slight paunch and a much friendlier look. He looked like the sort whose natural expression was a smile, despite the obvious grief in his eyes as he surveyed the remains in the alley. He wore square-framed metal glasses and also had a heavy salt-and-pepper beard above a blue StarCraft T-shirt and jeans.

There was a third man with them, hovering a step

behind, not quite as muscular or burly as the other two. He was built more along the lines of a long-distance runner. He also seemed younger. He didn't wear a beard like the other wolves and his dark hair was free of gray. But it was his eyes that attracted my attention. They were silvery blue and burning with anger when he looked at me. I wondered what I'd done to this man to make him hate me so, for it was obvious that he did.

The one on the right spoke, and it was his voice that I had heard before.

"What business have you here, Agent? I see no soul to collect."

The other wolves approached us he spoke. I could see them sniffing the air, their nostrils flaring.

"You smell like Lucifer," said the wolf in the StarCraft shirt. He had a deep, booming bass voice. The third wolf still hadn't said anything.

I raised my eyebrow at him. "That doesn't sound like a compliment."

"It's not," he said, frowning. "And you were at the other place, where Dagan died."

The redhead narrowed his eyes at me. "What were you doing there, Agent? If I discover that you had some hand in Dagan's death . . ."

He stepped forward, and before Gabriel could do anything I conjured up a ball of nightfire. I gave the wolf a steely-eyed look.

"Don't make dangerous assumptions, wolf."

He eyed the ball of nightfire with a sneer.

"Don't presume that a werewolf can be intimidated by an Agent's power."

I felt my magic rise to the surface, and I knew that my eyes had changed, become a field of stars on a canvas of black.

"What makes you think I am nothing but an Agent?" I replied.

The other wolves growled, and the air crackled with energy. I could see bones shifting beneath his skin, and for a moment I looked into a snarling canid face, and then he was a man again.

"Madeline," Gabriel said, and there was a warning in his voice.

"Let me handle this," I said quietly. I knew a little bit about wolves, having encountered them a time or two as an Agent. They respected strength, and they wouldn't respect me or allow me to help them if I cowered behind Gabriel.

"You don't want to make an enemy of me, Agent," the redheaded wolf said.

"And I don't want to be your enemy," I said steadily, still balancing the ball of nightfire on my hand.

The smaller wolf that stood just behind the other two looked like he might be calculating how best to leap over his compatriots and rip my throat out. I hoped that Gabriel would jump right into the fray if that happened, because the big guy seemed like he was working up a good head of steam.

I prayed that no one was looking out their back windows into the alley, because if they were, they were going to get a show. The last thing I wanted was a video of me throwing nightfire at a couple of werewolves to end up on YouTube.

The second werewolf cocked his head at me, doglike and curious. "What is it that you want, then?"

"To find out why these wolves are being killed," I said.

He gave me an appraising look. Then he laid a restraining hand on the first. "Jude, enough."

I realized that I'd gotten their relationship wrong. The redhead was beneath the second wolf in the social order. I'd assumed that since he had taken the lead and acted aggressively that Jude was more alpha than the other. Those kinds of prejudices could get me killed. The alpha was always the most dangerous wolf in the pack.

He studied me, sniffing the air as he did so. "You're telling the truth."

"Of course I am," I said, a little miffed.

"But the truth can hide evil intentions," the third wolf said, and I hadn't been wrong about the venom in his eyes. It was in his voice, too. "And you do smell like Lucifer."

"I'm his great-granddaughter," I said. This wasn't information that I usually liked to share with strangers, but they would continue to be suspicious of me without it.

The alpha raised an eyebrow at me. "Then you can only be Madeline Black, daughter of Azazel."

I mirrored his expression. "You seem to have the better of me."

He narrowed his eyes for a moment, then seemed to come to some decision. "I am Tyrone Jackson Wade, alpha of the Red Pack of Wisconsin. You may call me Wade. *En Taro Adun!*"

I was a little disconcerted by his odd greeting, but before I had a chance to ask him about it, he stuck a huge hand out for me to shake. I realized I was still holding the ball of nightfire. I quickly doused the fire and put my small hand in his.

Wade gripped it, and pulled me closer, his eyes searching. "Are you a true friend of the wolves?"

Something about the way he asked it made me think that this wasn't a casual question, and I'd been around the magical block enough to know that some words were binding. I saw Gabriel shake his head, ever so slightly, out of the corner of my eye.

I took a deep breath. I had no quarrel with the wolves.

Lord knew that Lucifer and Azazel probably had some master plan involving werewolves as they seemed to have for every race, but I wasn't privy to all of their machinations. And I wasn't about to let Gabriel dictate whom I could and could not befriend.

"I am," I said, and then I shivered a little as magic shimmered in the air.

Wade grinned, showing a row of white, white teeth. "Then the wolves are also friends to you, Madeline Black. Tell me, what interest have you in finding the wolf-killer?"

I hesitated. Wade seemed to know a lot about fallen angels, but I was certain that Samiel's existence was a closely kept secret. And as Beezle had pointed out, there was no way to be sure that Samiel was killing them. Even if I was a true friend of the wolves, there was no need to make them privy to every shadow in Lucifer's kingdom.

"I came upon the first murder site by accident after feeling a magical pulse in the area," I said. I felt it was important to tell the truth as much as possible, since Wade seemed to be able to tell when a person lied. "We followed the trail of magic to the body. I was . . . horrified by the murder, and wanted to find out who killed the wolf, but we were unable to discover anything concrete."

"And today?"

"I was grocery shopping at Jewel when the same thing happened."

Wade sniffed the air. I felt tense. I needed the wolf to believe me. I already had enough magical conflicts in my life without arousing the ire of a pack of werewolves.

"Very well," he said, and some of the tension drained out of me. "We would appreciate the assistance of Lucifer's granddaughter in this matter."

"How is it that you know Lucifer?" I said curiously.

"I have met with him before, as a representative of my people in negotiations with the fallen," he said, and grinned. "The werewolves of Wisconsin are sworn enemies of Lucifer. I am sure your great-grandfather will be happy to hear that you have reestablished good relations."

I felt the blood drain from my face. I'd just stepped in it, again.

"Never, ever play chess with a master, Maddy," Beezle mumbled from inside his coat.

Forget chess. I was still playing Candy Land.

A little while later we parted ways from my new pals, having discovered nothing especially helpful. Wade, Jude and the third wolf, whose name was James, had sniffed around the site and said that angels had been present, but also something that they could not identify. I'd carefully avoided Gabriel's glance when the men said that. There was no need to share any information about Ramuell or Samiel with the pack.

The three wolves gathered up the remains of their pack member in a black plastic garbage bag. I valiantly suppressed the urge to boot as they scooped completely unidentifiable bits of flesh and bone into the sack. Jude glared sullenly at Gabriel and myself all the while, like he would follow his alpha's orders but was reserving judgment on us. James tracked me constantly with his disconcerting gaze. Obviously the other two wolves did not share Wade's assessment of me.

As they departed, Wade called out, "We will meet again, Madeline Black. *En Taro Adun!*"

"What the hell does that mean?" I muttered to Beezle.

"Do I look like some kind of dog translator?" he snapped. He was feeling cranky because he'd missed out on doughnuts—I'd dropped the basket at Jewel—and he'd also missed his usual morning nap in his perch.

"No," I said vaguely. "It doesn't sound like werewolf language."

"And what would you know about werewolf language?" Beezle grumbled.

I ignored his jibe. Normally I enjoyed sparring with Beezle when he was grumpy, but I was worried about what Lucifer would say when he discovered that I had reestablished relations with the werewolves of Wisconsin. Would he be pleased? Would he be furious? I couldn't care less if he was pleased, since getting Lucifer's approval was not high on my to-do list. But I really didn't want him angry with me. I had enough problems without being in the soup with the Prince of Darkness.

Gabriel had tried to warn me. I'd seen the little shake of the head, telling me not to do what I was about to do. But I had done it anyway. I understood that I didn't know my way around this world yet, and that I needed guidance. But it chafed when I felt like someone else was always making my decisions for me.

"Of course, decisions don't seem to be my best thing," I muttered to myself.

"What? What?" Beezle shouted. "You'll have to speak up. I'm an old gargoyle and I'm feeling faint from lack of nourishment."

"Oh, for crying out loud," I said, rolling my eyes. "Gabriel, let's take this baby home so that he can eat."

"Popcorn!" Beezle said.

"We'll see," I replied, moving toward the place where the alley emptied back out to Nelson. I glanced behind me to see if Gabriel was following, and then stopped.

Gabriel wasn't there.

5

"GABRIEL?" I CALLED. MAYBE HE WAS JUST OUT OF sight, around the corner of the T-junction. "Gabriel, where are you?"

"That fool probably got distracted by something and wandered away. The two of you seem to think you're investigators," Beezle muttered. "He might have found a clue."

"He would have told me," I said, jogging down the length of the alley to the junction and looking down. He wasn't there.

"Maybe he followed the wolves," Beezle said. His tone said that he was supremely unconcerned with Gabriel's whereabouts.

"He would have told me," I repeated, starting to get angry. "He wouldn't leave me, not for a second. He's still feeling guilty for not being there when Antares attacked. And Azazel would have Gabriel's head on a shelf if he walked away from me and I got hurt."

I ran down the alley in the other direction, toward Belmont, calling Gabriel's name. How could he just disappear into thin air like that? We'd been standing there with the wolves. If something had happened to Gabriel, one of us should have noticed.

"He wouldn't leave me," I repeated, as I ran around the block, my head twisting this way and that. "Gabriel! Gabriel!"

I must have appeared a little unhinged because a couple of new moms walking their babies in the winter sunshine pulled their $800 Bugaboos out of my way as I went by.

"You're frightening the natives," Beezle said.

I stopped and glared down at him as I came back to the mouth of the alley. "Maybe they're scared of the ugly little monster hanging out of my coat."

Beezle looked affronted. "I'll have you know I am a very handsome gargoyle."

"According to wh—" I said, and then the breath was ripped from my body as something very large and very heavy crashed into me.

My attacker and I careened into the alley and smashed into a metal Dumpster. I cried out in pain as a protruding piece of metal pierced through my coat and into my back. Hot blood ran down my spine as I was punched in the face again and again by a heavy fist and I was nearly blinded by pain.

I didn't have time to think, to try to fight back. I had an impression of boundless strength holding me down, muscled bare arms, hot breath panting, mad green eyes . . . and wings. White feathers fell all around us as I tried to push with my hands, kick with my legs, to snap with my teeth, anything. But I could barely see; I could hardly breathe. Blood ran into my eyes as I was hit again and again without pause.

I tried to think, tried to focus my magic. I had to get this monster off me before he beat me to death. My magic flickered, then roared to life inside me. I didn't have the time or the inclination to focus it into something like nightfire. I just let the magic move through me, up and out, and have its own way.

There was an explosion of power that sucked the breath from my lungs, a burst of dazzling light like a firework. My attacker was thrown from my body and away like a cannonball, shooting through the air and out of sight. I tried to get a good look at him, but my eyes were stinging from blood and sweat and I had no clearer impression than before.

I felt like someone had pounded me all over with a meat mallet, especially my face. I shifted my jaw and to my horror felt a couple of loosened teeth on the left side in the place where I had been hit repeatedly.

I rolled to my side, slowly and painfully, and coughed out some blood.

"Fantastic," I muttered. "This day just can't get any better."

Then I remembered that Beezle had been in my pocket. I patted the place where I normally carried him and felt nothing but wool and lint. "Oh, gods. Beezle."

I forced myself to sit up, although as soon as I did I felt dizzy. I tried to focus my bleary eyes around the alley and found that I could see if I held my sleeve to my bleeding forehead. There was a small gray lump a few feet away from me, and it looked like Beezle, and it looked like he was breathing.

"Coming to getcha, Beezle," I said, and flopped over to my belly. Walking was absolutely out of the question, so I crawled to him, pulling my legs (which did not want to bend or function in any normal way) behind me like a slug as I heaved forward on my elbows.

My face throbbed with pain as I reached Beezle. I

picked him up with one hand and lightly patted his cheek with the other.

"Beezle, come on, wake up," I said, breathing shallowly. Everything hurt, and I didn't know if my attacker would come back. I had to get up, get away, but vigorous movement did not appear to be in my future.

Beezle's eyelids fluttered, and he sat up in my palm, rubbing a bump on his head with one clawed hand.

"What happened? Did we get hit by a tractor trailer?"

I kissed his forehead. Beezle might be a grumpy pain in the ass most of the time, but he was my grumpy pain in the ass and I loved him.

"I think," I said, remembering mad green eyes, "that we got hit by Samiel."

"Samiel, huh?" Beezle said, and he seemed to focus on my face for the first time. "When you make an enemy, Maddy, you do it right. You look like you got pounded in the face by a hammer."

I shuddered to think what I looked like. I never thought I was a great beauty to begin with, but I was sure that getting punched numerous times wasn't going to do anything for my dating life. I pillowed my head on my arms and breathed through my mouth. It hurt to move. It hurt to think.

I must have zoned out for a few minutes, because the next thing I knew, Beezle was hovering just above my ear.

"Earth to Maddy! You are lying in the middle of an alley and could get run over at any second," he shouted.

I rolled over to my back and whimpered. "I'm not sure getting run over at this point would make that much of a difference."

"Why haven't any cars come through this alley, though?" Beezle said thoughtfully. "We've been here for a while, finding werewolf bits and getting beaten up."

I knew that Beezle was saying something important, but I couldn't quite grasp the thread of it. It was weird that nobody had entered the alley, or seen me getting the crap pounded out of me. It was weird that nobody had seen the werewolf getting killed, or called the police when a bunch of suspicious characters had hung around the murder scene for a while in the middle of a weekday morning. This was important. I had to remember it so I could think about it later, when I didn't have forty anvils pressing on my brain.

But first I had to get up and get some medical help. Medical help. I felt around inside my jacket and found my cell phone, still intact. I kept a couple of throwaway cells on hand at home since I often lost phones when flying through the air, and I'd just lost one.

I managed to keep it together long enough to call an Agent Medi-Team and give them my location, and then I closed my eyes and went to sleep for a while.

My last thought before I conked out was of Gabriel. Where was he?

I woke to darkness in my own bed, and there was a figure snoozing in a kitchen chair beside me. For a moment my heart leapt, thinking it was Gabriel. Then a shaft of light came through the window and I saw that it was J.B.

I cautiously raised myself from the bed. I still felt sore all over. There was a large patch of gauze taped to my back where I had been cut by the Dumpster. A matching bandage was wrapped around my forehead. My fingers touched my cheek and I moaned in pain. My whole face felt puffy and tender, and the rest of me didn't feel that great, either.

J.B. shifted in the chair and opened his eyes blearily. "I'm not sure you should be sitting up in your condition. In fact, I'm not sure that you should be breathing in your condition."

I slumped back against the headboard, exhausted from

the effort of sitting up and taking stock of my injuries. "Is it that bad?"

He rubbed his eyes. "You've looked better. Like when you've come to work without showering and still wearing your house slippers."

I raised an eyebrow at him. "You are the soul of tact, J.B. No wonder all the women want you. What are you doing here, anyway?"

"Your gratitude is overwhelming, Black. I arrived with the Medi-Team and brought you home when they were done repairing you."

"This is repaired?" I said.

"Well, they can't do that magical healing thing that your guard dog can, but they patched you up as best they could. Where is your shadow, anyway?" J.B. asked.

I felt a pang in my chest when I thought of Gabriel. "He's gone."

"Gone, how?"

I explained about the body we'd found in the alley, and how Gabriel had disappeared without a trace a few moments before I'd been attacked.

"Do you think his disappearance had something to do with your attack?" J.B. asked.

"I suppose it could," I said slowly. "But it could also have something to do with the wolves. Or with Antares, for that matter."

And when I thought about it, Antares seemed a likely suspect. He had a whole host of magical tricks up his sleeve, and disappearing acts were a favorite of his.

"Are you saying that Antares is working with Samiel?" J.B. asked. "Isn't it enough that you've got enemies coming out of every nook and cranny? Do they have to be conspiring against you as well?"

"I didn't say they were conspiring. Antares may have taken Gabriel as part of some nefarious plot of his own and Samiel just happened to show up a few minutes later."

"I don't know," J.B. said doubtfully. "Coincidence sounds even more unlikely than conspiracy."

"Well, you figure it out, then. I'm feeling a little worn-out right now."

"No need to get cranky with me, Black."

"Oh, gee, why would I feel cranky, Bennett? It wouldn't have anything to do with the fact that I nearly got beaten to death a few hours ago, would it?"

J.B. sobered. "Yes, but why?"

"Why did I get beaten up? Because I killed Samiel's father, that's why."

"No, why did he beat you? Why didn't he use magic?"

Once J.B. said it, I realized that it was completely bizarre that Samiel had used such a mortal method of exacting vengeance. Ramuell had possessed magical abilities that had been terrifying in their execution, and Ariell had been an angelic being loaded with magic. Why had Samiel used his fists instead of his powers?

"Maybe he's powerless, like Antares," I said, although this seemed improbable. Completely powerless beings like my half brother were rare, especially when they came from such a notable magical lineage. Ramuell was Lucifer's son, after all. It seemed unlikely that Samiel would have no magic.

J.B. shook his head. "It would definitely stretch credibility to think that not only are two of your enemies conspiring against you, but both of them have no magic of their own."

"I'm not sure you are actually helping here," I said crossly.

He held his hands up. "I'm just saying."

"And I'm just saying that you're not adding anything very much useful to the conversation."

He looked as if he wanted to say something else, then paused and sighed. The moonlight reflected off the silver frames of his glasses. "No matter how hard I try, we always revert to our old patterns."

That made me pause as well. "You're right. I don't know why we always end up bickering like this."

"Because you have unfulfilled sexual tension?" said Beezle, flapping into the room and landing on my lap. He put his hands on his hips—or what stood in for hips, anyway. It was hard to tell that he had hips anymore since his belly had started expanding.

"Hmm," he said, eyeing my face critically. "It looks like you'll probably regain use of your jaw sometime by Christmas."

"I'm so glad that everyone is being positive and supportive in my time of need," I said, glaring at my gargoyle.

"Hey, we aim to please," Beezle said. "Now, what are we going to do about Gabriel?"

I shifted my hands restlessly on my lap. "I don't know. I don't even have a clue where to begin."

"Well, if you are interested in my two cents . . ."

"Which usually turns into two dollars," I said.

Beezle pressed his lips together briefly in annoyance and then continued on as if I hadn't spoken. "I think you should start with the wolves. They were there on the scene and they had the motivation to take him."

"What motivation would the wolves have? Their alpha had just stated that Maddy was a friend to them and vice versa. If they were truly interested in reestablishing relations with Lucifer, then why would they jeopardize that by taking Gabriel?" J.B. said reasonably.

"That's assuming the wolves actually do want to treat with Lucifer, which I doubt," Beezle said darkly. "Wolves generally keep a minimum of contact with the fallen."

"Why are you always so suspicious of everyone's motivations?" I said. "Maybe the wolves want to make peace and decided to take advantage of the opportunity."

" 'Take advantage' is the operative phrase here," Beezle said. "You have to stop trusting everything you hear or the fallen will eat you alive."

"And so will the faeries," J.B. said. "Believe me, there's nothing my mother loves more than turning naïveté to her advantage."

I felt myself getting annoyed. Sure, I needed some help with interpersonal relationships, and I was astonishingly sheltered for a woman nearing her thirty-third birthday, but I wasn't dumb. I didn't appreciate being treated as such.

"I think I can handle myself," I said.

They both said nothing but pointedly stared at my face, the very visible site of most of my injuries.

"What, you think that just because Samiel train-wrecked me that I can't maneuver among the intricacies of the courts?"

Their silence told me everything I needed to know about their opinion. I took a deep breath and told myself it would not be good to kill them.

"Let's not talk about me," I said, pinning a bright smile on my face, and then I winced. It hurt to smile, or to do anything more strenuous than talk through my teeth. "Let's try to figure out what happened to Gabriel."

"Why don't you just tell Azazel? He probably has the resources to find him," J.B. said reasonably.

I shook my head. "He might have the resources to find Gabriel, but when he found him Azazel would kill him."

J.B. looked astonished. "For being kidnapped?"

"He failed in his duty to protect me, and his life already hangs by a thread," I said grimly. "If Azazel finds out that Gabriel is gone, then that thread will be cut. We have to make sure that my father doesn't know about this."

I closed my eyes, overwhelmed by the amount of problems that had presented themselves in the last day. First I'd been assigned this crap job in the faerie court and Nathaniel was supposed to accompany me. Then Antares and Samiel showed up with the sole goal of grinding me into small pieces. I'd totally stepped in the middle of some long-standing problem between Lucifer and the wolves, and Gabriel had disappeared. And it was imperative, absolutely imperative, that Azazel not find out about that. I didn't know if I could live with myself if anything happened to Gabriel because of me.

"How are you going to make sure Azazel doesn't find out?" Beezle said. "The kidnappers may have contacted him already to ransom Gabriel. And even if they haven't, Azazel is in almost daily contact with him, checking up on you."

"How do you know that?" I said.

"I have ears," Beezle said. "He does live downstairs, you know, and sometimes his windows are open."

It annoyed me that Azazel was following my life that closely and that Gabriel hadn't said anything to me about it. But that was to be expected. I'd told myself time and again that Gabriel's first loyalty was to my father, not to me.

I had to stop thinking of Gabriel as a potential lover—a thing that was likely never going to happen—and instead as a potential enemy. Maybe J.B. and Beezle were right. Maybe I was naïve. I had to let go of these girlish dreams and focus on what was really happening around me.

And right now, Gabriel's loyalty was not the issue. His

life was. I had to find him before I could worry about anything else.

"And what are you going to do when it's time to go to the faerie court?" J.B. asked. "Wasn't Gabriel supposed to accompany you? How are you going to find him in two days without Azazel finding out, and in your condition?"

J.B. was right. Even without a clue to go on, I was hampered by my injuries. I needed some angelic healing, and there was only one place that I could get it. But it was risky—extremely risky. If there was anybody's loyalty in doubt, it was his. But maybe I could make it work. Maybe we could broker a deal that would make both of us happy.

"I think," I said, breathing deep and hoping that I wasn't making yet another horrible mistake, "that I need to give my fiancé a call."

"This is incredibly stupid," Beezle said the next morning as he primped the pillows around my head on the couch. J.B. had left after breakfast, promising to call later and check up on me. He'd also arranged to find substitutes for all of my pickups for the week, which definitely made my life easier. I had enough things on my plate without worrying about lost souls.

"Your opinion has been duly noted," I said dryly. "About eight hundred times over."

"You don't want Azazel to find out about Gabriel, but you've called the one angel who is likely to run straight to him and report? Did Samiel beat all of your brains out of you?"

"I've got to find some way to heal or else I'm not going to be able to find Gabriel, or negotiate with the faeries, or anything else," I said patiently. "Nathaniel is the only angel I can ask."

"But you can't trust him," Beezle said. "He only wants

to marry you because you're Azazel's daughter. He's not really a fiancé."

"Actually, I think it's more that I'm Lucifer's grand-daughter." I shook my head. "But maybe I need to start treating him as an actual betrothed."

Beezle's mouth dropped open. "Are you telling me that you are giving in to Azazel's will and accepting the marriage?"

It rankled when Beezle put it like that. "No. I most certainly am not. But maybe if I treat Nathaniel decently, he will do the same."

Beezle rolled his eyes. "Remember what I was saying earlier about naïveté?"

"I have to try, Beezle," I said. "And stop fussing with the pillows. I'm fine."

"Fine," Beezle said darkly. "Don't say I didn't warn you."

He flapped to the front window without another word and disappeared out to his perch.

I rested my head back against the pillows and closed my eyes. Beezle was wrong. I wasn't naïve. I knew exactly the risk that I took in asking for Nathaniel's help. I also knew that I would never find Gabriel in this condition, and that I couldn't afford to wait weeks to heal.

I must have fallen asleep for a while. When I opened my eyes, Nathaniel was kneeling beside me, his hand holding mine. There was an expression on his face that I couldn't define. I realized that my blood was burning hot, and I touched my face. The swelling was gone, the pain disappeared. He had healed me while I slept.

I rubbed my eyes and sat up, feeling remarkably hale and whole. My tongue touched the place where my teeth had been loosened by Samiel's punches and found them solidly implanted in the gum. Thank goodness. I didn't want to spend the rest of my life looking like a hockey player or a hillbilly.

"Thank you," I said, and I said it without begrudging Nathaniel his existence, the way that I usually did. I didn't know how I would have survived for this long in the angelic world without healing. The injuries that I had incurred from Ramuell alone would have killed me or crippled me for life if it had not been for Gabriel's abilities.

"Such a fragile thing," Nathaniel said softly, and it was like he could hear my thoughts. "That little strain of mortality. Small things hurt you so."

He rubbed my fingers gently as he talked. I fought the urge to pull away, the feeling that I was somehow being disloyal to Gabriel by letting Nathaniel touch me. I needed him on my side, and it wouldn't do to get his hackles up by acting like he had an infectious disease.

Nathaniel turned my hand over in his, touching the places where my hands were rough or dry from work. "The hands of a servant, not a princess."

This time I did pull my hand away, insulted. "I'm not the kind to fool around with manicures. And I don't have servants to do my dishwashing and bathroom scrubbing."

He folded his hand in his lap. "But you do not have to. You could live with Azazel in his palace. You could give up this life."

"And give up who I am, too," I replied fiercely. "I am not a toy for Azazel to play with."

Nathaniel raised an eyebrow at me. "Is that what you believe? That your father treats you like a toy?"

"I don't believe that my wishes are paramount in his view," I replied, trying to calm down.

This was not how I had intended to go on with him. I'd wanted to present my case simply, to get him to agree to a trade. If I lost my temper or made him lose his, then we would never get anywhere. Luckily, he had already healed me without my asking, so that was one thing I would not have to bargain over.

"Let's not talk about Azazel," I said firmly, swinging my legs to the floor and forcing him to back away. I indicated that we should both sit in the dining room. I wanted to be eye level with him, not lying prone with Nathaniel looming over me.

"No, let us discuss your injuries," he said as he followed me into the next room and sat down across from me. "How is it that you are so horribly injured and the thrall has not healed you?"

"His name is Gabriel," I said through my teeth. "Why do you always talk about him as if he were slime on your shoes?"

"And why do you always behave as though he were something more than that?" Nathaniel said. His voice was calm and reasonable but his blue eyes lit with anger. "You treat him as if he were your equal."

"Because he is. And you don't exactly endear yourself to me by acting like a prince."

Nathaniel smoothed the cuffs of his perfectly white shirt with his perfectly buffed fingernails before responding. He wore a trim-cut black suit, no tie, and his blond hair looked like it had been professionally coiffed. His glittering white wings were tucked neatly behind him, not a feather out of place. The overall effect was one of golden beauty, but that beauty was cold. And his natty dressing habits only made me feel worse about my lack thereof, particularly when I was wearing nothing but a white T-shirt and gray sweatpants. I could not see myself waking up next to this flawless creature every morning for the rest of my life. Did anything rumple him?

"But I will be a prince, when I marry you," he said calmly, looking into my eyes. "I do not think that you should be criticizing my behavior but looking at your own. You hardly behave in a way that is appropriate to your position."

My fingers curled into fists and I could feel my nails pressing into my palms. My magic rose up, hot and angry, and I could tell when Nathaniel sensed it. The atmosphere of the room changed. He sat up a little straighter, looked a little more wary.

I concentrated on controlling myself. *I will not blast my fiancé, I will not blast my fiancé, I will not blast my fiancé* . . .

"I hardly think that my behavior is any of your business," I said, when I felt like I could talk again.

"Of course it is. Your behavior reflects poorly on me in the eyes of the court."

I had to get this conversation back around to finding Gabriel or I was going to kill Nathaniel before he ever had a chance to help me.

I closed my eyes, took a deep breath, forced my magic down and said, "Enough already. I asked you to come here because I need your help."

He quirked one golden eyebrow at me in question.

"You ask why Gabriel hasn't healed me. Gabriel has gone missing, and I need your help to find him."

"And why should I assist you in finding the thr . . . Gabriel?" he amended, but Nathaniel said the name like it was poison dripping from his tongue. "His life is already forfeit since he has abandoned his duties to you."

"He didn't abandon me," I said angrily. "He wouldn't. There is nobody in this world who is more devoted to my safety than Gabriel."

Nathaniel spread his hands wide. "Then where is he?"

"I don't know," I said, my shoulders slumping. "I think he was taken."

I explained about the various incidents in the alley, from our following of the power signature to my attack. I left out the part where I had accidentally reestablished relations with the wolves, and pretended I didn't suspect the identity of my attacker. There was no need for Nathaniel to know anything about Samiel right now.

He looked thoughtful, something I hadn't expected. "How could the . . . Gabriel have been taken without your knowledge when he stood in such close proximity to you?"

"Exactly," I said. "Beezle thinks it was the wolves."

"Beezle?" Nathaniel asked.

"My gargoyle," I said, waving my hands impatiently. "Do you have any way of tracking power signatures? Gabriel could do it, but he didn't show me how."

Nathaniel's nostrils flared and his lips thinned. "That ability appears to be the exclusive provenance of the children of Lucifer."

I could tell that it cost him something to say this. He wasn't the type who enjoyed admitting weakness. But while it was an interesting fact for me to tuck away for later (being a child of Lucifer, I theoretically could manifest this power at some point) it didn't really help me with my immediate problem—finding Gabriel.

"Besides," Nathaniel pointed out, "if the kidnappers did not use magic, there would be no power signature to trace."

"You think something swooped in from the sky and plucked Gabriel out of the alley without me noticing?" I said doubtfully.

"You have not yet visited the courts of other fallen," Nathaniel said grimly. "There are horrors there that you cannot comprehend."

Horrors, I thought. Once more, a warning of horrors that I could not understand. I felt a prickling on the back of my neck. Nathaniel's eyes widened at something behind me.

"Down!" he shouted, his hand reaching across the table as something smashed into the dining room window and slammed into me.

6

THE BREATH LEFT MY LUNGS IN A TREMENDOUS whoosh as something heavy crashed through the chair, into my back and then fell to the floor with a thunk. The apartment immediately started to fill with smoke. I shook my head, trying to collect my thoughts.

A firm hand grasped my elbow and yanked me up from the table.

"You have to get out of here," Nathaniel said, dragging me away from the table and the source of the smoke.

I shook my arm free from his grip. "No, I have to get whatever is smoking out of my apartment before the whole building blows up."

I couldn't see his expression but I'm sure he disapproved. I dropped to the floor, coughing and covering my mouth and nose with the neckline of my T-shirt.

A hissing noise emanated from just behind the chair I

had been sitting in. I squirmed along the floor on my belly, feeling in front of me for the source of the noise. My vision was only slightly clearer than it had been when I stood up. The smoke was quickly filling the room. I could make out the vague shapes of furniture but nothing more.

"Open a window!" I shouted to Nathaniel. He didn't respond, so I assumed he had found the nearest exit and gotten out of the building. Which is what a smart person would do. But still, not very gallant of him, considering he was engaged to me.

The hissing noise grew closer. I belly-crawled toward it, fingers of my right hand outstretched, the other hand holding my T-shirt over my nose.

There was a blast of cold air on my back and the smoke seemed to lift temporarily. I glanced behind me and could make out the shape of Nathaniel in the front living room, opening all of the windows. Huh. So he hadn't left me, after all.

I turned back toward my goal, and saw that the smoke had dissipated just enough for me to see the source of the noise. I crawled toward it and carefully examined it without picking it up. It looked like a medium-sized black bowling ball with gray smoke emitting from a hole in the top. There did not seem to be any kind of incendiary device on it but I wasn't about to take chances.

I came to a crouch and then carefully lifted the ball into my arms. It is an unfortunate testament to my total lack of fitness that despite my newfound angelic strength, the ball felt heavy to me.

I began to move through the house toward the back door. A moment later, Nathaniel was next to me, taking the ball from my arms.

"Where?" he asked shortly.

"Down the back stairs, to the yard and into my rain barrel," I said. I was embarrassed that I was huffing and puffing, but it wasn't all laziness. The smoke had obviously affected my puny mortal lungs more than it had affected his.

Nathaniel disappeared into the kitchen, streaming a trail of smoke behind him. I walked through the apartment opening windows and letting the frigid November air inside. Luckily, we hadn't gotten into a period of deep frost so there should just be a thin coating of ice on the rain barrel. I just hoped that whatever was inside that ball would respond the way smoking things usually responded to water—by getting doused. If the item was magical, there was a good chance that it might blow up when it hit the water. You could never tell.

When I'd finished opening the windows and the air had cleared somewhat, I went back to the dining area to survey the damage. The ball had completely smashed the window—no surprise there—and rendered the back rest of the chair I had been sitting in to splinters. I put my right foot down and felt something sting. I stood on the opposite foot and looked at the oozing wound on the sole.

"Well, of course there would be glass on the floor, dummy," I muttered to myself. I hopped down the hall to the bathroom and sat down on the toilet. There was a small sliver of glass embedded in the ball of my foot. "I don't know how I survived this long on my own wits."

I reached down to the cabinet underneath the sink, pulled out my nail kit and collected the tweezers. Then I grabbed some rubbing alcohol and cotton balls, all while twisting around on the seat with my right leg crossed over my left and my right foot dripping blood on the blue tile floor. I dumped a little alcohol on the cotton ball and swabbed the tip of the tweezers. Then I added some more alcohol to the other side of the ball and applied it to the wound. I hissed as the alcohol stung.

You would think that after nearly being killed by a nephilim I would have more tolerance for pain.

I bent over my foot and began the business of trying to extract the glass. I grabbed at the sliver with the tweezers and pulled, whimpering as it came free from my flesh.

"I am so not cut out for a life of adventure," I muttered, wiping more alcohol on the wound to make sure it wouldn't get infected. My eyes teared up as the alcohol did its thing.

I finished bandaging the cut and stood up to test my weight on it. I would survive. A moment later, Nathaniel slammed the remains of my back door. I stepped gingerly into the hallway to meet him and had to cover my mouth with my hand to stifle my laughter.

Well, I'd wondered if he'd ever get rumpled, and now he was. He looked kind of like that cartoon coyote after the dynamite has gone off in his face.

Nathaniel's blond hair stuck straight up in front and had been blackened by soot. So had his face and his formerly pristine shirt front. As I sniggered into my palm, a couple of blackened feathers fell from his wings onto the floor.

He raised an eyebrow at me and I schooled my face into seriousness. Then he wordlessly thrust a piece of paper into my hand.

I turned the paper over and saw that there was a message printed on one side. It said, simply, *"I KNOW WHERE THEY ARE KEEPING HIM."*

I flipped the paper again, looking for further information. There was nothing but the message.

"Well, that's really freaking helpful," I muttered. "You'd think they'd have included a map or some flying directions or something."

I looked back up at Nathaniel, who appeared to be gathering the shredded remains of his dignity around him. "What happened when you brought the ball outside?"

"It exploded before I managed to get it to the rain barrel," he said tightly.

"I didn't hear anything," I said.

"It was a small explosion, and I held the bomb close to my chest so as not to cause property damage." He looked as though he were regretting this act of charity.

"Well, thanks," I said, touched by his thoughtfulness, however grudgingly given. "And where was the message?"

"Inside the bomb."

I rubbed my fingers on the paper. It felt like perfectly normal standard bond notepaper. "How did the paper survive the explosion?"

"Perhaps there was an enchantment on the paper," Nathaniel replied, shrugging.

He didn't seem as interested in the mechanics of the message-delivery system as he was in straightening and dusting the cuffs of his shirt. I, however, was very interested. An enchantment could only mean that the message had been delivered by a magical practitioner. Okay, fine. Most things that go bump in the night have some kind of magic. Not all of them had the kind of fine abilities that would allow them to keep a piece of paper safe inside an incendiary device.

So that narrowed things down to a witch or a faerie. Probably. There was still a lot I didn't know about the world, as I was discovering every day. But it seemed that your average Agent, demon, angel, vampire, et cetera, probably couldn't have performed this kind of spell.

Of course, one had to wonder why a witch or a faerie would send this completely unhelpful message inside a bomb. Was the being that sent the message a friend? And if so, was it their idea of a funny joke to send it in a way that could have potentially blown off a limb?

"Did you get a look at whoever lobbed this thing through the window?" I asked Nathaniel. "You were facing that way."

He shook his head. "I only saw the bomb approaching."

I frowned. "So whoever threw it could have flown past very quickly. Or thrown it from a great distance. Or possibly levitated it from the ground. Oh, hell. Maybe Beezle saw something."

"Where is your gargoyle?" Nathaniel asked. "Surely this commotion should have attracted his attention."

"You're right," I said, turning and hurrying toward the front of the house. Beezle kept his nest underneath the picture window, on the front porch roof. This ensured that he would not only see anything approaching the front door, but also that he could spy on anything that was going on in the street. Beezle is about as nosy as it gets.

"Beezle!" I shouted, throwing up the screen and leaning out until I could see his nest. The nest was a jumble of sticks, leaves, newspapers and the small piece of plaid wool that Beezle used to wrap around his ears. "Beezle!"

He didn't answer, and I felt a little ping of anxiety. Whoever had lobbed that bomb at my window could have hurt Beezle. I leaned farther, my hips balancing precariously over the sill, my skin coming out in goose bumps in the chilly November air.

"Beezle!" I shouted. "You answer me right now!"

Some neighbors walking by on the street below looked up in puzzlement and then quickly looked away when they saw me hanging out of the window and shouting like a lunatic.

"Beezle!" I repeated, my eyes searching every tree branch

and every roof shingle in sight. No sign of my cranky gargoyle.

"Beezle!" I said again, and I felt myself overbalancing,
my nose tilting toward the roof, and I had a second to wonder if I should call up my wings, when I felt Nathaniel's
arm around my waist, pulling me back inside.

I slapped at his arm, struggled against him. "Let me go!
I have to find Beezle!"

"You are not going to find him by shouting out the window. If the gargoyle were there, he would have come at
your call," he said reasonably.

I breathed long through my nose in counts of three, and
then did the same for the exhalation. I had to calm down.
I had to think. Beezle was missing. He could be lying hurt
somewhere out of sight.

"Okay," I said, tapping at Nathaniel's arm and looking
up at his stony face. He was probably pissed that my behavior had reflected poorly on him—again. "Okay. You can let
me go now."

"You are not going to do anything foolish?" he asked.

"Define 'foolish,'" I said, and then shook my head at his
look of puzzlement. "Sarcasm. Obviously not something
you are familiar with. Anyway, no, I am not going to hang
out the window and shout like the neighborhood crazy
anymore."

He released me slowly, like he wasn't sure whether or
not to believe me. I turned around and faced him.

"I need to find Beezle," I said. I tried not to think of how
alone I felt at this moment, with no Beezle and no Gabriel,
because if I thought of that, I might cry, and the last thing
I wanted to do was cry in front of Nathaniel. "You can head
back to court."

He raised his eyebrow, an expression that I realized I

would probably be seeing often since it obviously meant he was annoyed with me. "So I am dismissed, then, Princess?"

I felt the blood rise in my cheeks. "Sorry. I didn't mean to be so high-handed. But I have to go now. Beezle might be hurt."

"I will assist you," he said.

I tried not to look completely astonished but I am sure that I failed. Nathaniel was never going to be my first choice for company, but it would be good to have an extra pair of hands around in case whatever threw the bomb was still hanging around. "Um, okay. Let me grab some sneakers and a coat and we can head outside. Can you, um, hide yourself when your wings are out?"

"One of the first things an angel learns is how to disguise his nature from mortals," he said in an arrogant tone.

That snide remark made me feel more at ease. I could go back to disliking him and not have to struggle with the weird feeling of being grateful to him for healing me, and for helping me find Beezle.

I ran to my room, pulled on an overcoat and my black Converse sneakers, and then met Nathaniel by the front door. He was fixing his hair in the small mirror that hung over the table where I dumped my keys and spare cell phones.

"Come on, beautiful," I said, rolling my eyes. "We have work to do."

I let my wings out and winked out of sight. Nathaniel disappeared a moment later. Mortal eyes would not be able to see us, but to anything supernatural we would appear see-through, like ghosts.

We headed out the front window and started from the roof of the house down. I carefully checked every eave, every nook, every windowsill. I practically pinned my nose to the ground and crawled all around the front and back yards, calling down rabbit holes and peeking behind bushes. Nothing.

No sign of Beezle. No evidence of my attacker. Nothing.

I tried not to panic. Losing Gabriel was one thing. I had confusing, lusty feelings for him and didn't want to see him hurt. But losing Beezle was devastating. I had never, never been without him in my whole life. He had always been there—irascible, sometimes annoying, but he was mine. He'd been like a parent to me when I was young and alone and afraid, and a constant companion as I grew older. I could not even contemplate a future without Beezle in it.

I stood in the gangway between my house and my neighbor's and leaned against the outer wall of the building, rough brick against my check, my eyes closed. My stomach churned with anxiety. What had happened to Beezle? Who had taken him, and why? Were they hurting him? Would they ransom him?

I felt the brush of soft linen against my cheeks, and looked up to see Nathaniel standing before me. He tucked his handkerchief back in his pocket as I straightened.

"I wasn't crying," I said.

"Of course not," he replied.

"I'm just worried about Beezle," I said.

"Naturally," he said.

There was an awkward silence, and it only highlighted the nearly impossible distance between us. Gabriel would have comforted me, and I would have welcomed his comfort. Nathaniel didn't know what to do, and I didn't know if I wanted him to do anything anyway. And thinking these kinds of thoughts only made me feel more alone.

"I have arranged for repairmen to come and fix your back door and your broken window," Nathaniel said.

The door. I'd mostly forgotten about it. Gabriel and I

had pushed it back into the frame as best we could and nailed it shut yesterday morning—was it only yesterday? Why did it seem like ever since I'd discovered I was Azazel's daughter I had more and more days like this, days that seemed like lifetimes?

"How did you get out the back door when the bomb was in your hand? The door was nailed shut."

Nathaniel shrugged. "I tore it out of the frame."

"Ah. But it's going to be fixed now."

"Yes. I would not wish to take any chances with your safety."

He said this in a way that made me look up at him, and I thought maybe there was something like tenderness in his eyes. Maybe he meant it. Maybe he really did want to keep me safe. That didn't mean he cared about the person I really was as opposed to the person he wanted me to be. And no amount of tenderness would help me find Beezle or Gabriel. But I needed him to cooperate with me, in at least one way.

"Listen, Nathaniel," I said. "I really do need you to keep this business about Gabriel from Azazel."

He frowned. "Are you asking me to lie to my lord? Because the penalty for such a thing would be fierce."

As much I didn't like Nathaniel, I didn't want him to be punished. And I was sure that he wouldn't be willing to sacrifice his beautiful face for my sake. I'd have to play this carefully.

"I think that you would agree that something strange is going on here," I said.

He said nothing, only nodded so that I would continue.

"But I would not want to alarm my father unnecessarily."

"Surely in an event like this you would wish him to know? What if you incurred bodily injury while the . . . Gabriel was missing?"

"Well, in point of fact, I already have incurred bodily injury. And I'm okay, thanks to you."

"And what of the regular reports that Gabriel makes to Lord Azazel?"

I had thought this one through already, and I was pretty sure that I'd come up with a good solution. "What if you made the reports for a few days?"

Nathaniel's frown deepened. "You want me to deceive my lord by pretending to be the thrall?"

I decided to overlook his reference to Gabriel's status just this once. This part was going to be tricky.

"No, I just want you to call in to Azazel every day like Gabriel would. But I want you to edit your reports. Edit," I repeated, when he looked like he was going to argue. "Not lie. Just fail to mention certain information. And if Azazel is hearing from you, then surely he won't mind if he doesn't hear from Gabriel."

"But in order for me to report to Lord Azazel I would have to have daily knowledge of your activities and where-abouts," he said.

I nodded. This was the part that I really did not like. "Right, well, you would stay here for a few days."

He looked speculatively at me. "With you?"

"In Gabriel's apartment," I corrected.

Nathaniel appeared to be thinking it over. I found myself unconsciously holding my breath as I waited for his decision. There was no reason for him to help me, and really no reason for him to potentially put himself on the line for Gabriel. But this was the best solution I could come up with. My hope was that Azazel would be so happy that I wanted Nathaniel to stay nearby that he wouldn't wonder about Gabriel's radio silence.

What are the chances of that? I thought to myself, and

the voice in my head sounded a lot like Beezle's. Azazel didn't strike me as stupid, but I was hoping that I could pull a little sleight of hand. Maybe he wouldn't notice what I was doing with my left hand because he was watching my right.

"Your plan is not without risk," Nathaniel said.

I nodded.

"There is a strong possibility that my lord is already aware that the thrall is missing."

Beezle had mentioned this, too, but as I'd thought about it, I realized that it couldn't be true. "Wouldn't he have contacted me, then, to make other arrangements for my safety?"

Nathaniel thought about it for a moment. "Possibly. Or possibly he is waiting to see if you will call him. It is impossible to divine my lord's intentions."

Great. "Well, everyone keeps telling me that I am more important than anything else to Azazel, so I am going to assume that he would have gotten me another bodyguard by now. Surely my welfare would rank above any mind games."

"That would seem to be so, but it is not safe to assume anything with the Grigori."

I was getting impatient with Nathaniel's dithering. "Look, can we just assume that Azazel doesn't know, and that if we pull this off, he will never know? Are you going to help me out or what?"

Nathaniel looked disapproving. "You are asking me to make a decision that may materially affect my well-being, for the sake of a half-blood thrall and a woman who does not particularly like me."

I gritted my teeth. "It's just possible that I might like you more if you help me out."

"Very well. I will assist you. But I will want something in exchange from you at a later date."

I looked at him warily. "Something? Could you be more specific about that something?"

"I do not know what I might need at a later date, so how can I specify?"

I thought about it for a minute. "All right. It's a deal. But I have the right of refusal, same as you did. If I decide that the task isn't something I want to do, then you can ask me for something else later."

"It is a bargain, then," he said, and he held out his hand to me.

I wondered if this was how Faust felt when Mephistopheles held out the contract. I was getting something I wanted, but what price would I pay?

I put my hand in his to shake, and instead he raised it to his lips. When his mouth touched my skin, I felt a little thrill of attraction deep in my belly, and again felt like I was somehow betraying Gabriel. I tried to pull away and his fingers tightened on mine.

"Remember, Madeline Black, you are my betrothed. There will come a day when you belong to me, body and soul. And then there will be no bargaining between us. I will be master in my own house."

I narrowed my eyes at him and yanked my hand away, any hint of attraction doused by his attitude. "And you wonder why I dislike you."

"You have lived too long on your own," he said. "You will see my way is better, in time."

I clenched my fists at my sides. I would not lose control and blast him back into the Old Testament, which was apparently where he had collected his notions of marriage. I needed him to help me now. If he wanted to believe that one day I would be a meek little miss who would cleave unto him without a word of protest, then he could have his fantasies. There was no guarantee that the marriage would actually happen in any case.

"Whatever. Listen, do you think that we could go back to the alley where Gabriel went missing and see if you can pick up anything that I didn't? It seems like everything bad started there."

"And what of your gargoyle? Do you believe that he was taken by the same creature that took your bodyguard?"

"I have to believe it," I said. "Otherwise I have too many enemies to contemplate."

"I am sure that you do," he said. "Your lineage practically dictates that it is so."

"Way to comfort, Nathaniel."

We took off for the alley near the grocery store, the site of the second wolf murder, Gabriel's kidnapping and my strange attack from Samiel. I felt like I might be pressing my luck going back there, since an assortment of bad things had already occurred at that site. But it was the only lead that I had.

Late-afternoon traffic backed up on Ashland below us as we flew. The sky had a gray, wet look and the air was cold and damp. I shivered under my coat. I was still wearing only a T-shirt and sweatpants, since I hadn't really thought about dressing for the weather when I ran outside to search for Beezle. I couldn't be seen when my wings were out, but I could still experience the elements. I was invisible, not indestructible. Nathaniel, on the other hand, seemed perfectly comfortable despite his lack of gloves and hat. Yet another reason to dislike him.

We landed in the alley just as it began to drizzle.

"Wonderful," I muttered. "It's so great when the weather obscures every possible piece of evidence."

"The type of evidence that we are searching for would not be visible to the human eye in any case," Nathaniel said. "You are looking for traces of magic, or the evidence of a supernatural being."

"I thought you said that you couldn't trace a power signature?"

Nathaniel huffed, clearly annoyed that I had reminded him of a defect. "I cannot trace a power signature, but I can sense the evidence of magic. You would be able to as well, if only you would concentrate."

"So you mean that I don't need you at all?" I said, but softly enough that he couldn't hear. I hoped.

As Nathaniel walked around the area, I tried to focus my magic, to send out my will and look for the traces of other kinds of power. This wasn't like casting nightfire, or even the kind of magic that I used as an Agent to break a soul's binding to its body. It wasn't about destruction. It was a softer kind of magic, and soft magic was not my specialty. I could barely control my powers at the best of times. Fine control was pretty much beyond me.

Still, I made the effort, because I was heartsick at the loss of Beezle and because I wasn't about to let Gabriel disappear before I'd had the chance to figure things out between us. And, well, because I couldn't let Nathaniel be right about me. I wanted to be more than a blunt instrument of force, too emotional to control my powers.

I imagined my magic like a veil, a shimmering wash of power that blew away from me with a whisper. The veil extended away from me, gently settling on everything around me. I held that invisible net in place, searching all along the fabric of my magic with my mind, and was surprised to find that I could "see" Nathaniel's power inside the net. It was like finding a trace of heat on an infrared camera, I could clearly sense the pulse of magic and identify its source. Interestingly, Nathaniel seemed to feel my power settle over him.

"What is it that you are doing, Madeline?" he said. He was about five feet away from me.

I ignored his question. Emboldened, I pushed the veil away farther, trying to extend it over the breadth of the alley and then down to the T-junction where we had met the wolves. I felt beads of sweat break out on my forehead as it became much more difficult to keep the veil as light as a feather.

"Madeline, what are you . . ." Nathaniel repeated, but I held my hand up for him to stop.

I'd found something, and it was not at all what I'd expected to find. I'd expected to find traces of magical castings or, if we were lucky, an object that would somehow lead us back to Gabriel's kidnappers. Anything but this.

"Nathaniel," I said, breathing heavily from exertion. "There's a portal in this alley, not ten feet from where we are standing now."

7

"A PORTAL?" HE SAID BLANKLY. "THERE CAN'T BE A portal there. We would be able to see it."

I could see it very clearly, a swirling vortex of magical power trapped inside my invisible net. As I watched, the portal began to pull at the edges of my net, trying to suck the magic inside. Since I had no idea where the portal went or who had put it there I thought not getting yanked in was a good idea. I quickly doused my will and the net disappeared.

"That was close," I said.

"What was?" Nathaniel asked.

I explained about the vortex pulling on the edges of my power, and he shook his head. "This can't be."

"It can. I'm telling you that it's there."

"A portal does not operate in this fashion, like a secret door for club members only. It is always visible and always under the control of a master."

I thought back to something Gabriel had said to me once. "I thought that some portals were naturally occurring."

"Yes, but not in this plane. There has never been a naturally occurring portal on this mortal earth."

"So it's got to be under the control of a master, then," I said thoughtfully.

Nathaniel's lips pressed together. "Yes, it would have to be, if it were there."

"Oh, it's there," I said, getting annoyed. "In fact, this probably explains how Gabriel disappeared. He stepped into the portal by accident."

"In that case, why has he not returned?"

I glared at him. "Apparently when they were handing out the good stuff they forgot to give you brains to put inside that pretty head. How the hell should I know why he hasn't returned? I'm assuming it's because there is either something insanely dangerous on the other side of that portal or it's a trap. Or both."

Nathaniel gave me a long-suffering look. "Madeline, why would someone place an invisible portal—not that I believe in such a thing—in a throughway for mortals? Anyone could accidentally enter it."

I grabbed his wrist and dragged him in the direction of the portal. I was totally fed up with his if-I-can't-see-it-I-don't-believe-it attitude. Why the hell would I make up a portal in the middle of the alley? To get attention from him? I think not.

The portal was several feet inside the alley and close to the T-junction. As I approached the corner, I slowed, trying to remember exactly where it was located. Nathaniel smirked at me as I cast out my net again, this time trying to see two planes at once—the physical and the magical. It was less of a struggle to cast the spell a second time, but much more difficult to see the physical location of the portal behind the magical net. The real world was an indistinct blur, a vague procession of washed color and shadow.

I inched closer to the location of the portal, shuffling my feet in tiny steps. Nathaniel huffed out an impatient snort behind me. I would have made a smart remark at him but I needed all of my energy focused on the magical net. The portal had started trying to pull me in again, and I was exerting a great deal of effort keeping my power outside of the vortex.

When I was only about a foot and a half from the portal, I pointed my finger right at it and then dropped the net.

"There. It's right there. If you concentrate, you can see it," I said, throwing his words back at him.

Nathaniel looked at me doubtfully, but he got a steady, focused look, like he was searching for evidence of magic. I could see when he found the portal. His eyebrows shot up to his hairline.

"Extraordinary," he murmured.

"Don't apologize for doubting me or anything," I muttered.

He moved closer to the portal, and it seemed that he was feeling the edges of the vortex with his fingers. I wondered that the portal didn't try to suck his magic inside, the way it did for me. Maybe he was more powerful than I, or maybe he just had more control.

"What are you doing?" I asked curiously as he continued to move around the portal, seeming to examine it from every angle.

"Trying to determine the master of the portal," he said, not looking at me.

"Do portals have makers' marks?"

"Of a kind," Nathaniel said. "Most beings will leave a

kind of magical signature or a sense of their power behind with their casting. But the most extraordinary fact about this portal . . ."

"Other than the fact that it's invisible and it's not supposed to be there?"

". . . is that it seems to have been wiped clean of all traces of power."

I frowned. "But wouldn't the process of clearing the power signature leave a trace, too? I mean, it had to have been wiped clean by magical means."

"It would seem logical, but no. There are certain kinds of spells that can ensure that no trace is left behind."

"So we've got a portal with no way of knowing who cast it or why. That's just swell," I muttered.

I drifted closer to the portal, frustrated by everything that had happened and the total lack of leads.

". . . ddy!"

A voice, so small and faint I thought that I had imagined it.

"Maddy!"

I stood still, listening. It sounded tinny, like it was coming through a pipe, very far away.

"Maddy!"

"Beezle?" I called. "Beezle, is that you?"

No response.

"Madeline?" Nathaniel said, watching me with concern. "What is it?"

"Quiet," I said. "I heard Beezle."

"I heard nothing."

"Maddy!"

There, again, first quiet, then louder. Where was it coming from? Was Beezle trapped somewhere in the alley? Was he hurt?

"MADDY! GET AWAY!"

There. It was clear as a bell that time. I stared at the portal.

"He's there," I said to Nathaniel.

"Who is where?" he said.

"Beezle is inside the portal," I said, and I was sure of it, and I knew that it didn't matter how it had to be done but I was going to get him out.

I walked toward the portal, as if in a trance, my heart beating faster and faster until it was galloping in my chest. Beezle. I could get Beezle back.

"Madeline!" Nathaniel cried, and he sounded alarmed.

I felt his arm around my wrist, grasping, trying to yank me away.

I pulled my arm free, turned back to the portal. Nathaniel grabbed me again, twisted me around to face him.

"Madeline, what in the name of all the gods are you doing? You cannot just walk into that portal without knowing what may be on the other side." He shook me a little, his hands on my shoulders. "How am I to face Lord Azazel if you mindlessly walk into harm?"

I pushed his hands from my shoulders, furious. "Don't treat me like a child. You're only worried about how Azazel would punish you if I'm killed. Beezle is in there, and I need to find him."

Nathaniel's eyes were cold and furious. "Think, Madeline. The gargoyle may not be inside the portal. It may be a trap that is laid for you."

"I don't care," I said. "If he's there, I have to help him."

"You fool," he spat. "There are terrible things that you cannot even conceive of in other worlds. And contrary to what you may think, I would not relish the thought of your being devoured by a monster, or captured by a demon tribe."

My face reddened. Even if I didn't like Nathaniel, I should probably stop acting like he had no feelings. "All right, maybe you don't want me to get hurt. But if there is a possibility, even the tiniest possibility, that Beezle is in there, I have to go to him. I have to get him back."

He's the only creature in the world who has ever really loved me, I thought.

Nathaniel looked at me a moment. "You are going to go in there no matter what I say, are you not?"

I nodded.

"Then take my hand," he said.

There was a time when I would have done anything not to touch him. But for this, for Beezle, I put my hand in his willingly.

We stepped into the portal, and as we did I heard Beezle's voice screaming, "Maddy! NO! IT'S A TRAP!"

Well, of course, I thought. I knew it was a trap. I just didn't care.

And then the portal was pulling us through, and I was in agony. I had traveled via portal a few times to my father's house, and it was like having my head squeezed between two cinder blocks. Nathaniel gripped my hand tighter. My eyes felt like they were going to burst from my skull, and a moment later, we were out.

I felt Nathaniel's grip on my fingers loosen and I landed flat on my face in something soft and wet and foul smelling. I gagged and lifted my head, spitting out mud.

"Is there some reason why you can't follow the most basic of instructions? What don't you understand about, 'Maddy, no, stop, it's a trap'?"

I wiped mud from eyes, pushed myself back to my knees, and looked for the source of that very familiar and beloved voice.

Beezle was inside a tiny metal cage on a little grassy hillock about ten feet away from me. He didn't look much worse for the wear, but he scowled at me ferociously.

"Your gratitude is overwhelming," I said, picking myself up from the muck and looking around.

We seemed to have landed in a swamp. I stood ankle deep in rushes and lily pads, and enormous mossy trees dangled their branches over the water. The air was gray and misty and filled with a sulfurous odor. After a few moments my eyes began to water.

"And what did you bring him for?" Beezle said, jerking his thumb toward Nathaniel.

I looked in the direction that Beezle had pointed and realized that Nathaniel had flown out of the portal. He hung just above the water, angelic white wings outspread, not a speck of mud on him.

"I hate you," I said, and the bastard had the audacity to smirk.

I began to slog toward the shore and the little cage in which Beezle was trapped. Nathaniel fluttered ahead of me and landed next to Beezle's cage, examining it carefully.

"So where's the big reveal? How come you were so all fired up that I shouldn't come and get you?" I said.

Beezle sighed, closed his eyes for a moment, and pointed behind me. "Because of that."

As he said it, I became aware of fine earthquake tremors in the ground, and the water lapping against the backs of my legs. The scent of sulfur grew stronger, and Nathaniel stood up, eyes hard and watchful.

I huffed out a deep breath. "It's something huge, isn't it?"

Beezle nodded. "Yup."

There was a sound of several limbs splashing in the water. "Is it all squishy and tentacly?"

"Yup."

"I hate my life," I said, and as I turned I conjured a ball of nightfire and threw it.

I had a sense of something massive, an enormous two-story shadow that trembled and pulsed and oozed, and then the ball of nightfire hit it and it opened its enormous maw and howled in rage.

Its howl created a gale force wind that tossed me back several feet. I landed on the hillock beside Beezle's cage. He seemed nonplussed.

"I think that just made it madder," he said.

I pushed up to my elbows as the creature came forward, sniffing for me with a long, elephantine nose. It had several small eyes but the orbs were covered in a milky white film—the creature was blind. The nightfire did not seem to have damaged it in any way.

"Do you think you could manage to defeat this thing quickly so we can get home?" Beezle said. "I never did get my doughnut."

"Only you would think of doughnuts at a time like this." I came unsteadily to my feet and pushed out my wings. "Where's Nathaniel?"

"Got tossed that way when the monster started yelling," Beezle said, pointing behind him. "Not such a smarty-pants with those wings now, is he?"

There was no sign of the angel. Behind the hillock was a tangle of trees and darkness, surrounded by mist.

"How come your cage didn't get tossed, too?" I asked.

"It's attached to the ground. Um, maybe you want to direct your attention to the giant monster squishing toward us? It seems to have caught your scent."

"Yup, right on that," I said.

I tried to get a good look at the creature as I readied my

magic. The shifting clouds of mist made it difficult to get a clear view. There was zero sense in trying to overpower it—the creature was the size of a building and had about twenty tentacles with which to grab and crush me. I couldn't blind it, because the monster was already blind.

"Any idea what this thing's weakness is?" I asked Beezle.

He put a claw on his lower lip like he was thinking. "I'm not sure, but I think most monsters dislike fire."

"Fire. Right. I don't know how to make regular fire."

Beezle snorted. "Are you sure about that? You do have a heartstone now."

"What does that have to do with anything?"

"Umm, heartstone? Power of the sun inside you? Did you get denser while I was away?"

The monster squished closer. I tried not to gag at its scent. If I still had the abilities that I'd had when Evangeline possessed me, I'd be able to take down this creature without blinking.

I knew that I had a heartstone, but I didn't see how that would help me. I didn't know half of what I was capable of doing. If Gabriel were with me, he could help me. But Gabriel was gone, and Nathaniel had disappeared, and the only being around to help me was a snorting little gargoyle who seemed to think that I was acting dumb by not using a power that I didn't even know I had.

Beezle huffed. "Whatever you're going to do, I'd advise you to do it now."

"Better to try than to be eaten, I guess."

Lucky for me the monster moved at the pace of a slug. I gathered up my magic, and then I did something that I had only done once before. I thought about my heartstone, about the pulse of sunlight that burned in the core of me, and I drew on that power. As I did, I felt heat burn inside, a beam of sun that traveled through my blood and veins and muscles and penetrated the source of magic inside me.

My magic burst open like a flower blooming at its touch. I knew what to do, knew as easily as if the knowledge had always been inside me and was simply waiting to be awakened—as maybe it was.

The monster crept closer. Its tentacles lashed out, seeking me. It opened its horrible mouth, a mouth filled with rows of tiny serrated teeth that shifted back and forth like the blades of a power saw.

I held out my hand in front of me, pushed the power down my arm and through my fingers. An arrow of flame shot from the tips of my fingers into the creature's mouth and disappeared into its throat.

"Bull's-eye," I said, satisfied.

"Nothing appears to be happening," Beezle said.

"Wait for it," I replied.

The monster had stopped, and if a horrible, squishy, tentacly thing with a dozen blind eyes could look confused, then that was the look on its face. Its arms waved about listlessly.

"Still waiting," Beezle said.

I looked at him. "Have a little faith."

And just as I said that, the monster emitted an enormous sulfurous belch, and then burst into flames.

It screamed in rage and pain, and the smell of its burning flesh was horrible. A flaming tentacle lashed out, and I was forced to run backward toward the trees in order to avoid it.

"Oh, sure, just leave me here!" Beezle shouted after me.

"You're safe enough," I shouted back, but as I retreated a little ways into the cover of the trees, I wasn't sure about that. I was hoping that the cage would provide some protection should one of the monster's burning arms smash into it, but maybe the force of the tentacle would knock Beezle's cage off its mooring and into the swamp.

I turned back, trying to see if I could free Beezle from a distance. The thick, greasy smoke pouring off the now-dead monster made it impossible to see. I inhaled shallowly but I still coughed and choked as the smoke filled my lungs. A heavy, oily residue filled my mouth and nose.

"Why can't anything ever be easy?" I muttered.

I dropped to the ground and tried not to think about what I was crawling through. My fingers clawed in moss and mud, and I could feel my knees sinking in the muck as I pushed forward. Sweat and smoke stung my eyes and made them water.

"Beezle, shout out, would you?" I called. "I can't find you in this mess."

"To your right," a growly voice said in a long-suffering tone, and it was not three inches from my ear.

I turned my head to see Beezle watching me frog-crawl through the mud.

"That look really works for you," he said.

"Why is it that I wanted you back again?" I said.

I came to my knees, inspecting the cage. There didn't appear to be any kind of door or lock.

"How does this open?" I asked.

"Antares sealed it with one of his momma's spells," Beezle said.

"Antares took you?" I asked. "Did he throw the bomb through the window, too?"

"Yup," Beezle said. "He came up on the house under a cloak of invisibility and then manifested in front of me. Before I had a chance to warn you he had me magically bound and was tossing the bomb."

"Then he came back and took you to the portal in the alley," I finished. "Do you know if he was the one who put the portal there?"

"I don't think that he did," Beezle said thoughtfully. "It seemed like, from the many evil-villain mutterings that I could catch, he was using someone else's portal for his own device. He seemed to think he was being pretty clever."

"He usually does," I said. "But why would he send me that note when he clearly wants me to get blown up? What's the point?"

Beezle frowned inside the cage. "What note?"

"The one that said, 'I know where they are keeping him,'" I replied, running my hand around the seam of the cage. I could sense the spell that Antares had used to seal the cage shut. It was imperfect, and when I prodded it gently with my own power I could feel the spaces in the magic where it would give way. The only thing that I was afraid of was a booby trap. "Do you know if Antares wove anything dangerous in with this seal?"

"It didn't seem that way, unless there's a trap already inside the spell. He was in kind of a hurry."

"Trying to avoid the big monster that lives in the swamp, I bet. Well, there's nothing for it but to try."

"Says the woman who's probably not going to get splattered into a million pieces if you're wrong."

"Do you really think I'd let you get splattered into a million pieces?" I said, and tried to keep the uncertainty that I felt out of my voice. I wasn't going to let Beezle get blown up if I could help it.

I carefully found a weak spot in the spell and pushed my power through it as gently as I could. The top of the cage flew off with a surprising amount of force and clocked me in the chin.

Beezle snorted a laugh as he flew out of the cage.

I rubbed my chin. "And I say it again: why was it that I wanted you back?"

He shrugged as he hovered in front of me. "Because you'll never survive without me?"

I pushed wearily to my feet. "I may not survive with you at this rate. Now, what the hell happened to my useless fiancé?"

Beezle pointed into the woods. "Like I said, he went that way."

"I wonder if he got knocked out," I said as I squelched my way through the mud toward the trees. "Nathaniel!"

He didn't answer. The heavy mist and the shadows of moss cascading from the branches made everything look eerie. I kept thinking that I saw a person in the mist, but when I looked closer I would see that it was nothing but the twisted claw of a tree or a shifting bit of moss.

After a few minutes I stopped. Beezle, who fluttered just next to me, took the opportunity to rest on my shoulder.

"Why are we stopping in this creepy place?" he asked.

"Because I don't think I should go any farther and get myself hopelessly lost. As it is, I'm not sure that I could retrace my steps back to the swamp."

"Just follow your nose," Beezle said. "I'm sure the stink of burning monster carcass will lead the way."

"Nathaniel!" I called again.

We waited in the silence, and as we did I realized something. There was no noise in this place. No buzzing of insects, no chirping of birds, no slosh of toads as they leapt from lily pad to pond.

I stepped back, all of my self-preservation instincts coming to the fore. If you walk in the woods and you hear no noise, it's usually because something big and scary is on its way. "I'm not sure that we should stay here any longer."

"What about Nathaniel? Azazel won't like it if we leave him here."

"He's an angel. I think he can take care of himself," I said, and turned on my heel. And stopped.

Standing in front of me were three people aiming bows and arrows at us. They were all male, tall and thin and dark haired, and the tips of their ears were just slightly pointed. They were dressed like refugees from Peter's Lost Boys—animal-skin pants and leaves woven into shirts.

"Faeries," Beezle mumbled.

"Got that much figured out, thanks," I said.

The faerie in the middle, a middle-aged male, spoke. "Who are you that dares to breach the realm of the most glorious Queen Amarantha without permission?"

"Amarantha," I repeated in a monotone.

Of course. Antares had led me right into the kingdom of the woman I was supposed to negotiate with as Lucifer's ambassador. I really should give Antares more credit. Looks like my half brother knew what he was doing after all.

8

"DO YOU THINK YOU'LL GET YOUR HEAD CHOPPED OFF in front of the whole court, like Lucifer's last ambassador?" Beezle asked quietly.

"Can we not talk about separation of my extremities? It gives me the queasies," I said out of the corner of my mouth.

"Answer me, intruder, or you will be executed here and now for your crime," the middle faerie said, and he tightened his grip on the bowstring to show me he meant business.

I held my hands up. "Peace. I am Madeline Black, Agent and daughter of Azazel. I came here unwittingly through a portal looking for my gargoyle."

I jerked a thumb at Beezle, who was still perched on my shoulder. He gave the three faeries a little finger wave.

The faerie frowned. "Daughter of Azazel? You are Lucifer's ambassador?"

"Yes," I said warily. "And who are you?"

"I am called Ivin. If you are the ambassador, then why are you here instead of at court?"

"I didn't come here with the intention of negotiating today. Like I said, I didn't even realize this was Amarantha's kingdom. I was looking for Beezle and kind of ended up here by accident."

Ivin's face hardened. "Accident is no excuse. And besides, we are well versed in the duplicity of your kind. How am I to know that you did not come here with the intention of spying and gaining some advantage before the negotiations begin?"

"I give you my word as an Agent that I did not come here to spy," I said. I was starting to get a little nervous. I knew that whatever happened here would probably make my task as negotiator that much more difficult. But even more than that I was wondering whether I could outdraw three archers with my magic should they decide that the best option all around would be to shoot me then and there.

"The word of an Agent may be worth something, but the word of the fallen is less so," the faerie said.

"I've never fallen from anything," I said.

"Your father is one of the Grigori, and thus you are one of their kind."

Just then there was a rustle of leaves in the trees a few feet away, a thump, a cry. It sounded like there was a struggle going on just out of sight.

Ivin, who was obviously the leader, gave a hand signal to the faerie next to him and that man disappeared into the woods. A few minutes later he and a fourth faerie appeared holding Nathaniel between them. My fiancé's hands were tied in front of him with a thin cord that looked like vine, his hair was rumpled and filled with feathers and his pale blue eyes were icy with fury.

I sighed. I didn't know if Nathaniel had been trying to sneak around and save me from the faeries or sneak around to the portal and save himself, but either way it was apparent that reconnaissance was not one of his skills. I really, really, really missed Gabriel. In a survival situation, he was significantly more competent than Nathaniel.

"I found this angel attempting to slip past us," the fourth faerie said to the leader.

"Nathaniel ap Zerachiel?" Ivin said, and his voice was astonished. "You, who have always come to Amarantha in good faith?"

"Ap Zerachiel?" I muttered to Beezle. "What's that all about?"

"Zerachiel is his father," Beezle whispered back. "One of the archangels, before the Fall."

No wonder Azazel wanted me to marry Nathaniel. Azazel probably wanted me to make some kind of super-angelic baby. Between my mother's bloodline as a direct descendant of Lucifer, Azazel's own power and Nathaniel's heritage, we would probably make a monster. I shuddered involuntarily. Just one more reason to make sure this marriage never, ever happened.

Nathaniel bowed his head curtly. "And I continue to negotiate with your queen in good faith on behalf of my lord. I had been separated from Madeline and was attempting to reconnect with her."

"But what were you doing here in the first place?" Ivin asked.

"I believe Madeline told you we were here to rescue her gargoyle."

"So you lurked in the woods to spy on our conversation? If your conscience is clear, why not simply rejoin your party?"

Just as Nathaniel was about to open his mouth and

respond, yet another faerie came trotting out of the woods from the direction of the swamp. This one, too, was tall and thin and dark haired. They all pretty much looked the same, like they'd been cloned.

The new arrival stopped in front of Ivin and reported. "The leviathan has been killed. Burned to death."

Ivin's eyebrows winged up to the top of his forehead. He turned to look at me accusingly.

"It was going to eat me," I said. "What did you want me to do?"

His eyes hardened. "I should kill you here and now for this offense, but since you are Azazel's daughter I will take you to the queen for judgment. Bind her hands."

I wasn't willing to jeopardize all of our lives by doing something foolish, and I didn't think Lucifer would appreciate it if I spoiled his negotiations before they even began by knocking all these idiots out with my magic and running away. But there was no way in hell they were going to bind my hands. I would not be brought before Amarantha like a prisoner. I may have been covered in mud and dressed like a homeless person, but I was still Madeline Black. I had *some* pride.

One of the faeries came forward with the vine cord. I stepped back and conjured a ball of nightfire, holding it in front of me. The other four faeries made ready to fire their bows.

"You're not putting those on me," I said softly, and I felt Beezle on my shoulder twitch in surprise. I didn't look at him. If I did, I would doubt myself, because I was sure he had a what-in-the-four-hells-do-you-think-you're-doing look on his face.

"You are to be brought before the queen for judgment," Ivin shouted.

"And I'll go. But you will not treat me like a criminal," I responded. I wondered if I could make the nightfire scatter, like a shotgun blast. Of course, maybe now was not the time to be contemplating new and exciting ways of using my power.

"In my eyes you *are* a criminal. You have trespassed on Amarantha's kingdom with foul intentions," Ivin responded.

I drew my power around me like a cloak, pushed it up and out so that all in the clearing could feel it. I wanted them to know just who they were messing with. All the faeries took a little sidling step backward, not a lot, but just enough for me to know that they felt my magic, and it gave them pause.

"You will not bind my hands," I repeated. "You will treat me with all due respect accorded to an ambassador from Lucifer's kingdom."

"I could kill you before you wielded your spell," Ivin said, and he pulled his bowstring tighter.

I narrowed my eyes at him and pushed more power into the ball of nightfire that hovered above my palm. "Care to try me?"

I knew that I put Ivin in a bad position. He was the authority here, a representative of the queen, and it would be difficult for him to back down in front of his men. On the other hand, my sympathy only went so far. I had enough sense to know that I needed to come to the queen on my own terms or else she would never respect me.

Everyone in the clearing was still. Ivin and I had our eyes locked on each other, each waiting for the other to make a move. The faerie who had approached me with the vine cord seemed to be holding his breath. I wanted to look at Nathaniel, to see if he would help me if it came down to a firefight, but I didn't want to release Ivin from my gaze.

A minute passed, two. I readied my power. He wasn't going to give in. I wondered how many of them I could take down, and if I could avoid ending up looking like a pincushion filled with arrows.

Ivin abruptly dropped his bow. The other faeries paused a moment, as if in astonishment, and then dropped their weapons to their sides.

He gave me a little bow. "Welcome to the kingdom of Queen Amarantha, Ambassador Black. We would be happy to escort you to our queen."

I closed my hand and the ball of nightfire disappeared. I gave Ivin a regal nod. "Would you please unbind the hands of my escort?"

Ivin looked like it would pain him to do such a thing, but since he'd already embarked down this path he had to see it through. He nodded at one of the other faeries and the cord on Nathaniel's wrists was cut. Nathaniel gave the faerie who had fought him in the woods a look of venom. If I were that guy, I would avoid being caught alone at night by Nathaniel.

Nathaniel came to my side. The leader stepped around us, another faerie next to him, and indicated that we should follow them through the woods. We walked behind them in silence.

Even though Ivin had spoken the correct words and released Nathaniel, it still felt like we were prisoners. Two faeries walked in front of us, one behind and one on either side. Their weapons had been returned to their backs but all five faeries were tense and watchful. It was clear that they didn't trust us and that any false move on our part would result in someone getting bloody.

The terrain did not improve significantly as we moved away from the swamp. The woods became thicker, the trees larger. The way that we followed didn't really seem like a path. There was no tramped-down dirt to indicate the crossing of many feet. Gigantic roots jutted from the ground; large branches reached into our way. Small bushes with prickly thorns scratched and caught at my clothes.

The faeries leapt lightly from root to rock, easily avoiding creeping branches and reaching thorns. They seemed to slide through the woods like water. I was more like a stumbling rhinoceros. I tripped over every obstacle, got grabbed by every jutting piece of greenery. After about twenty minutes I was sweating like a pig under my winter overcoat.

I might technically approach Amarantha like an ambassador, but I was certainly not going to look like one. I don't generally think of myself as vain or girly, but I was sweaty, bruised and covered in dried mud from head to toe. Nobody wants to appear before a queen like that. I shuddered to think of what my hair looked like.

We walked for what seemed like an hour. After I'd tripped over my nine hundredth tree root, I decided to break the silence.

"How much longer?" I asked Ivin.

He looked back at me. "The court of Queen Amarantha is approximately a day's walk from here."

I stared at him. "A day? Are you crazy? I can't take a day to walk to court. For chrissakes, Nathaniel and I can fly. Surely there's a quicker way than walking."

"You can fly but we cannot," he said. "You entered the queen's kingdom at the very borders of her authority. It is not my fault that you chose to come that way."

"Believe me, it's not a choice I would have made if I had known," I grumbled. "What about a portal?"

"We do not have the ability to create portals. That is solely the province of your kind," he said.

"Then Nathaniel can make one. This is ridiculous. Do you seriously think that I am going to . . ." I trailed off as the ground beneath me trembled and all the faeries went still. "What is it now?"

The leader looked alarmed. "We must go now. As quickly as you can, follow me."

"What is it?" I asked again, but all the faeries had disappeared into the brush.

The ground shook. I heard something chittering and clicking in the darkness of the trees. It sounded like several legs thumped on the ground. Dead leaves crackled and twigs snapped as the creature approached. There was a heavy scrape of furred body on bark as it pushed through the woods.

"That sounds like a—" Beezle began, but I cut him off.

"Don't say it. It's not allowed," I said, and I pushed my wings out. I have a mild to moderate case of arachnophobia. If that thing was what I thought it was, then I would probably pass out right there and wake up to find myself in a cocoon hanging from a tree. "Come on."

Nathaniel and I flew up toward the top canopy of trees, but the branches were tightly woven and it was impossible to get above the tree line. My clothes and wings snagged on everything and my face was horribly scratched after a few minutes.

The chittering and clicking came closer. Nathaniel looked at me in alarm.

"We can't get through," he said.

"Tell me something I don't know," I muttered. "Beezle, can you squeeze through here and try to get above the trees, maybe find a place where we can fit through?"

Beezle looked at me doubtfully. "I can try. But how will I direct you from up there? You'll never hear me, and you certainly won't be able to see me."

Nathaniel broke a small branch off one of the trees. He snapped it in half, muttered a word, and the ends of each branch started to glow.

"Take this," he said, handing it to Beezle. "It will send a signal to us and guide us to where you are."

"Magical GPS," Beezle said, and he sounded impressed. "Okay, don't get eaten by the giant sp—"

"Don't say it," I repeated. "Just go, and be careful."

"I'd rather go up than down," Beezle said, and as he disappeared into the branches, I had to agree.

The creature-that-shall-not-be-named in the woods seemed to have paused. We still couldn't see it but it seemed frighteningly close. The air was dense with a strange green miasma that slowly filled the clearing. I wondered if the gas was emanating from the creature, or if it was yet another obstacle generated by the forest for me to deal with. Amarantha had a pretty effective defensive system here in the outlands. I'd probably appreciate it more if her system would stop trying to eat me.

"What do you think?" I asked Nathaniel.

"I think we should stay as high as possible," he said grimly.

"I'm on board with that," I said. "But I don't think we should move too far until Beezle . . ."

I stopped as a wave of dizziness overtook me and I almost fell out of the tree. I rested my head against the bark for a minute, then resecured my grip on the branch I was seated on. It didn't seem to help. Nausea rose up in my stomach and I gagged, trying not to boot.

"What is the matter?" Nathaniel asked. His eyes scanned the immediate area. The creature seemed to have either fallen asleep or left, because there wasn't a sound to be heard.

Sweat trickled down my face and spine. My T-shirt was uncomfortably wet in a few moments. I folded myself over the branch so that I rested on it from face to belly, my legs straddling it like a horse. I turned my head to one side and tried to breathe through my nose. Unfortunately, breathing seemed to make it worse. My stomach twisted in knots of pain, and my chest felt tight.

"Are you sick?" Nathaniel asked. He floated down to my side, his face level with mine and his body hanging below as he flapped his wings gently in place.

I nodded a very tiny nod and closed my eyes. Looking at him hanging there was making me feel sicker.

He frowned. "It must be this fog. It's affecting your human body."

"Great," I said through clenched teeth. "As if I don't have enough to deal with. Now there's poison gas."

"We must get you away from here before it affects your brain," he said.

"Bad news," I said. "My brain's already affected. It's doing the tarantella with my stomach."

Just then the creature began to move again, and it seemed to be moving a lot faster than it had before. Nathaniel reached for me.

"Carefully . . . unless . . . you . . . want . . . puke . . . all . . . over . . . your . . . jacket," I slurred. My tongue felt heavy in my mouth and it was getting harder to think.

"I will risk it," he said, and lifted me off the branch. He placed my head on his shoulder like I was a baby and put my arms around his neck. "Wrap your legs around my stomach and don't let go."

"Ooookay."

I just wanted to go to sleep. I could hear, in a far and echoey way, the resumed chittering and clacking of the monster in the woods. It just didn't have any urgency for me anymore. Sleep was the thing. Sleep was good.

"Madeline, do not go to sleep," Nathaniel ordered.

"Tired," I murmured.

"Do not go to sleep. You must listen to me. I am your husband."

"Not yet, you aren't," I said, or maybe I thought it. It was hard to remember how to talk.

The monster crashed into the clearing. I heard branches breaking and the high-pitched whistle it emitted as it saw us. From my resting place on Nathaniel's shoulder I could see his eyes grow wide.

"Hold very tight," he said, and he let go of me so that his arms were free. I hung off the front of his body like a baby gorilla. "I must attempt to fight this creature."

"Is it a giant spider?" I mumbled.

"Yes," Nathaniel said, and then he threw a bolt of lightning at it.

The lightning sizzled as it hit the spider's skin and the clearing filled with the scent of ozone. The spider screeched in anger and thumped its legs on the ground.

"Did that help?" I asked.

"No. Do not let go," Nathaniel repeated, and he began to try to fly away from the creature.

Pretty quickly he came up against the same problem that we'd had before—the woods were too dense to fly. He hadn't made any kind of headway and the creature was coming up on us with alarming speed. I looked over Nathaniel's shoulder and wished I hadn't.

The spider was fourteen feet tall, with long, tufted gray hair and about a million spinning red eyes. I wasn't going to be able to sleep for weeks if we got out of this alive.

"Portal?" I asked.

"The elements here are not correct," Nathaniel said, turning to face the spider and lowering to the ground. "The trees would suppress it. We need an open clearing."

"Where's Beezle?" I asked, and slipped from his shoulders to the ground. I landed and sprawled at his feet just as the spider came close enough for me to smell the stink of its blood-scented breath.

"I told you to hold on," he said, and blasted the spider with nightfire.

The animal reared back, emitted a high-pitched screech. Its teeth clicked together as it retreated a few feet and hissed at us.

I looked up at Nathaniel from my prone position in the dirt. Now that we were away from the cloud of green gas, I was feeling a little better. The bands of tightness around my chest loosened and some of the nausea subsided.

"Nightfire help?" I asked.

"Apparently not," Nathaniel said. "It seems to be impervious to magical means of destruction."

"A very wise gargoyle recently told me that most things don't like fire," I said, and sat up just as the spider made another run at us.

I pulled up my magic, pushing through the lingering feeling of wrongness from the miasma. Eight legs pounded into the ground, coming closer. I heard Nathaniel muttering to himself, preparing some assault of his own.

The spider's crazy whirling eyes were too close. It let out a scream of triumph.

I pushed the spell through my heartstone and let it fly, the same spell that had destroyed the monster in the swamp. The spider ignited immediately. It howled as it went up in flames, thrashing its burning legs all around the forest. The stink of scorched meat and burned hair was everywhere.

Some of the trees caught fire and the area quickly filled with smoke.

Nathaniel yanked me to my feet and pulled me forcefully away from the smoke and flame. After a few moments of caveman dragging I disentangled myself from his grip, slapping his hands away in irritation.

"I can walk, for crying out loud." I couldn't walk very steadily, but I was sick of being yanked through the flora.

Nathaniel gave me a stiff-faced look. "Forgive me. A few moments ago you were helpless and needed me to help save you from the giant spider."

I brushed some imaginary lint off my filthy clothes, keeping my eyes down. "Yes. Well. Thanks for that."

He put his hand beneath my chin and forced my gaze upward. "Can you never look me in the eye when you are being civil to me?"

I arched an eyebrow at him and gave him a small grin. "It doesn't come naturally."

He let go of my chin, leaving a little warm spot where his fingers had been. "Perhaps it will one day."

We stood there for a moment, staring at each other. Then I became aware of the heat of flame crackling closer.

"Better move," I said. "I wonder what the hell happened to Beezle."

Nathaniel looked surprised. "I forgot about the gargoyle."

He reached into his pocket and pulled out the twig that matched the one he had given Beezle. The end glowed blue.

"He has found a clearing for us," Nathaniel said. "This way."

He turned to the right and began to cut through the woods. Behind us there was the enormous crash of a tree as it was consumed by fire. I winced.

"Amarantha is not going to be happy with me," I said. "First I barbecued two of her best monsters, then I burned down her forest."

"Let us worry about Amarantha at another time," Nathaniel said. "The important thing is to leave this area before we are barbecued ourselves."

We hurried through the forest toward Beezle. It seemed to take forever, particularly with the forest burning to the ground behind us. It is not comfortable to feel flames literally licking your heels.

About ten minutes later we reached an open clearing. Beezle sat on a large, pointed rock that jutted up several feet from the ground. He looked terribly smug.

"Check it out," he said. "Forget getting above the tree line. You can set up a portal here and get us straight home."

"I'm all for that," I said, turning to Nathaniel. "Portal us out of here."

He gave me a surprised look. "But what of your mission? The faeries in the woods will surely report to Amarantha that you were here and that you left without paying her notice."

"Those guys abandoned us," I said. "And if Amarantha asks why we left, that's what I'm going to tell her. They took off through the woods and we were stuck dealing with the giant spider. Anyway, excuse me if I'm not too worried about what Amarantha will think right now. The forest is on fire and I want to get out of here."

Beezle looked behind us and his eyes widened.

"What, you just noticed the smoke and the flame?" I asked.

He glared at me. "Good work, Maddy. You came, you saw, you burned everything to the ground."

"You were the one who told me that most monsters don't like fire."

"Children, please," Nathaniel said. "I cannot concentrate while the two of you are bickering at one another."

Beezle and I gave each other identical looks of annoyance while Nathaniel worked his hocus-pocus. I really needed Gabriel to show me how to make a portal. It would definitely be handy for quick getaways.

A few moments later the portal was up and running, and not a second too soon. The trees that ringed the edge of the clearing had started to come down in a crash of sparks and ash.

"I hope you know what you're doing, leaving like this," Beezle said, his tiny arms wrapped around my neck.

"I hope I know, too," I muttered, and stepped inside the portal behind Nathaniel.

We landed on my back lawn. It was late in the day already and the sun was slanting weakly through the trees on its way down. It would be full dark soon, and another night would pass without Gabriel at home.

What was I going to do? It didn't take a genius to know that Lucifer was not going to be happy with me for this. And Amarantha had beheaded Lucifer's last ambassador just for some lapse of court etiquette. Not only had I jeopardized my mission to court and possibly Nathaniel's life, but I hadn't even managed to find a clue as to Gabriel's whereabouts.

Not to mention Antares had managed to sneak up and take my gargoyle unawares, so who was to say that he couldn't sneak up on me and yank my intestines through my nose?

My brain was tired; my body was tired. I just wanted to crawl into bed and pull the covers up and pretend that everything was normal, but my life was getting less normal every day.

"I need something to eat," Beezle announced.

"Of course you do," I replied. "Pizza all around, then."

Beezle pumped his fist in the air. "Hawaiian?"

Not my favorite, but it was Beezle's. And I had missed him. He'd only been gone for a few hours, but I had missed him.

"Hawaiian," I said, and went inside to call for delivery, Nathaniel following silently behind.

9

A COUPLE OF HOURS LATER I WAS SHOWERED, FED and ensconced on the couch with Beezle watching one of our favorite movies—the one where the alien attaches itself to this guy's face and then bursts out of his chest and eats everyone on the ship. You would think that, given the large quantities of actual monsters in my life, I would prefer preschool cartoons, but for some reason this film still entertained me. Maybe it was because Beezle felt free to comment on the total stupidity of the characters who got eaten.

"Move, lady, move!" he shouted at the television. "The big monster is standing right there. Don't cry. Run!"

Nathaniel had gone downstairs to Gabriel's apartment for the evening. I hoped that he wasn't poking around in Gabriel's private things. I felt bad about letting Nathaniel sleep in Gabriel's space but I definitely didn't want him up here, even on the couch bed. I did not want to get into an argument about husbandly rights.

I also felt more than a little guilty about being happy that Beezle was home when Gabriel wasn't. The lack of his presence was starting to press on me, like a niggling headache. Even when I was engaged with something, I was always aware of the fact that Gabriel wasn't with me.

The front doorbell rang just as the heroine of the film was making her escape from the ship that was about to self-destruct. Beezle and I glanced at each other, then at the clock. It was past ten.

"Who could it be?" I asked.

"J.B.?" Beezle guessed. "Gabriel, tied up in a burlap sack?"

"Antares, Samiel, an emissary from Amarantha come to take my mortal remains back to her . . ."

"Lucifer with a great big stick to beat you with for jeopardizing his negotiations . . ."

I stood up. I didn't want to contemplate Lucifer being angry with me. For all of my bravado where he was concerned, he scared me. I generally tried not to think too intently about him or I would feel sick to my stomach. It seemed that he had far too much power to affect my fate.

"Okay, let's not speculate and say we did."

"Can I go out the front window and see who it is?" Beezle asked.

"Absolutely not," I replied as I went down the front stairs. "What if it's Antares again?"

"Are you going to keep me in the house forever?" he whined. "I'm a gargoyle. I have guardian duties."

"Oh, excuse me. It must have been torture to sit on the couch and eat pizza and watch a movie. I'll be sure to send you outside the next time I'm thinking of doing such a crazy thing."

I peeked through the curtain on the door at the bottom of the stairs. J.B. stood in the foyer with his hair sticking up all over the place and a haggard look in his eyes.

"It's really J.B.," Beezle said.

"I know that. He wouldn't be able to stand in the foyer otherwise," I replied.

I swung the door open. "Can't you ever show up during regular visiting hours?"

"Feeling better, I see," J.B. said. "Well enough to burn down about forty acres of outland forest and kill two of my mother's favorite pets."

I rolled my eyes and turned around, indicating that he should follow. J.B. slammed the front door shut behind him.

"How many times do I have to say that those pets of hers were trying to eat me?"

"That's what they're there for," J.B. said.

"Well, was I supposed to let them do their job?" I opened my front door and waved him inside ahead of me.

He turned on me, his face full of anger. "Of course not. But why the hell were you there in the first place? I thought that you were going tomorrow as part of an official envoy. You have no idea how bad this looks. The queen was ready to demand your head as compensation from Lucifer and call off the negotiations entirely. I've spent the last several hours trying to convince her not to do so and to let the negotiations proceed as planned."

"Well, thanks for that," I said grudgingly. "But how did she find out so quickly? Those faeries that we saw in the forest said it was a day's walk from where we were."

J.B. looked at me pityingly. "It was a day's walk. But they have magic, you know. They were at the queen's court a few minutes after they left you."

"Those little bastards," I said, and then I latched onto

something that J.B. had said. "Yeah, wait a minute. They LEFT me. Us. Me and Beezle and Nathaniel. As soon as the spider showed up, they took off without a by-your-leave. So I didn't see any reason why I should chase them down again."

J.B. looked interested. "The guards abandoned you?"

I nodded. "Ran right through the woods without waiting to see if we were following."

He ran his hands through his hair. "All right, we might be able to work with that. It was a breach of conduct for them to leave you to danger. But what were you doing there in the first place?"

I explained about Antares, the bomb, Beezle's kidnapping and the invisible portal in the alley.

"I'm sure that my mother doesn't know anything about an invisible portal," he said, frowning. "I wonder who put it there. And why."

"That's just what we've been trying to figure out," I said. "And I'm thinking it must have something to do with Gabriel's disappearance."

"Why would anyone take Gabriel through a portal to the queen's lands?" J.B. asked.

"I'm not sure," I said. "I keep feeling like I'm missing something. There are all these disparate factions floating around causing problems. Any one of them could have taken Gabriel."

"I still think it was the wolves," said Beezle.

"I still think you have wolf prejudice," I replied.

"Why are you defending the wolves?" J.B. asked. "It's not like you have a relationship with them."

"Well, I do now, sort of. They said that I was a friend to them and vice versa. Plus, I don't know—I've always kind of liked the wolves. They're straightforward. They don't play games like the courts of the vampires or the fallen. With the wolves, what you see is what you get."

"That doesn't mean that they weren't involved in Gabriel's disappearance," J.B. said. "Don't kid yourself. They have an agenda, too. They're trying to negotiate with Amarantha right now for some ancient lands of theirs that currently belong to her, and they don't want the faerie court to strike any new deal with Lucifer's kingdom."

"Why not?"

"The wolves have a long-standing argument with Lucifer. They don't want Lucifer to gain any leverage with Amarantha that might affect their land claim."

"Is there anyone not negotiating with Amarantha right now?" I said, annoyed. "Just how many players are in the pond here?"

"She just signed a new treaty with the vampires regarding right-of-way access, so they're out of the picture right now," J.B. said. "Other than that, pretty much everyone is in and out of the court for one reason or another."

I blew out a breath. "Just why the hell did Lucifer think that I could handle this?"

Beezle and J.B. looked at each other.

"Yes, I know, that's what you two know-it-alls tried to tell me yesterday. I'll figure it out. J.B., go home and get some sleep. If you keep doing that to your hair, it's going to fall out."

"I'm overwhelmed by your gratitude. 'Thanks, J.B., for making sure that your mom didn't send her assassins to remove all my limbs one by one.'"

I kissed him on the cheek. "Thanks, J.B. Now, come back tomorrow morning around ten so you can escort me to the court. Surely she won't chop off my head on sight if her son is part of my entourage."

"Don't count on it," he said, and disappeared out the front door.

"Can I sleep in my nest?" Beezle asked.

"No," I said. "You can set something up on my dresser."

"Your dresser is hard," he complained.

"So get a pillow," I replied. "You're the one who's always going on about how cold it is outside."

After about fifteen minutes of grumping and grumbling, I finally got Beezle settled. I collapsed on the bed and closed my eyes in an instant. And when I slept, I dreamed of Gabriel.

It was dark where he was, so dark and cold, a pit of frozen stone. The stone was black as night and shone in the faint gleam that emitted from the top of the pit. Gabriel's eyes gave off a slight glow from the shadows.

He was naked and shivering, and in the light I could see long welts clotted with blood on his back, his arms, his shoulders. He had only been gone for a little more than a day, but his face had a gaunt, haggard look, as if he hadn't been eating. Since I couldn't see any sign of food or water, he probably hadn't been.

He hunched over his knees, arms wrapped around his legs, his wings enclosing his body in a makeshift blanket. Gabriel was always so calm, so self-assured, and it hurt my heart to see him trembling on the ground like a lost child.

I held my hand out to him, knowing that I could not touch him, that this was only a dream, when suddenly he looked up.

"Madeline?" he said. His face was alight with hope.

"Gabriel," I replied, and I brushed my hand over his cheek, expecting to feel his skin beneath my fingertips, the dark stubble that grew there. But of course I couldn't. I wasn't really there.

"Madeline?" he asked again, and his eyes searched for some sign of me. Disappointment crept over his face.

"I'm here, Gabriel," I said. "I'm here. I'm coming for you."

But he dropped his head to his knees. He didn't see me. He didn't hear me. I felt a moment of despair. What good was I to him, or to anybody? How had I let this happen in the first place?

Then I realized I could at least try to find out where he was. I drifted upward through the pit. There was a long channel above the hole where Gabriel was held. The channel was far too narrow for Gabriel to fly through, and too smooth to climb. His captors must have found some way to suppress his magic as well, or no prison would be enough to keep him there.

I wondered if they'd simply dropped him into the hole or if they had cared enough about broken bones to lower him gently. Judging from the whip marks on his back, it was probably the former.

I floated through the open hole at the top of the pit and emerged in a cave. There was no sign of Gabriel's captors, no sign of life of any kind. There was only black volcanic rock and gray sand. I couldn't smell anything or feel heat or cold, so from my point of view it was a basically a nondescript cave. It could have been anywhere in the world.

I let myself drift along, toes just brushing the fine sand that covered the ground everywhere I looked. After a few minutes I came to the end of the cave. The tunnel turned abruptly and opened out over the edge of a cliff. I went right up to the edge and looked down.

Even though I was some kind of ghost or floating aspect here, I still had a moment of vertigo. The cliff dropped away to a sheer face that fell maybe two hundred feet to a thin creek bed, long empty of water. There was a wide expanse of open plain on the other side of the creek, gray sand and gray sky and clouds exploding with lightning.

I had a foreboding feeling as I looked around this dead place, gray as far as the eye could see. I looked and looked and finally found what I expected.

Far in the distance I could see the clawed outline of a tree, white as bone, scraping its branches like talons across the sky.

"The Forbidden Lands," I said. It was a place that I had never wanted to see again, the place where Lucifer and the Grigori had imprisoned the nephilim. It was the place where Ramuell had torn out my heart, the place where I had died once—for a little while.

Who had brought Gabriel here and dropped him into that oubliette? If they wanted him for some purpose—as a ransom or a slave—then why leave him here to be forgotten?

Suddenly there was a movement on the plain below. From the right of the cliff that I stood upon came a single individual. At this distance I could detect only the gleam of golden hair and of white wings, marking him of angelic descent.

From the left came a small group, knotted tightly together and moving almost as one body except for the leader. He strode ahead to meet the individual coming from the other direction. All I could see of the leader was that he was tall and horned—that plus the multicolored glob of beings behind him told me that he was a demon.

I needed to get closer and find out who these characters were and if they had anything to do with Gabriel's kidnapping. I knew that my physical body was not here, and that even if it were here, I could fly. But it still took everything I had to step off the edge of the cliff.

I fell slowly, floating downward like a dandelion seed drifting on the breeze. It seemed to take an eternity before

I met the ground. I landed softly in the sand, and my bare feet made no impression. It was only then that I realized I wore nothing but my only white nightgown—a favorite of Gabriel's—and it wasn't even what I had actually put on to sleep in. I felt suddenly vulnerable, that if I presented myself like this in the sight of those demons, they would fall upon me and devour me.

But that was absurd. Gabriel couldn't see me. I was dreaming, or having a vision, but I wasn't really here. This might be my only chance to find out who took Gabriel, and why, and to try to figure out how to get him back.

I had landed several feet behind the angel. His wings were up and outspread and obscured his face from the angle at which I stood. I approached cautiously, hugging the cliff face even though one of the demon entourage would surely raise a cry if I could be seen.

The demon in charge, the one speaking with the angel, looked a lot like my half brother. He so resembled Antares that I had to do a double take to make sure that it wasn't him. The leader was about nine feet tall, with red skin, oversized bat wings and gleaming black horns jutting from the top of his forehead. He had a strange sigil, almost like an ampersand with the bottom curl cut off, branded on his face.

The sight of that sigil gave me a flash of memory. Antares tossing me down the stairs, telling me that he would be honored above all others when he brought my heart to his master. He showed me the same sigil on his hand, the sign of Focalor. Focalor was one of Azazel's enemies, but he could not openly declare war against Azazel because that would be tantamount to declaring open war on Lucifer. Was this creature Focalor, or another one of his toadies like Antares?

I crept carefully toward the angel and the demon, who were deep in conversation, in order to hear what they said.

Unfortunately, I was doomed to disappointment. They seemed to be speaking some kind of language that involved a lot of grunting and gesturing. The demon was annoyed with the angel, and as they talked his face grew thunderous. The band of demons behind him moved restlessly as their leader became more fractious. I still could not see the face of the angel, but his body language was unyielding. There would obviously be no negotiations with him.

I studied the demons, looking for a familiar face. The only other demons that I had ever seen had been with Antares, and if I saw one of them in this group, then at least I would have some kind of lead to follow. Tracking down Antares wasn't too hard. He showed up at my house every chance he got.

I moved a little closer, hoping to at least see the face of the angel dealing with a demon as if it were his equal. This was a big no-no in the courts of the fallen. There was a pretty strict caste system there, with the Grigori—the first fallen—at the top, then other angels, then demons, who acted almost as servants to the castes above.

Certain crossbreeds were tolerated at higher levels— like me, because I was pretty much descended from fallen royalty—but others like Gabriel ranked below the lowest demons. Within the general groups there were even stricter breakdowns of hierarchy, which had a lot to do with how much power you had, who was in your entourage, who your parents were, or all of the above. It was pretty extraordinary to see an angel treating a demon this way.

I drifted over the sand as the discussion grew more animated. Because of the position of the party I had to approach the angel almost directly from behind. As I drew within a few feet of him, he suddenly stopped speaking and turned around.

His eyes widened, green eyes filled with malice.

Samiel.

It was as if he saw me floating there when no one else could. I heard a voice in my head say, "Enemy."

He reached for me, his fist uncurling to tear out my heart, just like his father had done.

"No," I whispered, and my body filled with terror. How could he see me? How did he know that I was there?

"Madeline!"

Gabriel's voice. Gabriel. I had to get away. I shot upward, away from Samiel's clawing fingers, up the side of the cliff, back into the cave. Samiel came right behind me, a relentless machine, wanting only one thing—vengeance for the deaths of his mother and father.

I turned around and around in the cave, realizing I'd fallen into a trap. Now I *would* be torn to pieces by demons.

"Maddy!"

Samiel bore down on me, his face unyielding, his eyes furious.

"Enemy."

"Maddy!" A gravelly voice, one that I knew very well.

"Madeline!" Gabriel calling from the oubliette.

"Enemy."

Enemy, enemy, enemy.

"Maddy!" Beezle shouted, and he sounded so angry with me, and I woke up.

Beezle crouched at my shoulder, looking scared and annoyed. I shifted onto my elbows and realized the bedsheets were soaked in sweat.

"You were having a nightmare. It was keeping me awake," Beezle said. "What were you dreaming about? You kept screaming 'enemy' over and over again."

I sat up farther and rubbed my face with my hands. "It wasn't a dream, I don't think."

Beezle held up his hands. "Oh, no. No more visions. Remember the last time you had visions? You were possessed by Evangeline and tricked into the nephilims' prison."

"Well, that turned out okay," I said, annoyed. "I did defeat Ramuell in the end."

"And lost some of your humanity in the process," Beezle reminded me.

I put my hand over my chest to the place where my heartstone pulsed in place of my human heart. It felt warm there, like the sun. Samiel had wanted to tear out my heart, just like Ramuell had. I shuddered and threw the blankets off, nearly tossing Beezle across the room in the process. He scowled at me as he fluttered above the bed.

"All right, let's hear it," Beezle said. "Tell me about this latest complication."

I told Beezle about the vision—Gabriel in the pit, Samiel and the demon. He looked troubled.

"It sounds like they might be arranging a trade for Gabriel," Beezle said.

"That's what I thought, too. The only question is, which of them took him in the first place and which of them wants him badly enough to trade?"

"Actually, there's a more serious problem here. If a representative of Focalor is dealing for Gabriel, that's tantamount to declaring war on Azazel's court. Gabriel is Azazel's servant and he's your bodyguard. Even though he's a half-breed, everyone in the courts knows of his importance to Azazel. And if Focalor is making such a bold move, that means he is prepared for the consequences."

I stared at Beezle. "The whole power structure that Lucifer has built could collapse."

Beezle nodded. "If Focalor attacks Azazel's court openly, then other courts with grievances will see it as an opportunity to attack their enemies as well. The whole of Lucifer's kingdom could fall to pieces in a few days. This is why Lucifer and the Grigori keep such a ruthless hold on the courts."

"It only takes the tipping of one domino for the whole run to be knocked down," I said. "I had no idea that the kingdom was so fragile."

"Lucifer has kept control of some of the most dangerous creatures in the world for millennia. A lot of those creatures would be unbelievably deadly to humans if they did not abide by his rules and stay within his confines, and I'm not just talking about the demons, either."

I couldn't imagine what would happen to the world if Lucifer's control was broken. Would there be demons running amok? Open warfare among the angels? Would demons rise up against their masters? All of those things would probably happen, and more. It would be horrible beyond imagining.

"Horrors beyond your comprehension . . ." That was what Antares had said. Had he known about this? If he was close to Focalor, he probably would have known of his master's plans. And Antares certainly would relish an opportunity to get back at Gabriel, who had humiliated him in front of his demon buddies. Had Antares taken Gabriel in the alley for Focalor? Why would Samiel want him?

And was any of this connected to the hidden portal in Amarantha's kingdom? I still didn't know who had put that portal there, or why, although Antares had done a good job of using it to his advantage and destabilizing my relations with the faerie court before I even arrived.

I put my hand to my head in the place where a stress headache was rapidly forming. As if I didn't have enough on my plate, I needed to prevent the total collapse of Lucifer's kingdom as well?

Beezle watched me silently, and I'm fairly certain he guessed most of what I was thinking. He can be a pretty perceptive gargoyle when he wants to be.

The problem was that I wasn't exactly sure what I should do with this knowledge. If I went to Lucifer, he might be able to stop Focalor before his plans unfolded but that would be a guaranteed death sentence for Gabriel.

I could try to rescue Gabriel. But, one: he had probably been moved by now. And, two: even if he hadn't been moved, I wasn't sure I could find the oubliette. It wasn't as though I was an expert in the geography of the Forbidden Lands.

I wasn't sure who might have him now, and what purpose he might serve for their plans. Basically, I wasn't sure of anything except for the fact that it was half past five and there was no way I was going to be able to sleep again after that vision.

"Oatmeal?" I asked Beezle.

He made a face at me. "You've got to be kidding."

"Chocolate-hazelnut spread on toast?" I guessed.

"Now you're talking," he said, and followed me into the kitchen.

After breakfast I was no closer to a solution than before. I felt that Gabriel's safety was paramount, but Beezle argued that if there was a war between the courts, Gabriel probably wouldn't be much safer than the rest of us. On top of everything, my trip to the faerie court was today, and there was no way that I could put it off after the burning-down-the-forest debacle.

So I packed my things with a heavy heart and made an effort to dress like a grown-up. I usually wear black boots, blue jeans, and black sweaters every day in the winter, but buried in the back of my closet were a couple of suits and a nice skirt and blouse. I tried everything on to make sure that it fit okay. The suits were a little tighter than they used to be—my curves were a lot curvier than I remembered. Beezle opened his mouth to say something and I glared at him.

"Not one word," I said. "You're the one who makes me keep all the junk food in the house."

"I'm a growing gargoyle," Beezle said.

"Yeah, growing horizontally," I muttered, but not loud enough for him to hear.

Nathaniel came upstairs a little before ten. He was all spiffed up in a dark suit and a blue tie that made his eyes look electric bright. He looked over my gray pencil skirt and black blouse with a critical eye.

"Don't you have any colors that are not drab as winter?" he said. "Amarantha is not going to be impressed by your appearance."

"She doesn't have to be. She just has to listen to me," I said, my pride stinging. I'd actually made an effort to fix up my hair, put on makeup and heels, and generally look neater than usual. He could at least have offered a token "You look nice."

He frowned. "I'm not certain that she will take you seriously when you look like someone's secretary."

I actually felt the blast of nightfire crackling under my fingertips before Beezle laid a restraining claw on my shoulder.

"You can kill him later," he said, and I eased down. I didn't need Nathaniel's opinion to validate me, anyway.

The doorbell rang right at ten.

"That's J.B.," I said. "Let's get this party on the road."

10

AS SOON AS I STEPPED ONTO THE PORCH, J.B. WHISTLED at me.

"You look awesome," he said, looking me up and down several times.

I said nothing but gave Nathaniel a pointed look.

"I still think you look like a secretary," he said in reply.

"Yeah, but a *sexy* secretary," J.B. said. He wore an extremely expensive-looking tailored suit under an equally tailored coat, and he'd tucked his glasses away somewhere. His eyes were a brilliant green.

"Okay, enough with the compliments, or lack thereof," Beezle said. "Let's get a move on, here."

"How are we getting there?" I asked J.B. "Portal?"

"Nah. Mom's sending a car," he said. "It'll pick us up in the alley."

So we tramped down the gangway to the backyard with

our luggage, Beezle fluttering behind me. It was kind of amazing that none of our neighbors had ever seen him, especially since we hadn't exactly been secretive about his presence lately.

We stood in the alley, blowing our breath on our hands and stamping our feet. It felt about ten degrees colder than the day before. At least this time I was properly dressed, with a hat and gloves and scarf in addition to my long wool coat. I noticed some dried mud that I had missed in my hasty cleaning this morning and tried to brush it off with my glove. Nathaniel shook his head at me pityingly.

"This negotiation is doomed before we even begin," he said.

"Will you stop acting like I'm dressed like a peasant?" I snapped.

"You're covered in mud."

"Do you want to be covered in blood?" I said. "Because that can be arranged."

"Children, children," J.B. said.

Just then a long black limousine rounded the corner and came toward us.

"Why did we have to get picked up back here?" I asked J.B.

"Because the driver is part troll," he replied as the limo came to a smooth stop in front of us. "He's a little conspicuous. Try not to stare."

Trolls mostly lived in isolated wilderness areas because of their size, which could reach well over twenty feet. Since wilderness areas weren't generally in my pick-up range I'd never had the opportunity to see one. I'd heard a lot of stories from Agents who'd transferred from rural areas— apparently trolls tended not to cooperate with the Agency very well. I was a little curious about how a troll half-breed had happened. They were so big I didn't think they would be able to crossbreed with anything humanoid. Then I realized that the breeding process was probably horrible for the non-troll, and decided to stop thinking about such things. They were not conducive to an easy mind, and I was more than a little nervous about this meeting.

Lucifer was counting on me, and aside from the fact that I really didn't want him upset with me, I wanted to have my debt to him cleared. This job was a repayment for killing his son. Now, his son had done his damndest to kill *me* several times and was a monster by any calculation, but Lucifer was still bothered by it. I owed him a boon, and this was it. Once I got clear of this, then we were back on an even footing, or as even as one could be with the devil himself.

The driver of the limo got out and came around to open the door for us. I tried to take J.B.'s advice, but it was hard not to stare. The troll was dressed in a typical chauffeur's outfit—black suit, white shirt, black hat. He was roughly human-sized, about six feet tall with the bulging muscles of a bodybuilder straining the fabric of his suit. All this would not have been in the least notable except that he had the face of a furless boar.

He had a pig's snout, longish pointed ears with tufts of hair at the end, small cunning eyes, and fangs that jutted over his upper lip. The effect was so disconcerting that it was difficult to look him in the eye as I stepped into the car ahead of J.B. and Nathaniel.

"Ambassador Black," he said, and his voice was low and growling.

I nodded at him—it seemed like the appropriate thing to do—and then settled myself on one of the plush seats.

J.B. managed to slide in next to me, cutting Nathaniel out so that he was forced to sit on the opposite seat. Nathaniel glared at J.B. as the latter slung a friendly arm around my shoulders. Apparently Nathaniel's fawning respect for J.B. had evaporated in the face of male territoriality.

J.B. leaned over to whisper in my ear. "I'm sure I don't need to tell you . . ."

"Don't eat or drink anything while we're in the court," I whispered back. "I know. I don't want to be trapped in the faerie court for the next hundred years. I have enough problems. I packed plenty of snacks."

"Did you pack enough for you and Beezle? Because I've seen the way your gargoyle eats. And don't speak too freely in front of Tyree—the driver," he said. "He reports everything right back to my mother."

"Got it," I said.

I glanced over at Nathaniel. His face had turned brick red with annoyance. I wanted to tell him that J.B. and I weren't flirting—it only looked that way. But then I remembered that I didn't want to marry him anyway. I don't know why I kept having these concerns for his feelings. I didn't want to think that Nathaniel might be growing on me, especially when he hadn't even said anything nice about my outfit.

J.B. kept his arm around my shoulders, but I resisted the urge to sink back and relax. I had too many things to worry about, and most of all I missed Gabriel. He had only been a part of my life for a few months, but nothing seemed right without him. And I hated to think of him being harmed and unable to defend himself.

I looked out the window and let my thoughts drift— Amarantha, Lucifer, the wolves, Samiel, Focalor, Antares. So many players, so many pieces on the chessboard. The question was—was I pawn or player? I wasn't sure yet. I wasn't even sure what Lucifer wanted me to negotiate with Amarantha. He'd said he wanted to reestablish relations, but once I did that what else was I supposed to do? I wasn't privy to Lucifer's needs and wants, and I wasn't sure if furthering his agenda was the best thing for the world in any case.

After a while my eyes closed of their own volition. I don't know how long I slept, but when I opened my eyes again I was curled into J.B.'s chest and it was dark outside. I looked sleepily up and saw that J.B. had a very satisfied smile on his face. Beezle was coiled into a sleeping ball on the other side of the seat from him. Nathaniel stared out the window, his face frozen.

I pushed away from J.B. and stretched. "How much farther?"

"You actually woke up just in time," he said. "If you look out the window, you can see the castle as we approach."

"The castle," I said. I don't know why I thought that Amarantha would live in an ordinary house. My own father lived in a rather palatial home.

But when I glanced out the window I saw that Amarantha lived in a real, honest-to-goodness faerie castle, with high towers, winding turrets, catwalks—the works. The whole thing was about the size of five or six city blocks, and it was surrounded by a genuine moat. As we approached the castle, a drawbridge came down to allow us access into the courtyard.

"Grog and meat, anyone?" I muttered. I noticed that several faeries carrying bows and dressed like the warriors we had met in the woods patrolled the catwalks. Apparently these were Amarantha's soldiers. I wondered why she felt she needed them when her forest was full of freaky things that ate intruders. Was her kingdom that threatened, or was she just that paranoid?

The limousine pulled to a stop in front of a huge arched

doorway. Tyree shut off the car and stepped around to open the door for us.

"Remember," J.B. said. "The court follows very strict rules. Do not show any disrespect to the queen."

"And do not treat the servants as your equals," Nathaniel said.

"And don't eat or drink anything that's offered, but refuse it politely," Beezle reminded me.

"And also . . ." J.B. began.

"I don't need three babysitters," I said. "I know to be careful."

"But you don't know when to stop running at the mouth," Beezle said.

"Look who raised me," I said pointedly.

"What are you trying to say?" Beezle said, looking offended.

I rolled my eyes and stepped out of the car behind the others. Beezle fluttered down to my shoulder and landed with a grunt. I decided to start practicing my tongue biting now and withheld the comment about his weight. Best to begin as I meant to go on.

J.B. led the way to the front door. Before we reached it, the door swung open wide without a sound. A glitteringly perfect faerie stood there with a fake smile of welcome on her face, and suddenly I understood why Nathaniel had said I was underdressed.

She was about five foot ten with the body of a lingerie model, and she wore a floor-length purple silk gown that clung to every curve on the way down. Her blond hair was piled artfully on her head and she wore jewels everywhere they could be worn. She held her hands out to J.B.

"My prince," the faerie said, and of course she had a

breathy, Kathleen Turner–type voice on top of that body that screamed sex.

"Lady Violet," he replied, kissing her fingers.

I felt a weird little flutter, almost like jealousy, but I decided that couldn't be it. I did want to ask J.B. when he had suddenly turned into Rico Suave, but the skinny bitch clinging to his arm gestured for us to join them.

"Ambassador Black, I am Lady Violet, the queen's right hand," she purred, giving me the once-over and finding me not worth her time. "My queen is awaiting your arrival in her court. Lord Nathaniel ap Zerachiel, you also are welcome as a member of Ambassador Black's party. And who . . . is this?"

Violet couldn't keep her nose from wrinkling in distaste as she looked at Beezle, still perched on my shoulder.

"This is my gargoyle, Beezle," I said.

"A gargoyle. How . . . quaint."

"I'm assuming he's as welcome as everyone else in my party," I said pointedly.

J.B. widened his eyes at me, but I wasn't going to let her or anyone be rude to Beezle. And really—I was a princess, not just an ambassador. I outranked her, and from everything J.B. and Beezle had told me, rank was everything with these faeries. Best to remind her of that.

Violet's face had reddened slightly at my rebuke and she flashed me a venomous look before she had a chance to hide it under the smooth mask of welcome. Oh, well. I didn't think we were going to be BFFs anyway.

"Of course. You are welcome to Queen Amarantha's court . . . Beezle."

Beezle gave her a regal nod from his perch, like he was a king deigning to acknowledge a peasant. High color flared in Violet's cheeks. I wanted to give him a high five but that seemed like it would be bad form.

I felt rather than heard Nathaniel give a little sigh next to me. Whatever.

Violet turned on one spiked heel, her arm still firmly curled around J.B.'s.

"If you will come this way, please, Ambassador. Your coats and luggage will be brought to your rooms."

We pulled off our outer things and handed them to more faeries who appeared out of nowhere. They didn't speak, simply took our coats, bowed, and slipped away again.

"Passages in the walls, you think?" I whispered to Beezle.

He nodded thoughtfully, then took off from my shoulder to fly ahead a little. I think he wanted to eavesdrop on the conversation between J.B. and Violet. The two of them were having quite the little tête-à-tête as we strode along.

If there were passages in the walls, that meant there was always a chance of our conversation being overheard. I made a mental note not to speak too freely while we were here.

J.B. and Violet walked ahead of us down a long stone corridor lined with medieval armor. Amarantha apparently really enjoyed playing queen of the castle, down to all of the accessories. Then I got a closer look at one of the helmets on the suits. Inside was a human face, frozen in terror, mouth open, eyes wide. I gulped.

Nathaniel noticed the direction of my gaze. He leaned close to me as we walked.

"Those are soldiers from the War of the Roses in 1460," Nathaniel whispered. "Amarantha kept them as trophies when she helped the Earl of Warwick defeat the Lancasters at the Battle of Northampton. She added the armor later."

"Isn't that in England?" I said.

"Yes. Amarantha had her castle moved brick by brick when she migrated here two hundred years ago."

"Just how old is she, anyway?" I asked. This corridor

seemed to be taking forever, especially now that I knew the suits of armor were filled with bodies.

Nathaniel frowned. "I am unsure of her precise age, but I believe she has recently entered the 1107th year of her reign as queen."

"Wonderful," I said sotto voce. "How come everyone I meet is a kajillion years older than me? They've all had centuries to practice being crafty. Me, I'm just a thirty-something thrown in the deep end of the pool without a floatie."

"I am your floatie," Nathaniel said.

I giggled. I couldn't help it. Nathaniel looked so stiff and formal, as he always did, even when he said the word "floatie."

"You do not believe my assistance will be valuable? I assure you, I have had many dealings with Queen Amarantha," he said, his voice frosty.

"Of course I believe you'll be valuable," I said, not wanting to deal with one of his hissy fits right now. "It's just that—"

I was cut off as we finally rounded the corner at the end of the corridor and we were greeted by a set of polished oak doors. Violet finally took her claws off J.B.'s arm and turned to face us.

"If you will wait here for a moment, I will alert the queen to your presence."

She disappeared inside the double doors so quickly that I didn't have a chance to peek at the throne room behind them. Based on the rest of the castle, though, I was sure that Amarantha's court would be dazzling, ostentatious and probably a little scary. I took a deep breath and steeled myself. Beezle fluttered back to my shoulder and gave me a reassuring squeeze of his claws.

A few minutes later the doors swung open and I heard a voice announce, "Ambassador Madeline Black ap Azazel, on behalf of Lord Lucifer. Lord Nathaniel ap Zerachiel, escorting. Prince Jonquil of Queen Amarantha's court, escorting."

I gave J.B. a sideways look. "Jonquil?"

He took my arm very firmly and pressed his lips together. "Not a word."

"Oh, no," I whispered. "I am definitely not going to forget this."

We stepped into the breach, J.B. on one side of me and Nathaniel on the other, both of them holding my arms. I felt like Dorothy skipping down the yellow brick road between the Tin Man and the Scarecrow. Too bad I didn't have a basket to put Beezle in.

The throne room was pretty much what I'd expected, although from a slightly different era. Rather than sticking with the medieval theme here, Amarantha had gone for Baroque. The ceiling was high and covered in gold foil and curlicues. The windows were draped with pink velvet and gold tassels. The parquet floor was polished to a high gloss. I half expected to see Louis XIV come striding down to meet me.

The room was the size of a ballroom rather than a throne room, and it was packed to the gills with faeries dressed like they were at a black-tie wedding. Amarantha's throne was on a raised dais at the opposite end of the doors, so that we had to promenade in front of the assemblage in order to reach her.

As we entered the room, there was a momentary hush, and then the murmur of voices started up again, many of them declaring in disparaging tones that I looked terribly ordinary and other things to that effect.

I was reminded of the first time I entered Azazel's court, when so many of the angels had found me wanting. I just hoped that this visit wouldn't end the way that one had—with someone getting their head chopped off. I still had nightmares sometimes about Greenwitch's head rolling to my feet, her pale eyes staring forever into the void.

J.B. patted my arms reassuringly. "You're better than they think."

I smiled at him. "I know that, but thanks for saying it anyway."

He smiled back, and I felt that little flutter again, this time in the vicinity of my heart.

The crowd parted before us in ripples, and I finally got a look at Amarantha. She was looking pretty damned good for a woman over a thousand years old. She didn't even look old enough to be J.B.'s mom. Of course, Azazel looked like he could be my handsome older brother. That was just a symptom of being the half-human child of an immortal.

Amarantha had mahogany hair pulled to a low knot at the base of her neck, the same glittering green eyes as J.B. and a perfect heart-shaped face. Rather than go overboard on the fashion front (as I'd expected, given the crazy gold and velvet all over the room), she'd chosen to set off her flawless skin with a simple, fluid dress the color of champagne. It left her shoulders bare and highlighted the diamond the size of my thumb that she wore nestled between her perfect breasts.

We drew to a halt in front of the dais, and the queen rose from her throne to greet us. She did not, however, step down to our level. Point taken. Her eyes were hard and watchful, and I could almost see the calculations moving behind those green orbs. She was taking my measure and, like so many others, finding me to be less than she'd expected. Well, that was fine. When people have low expectations of me, I find that it's easier to take them by surprise.

"Ambassador Black," she said, and as she spoke I heard conversations hush all over the room. Nobody was going to miss this one. "You are welcome to my court as a representative of Lucifer."

I gave a tiny nod of my head. I wasn't going to bow and scrape. I knew my place in Azazel's court and she wasn't ranked that far above me. I also wanted to avoid showing this woman my neck, just on principle.

"Queen Amarantha, I come to you as a representative of Lord Lucifer's court for the purpose of reestablishing relations between the kingdoms of the fallen and the faerie," I began, quoting directly from a speech Lucifer (or one of his flunkies) had written out for me. I'd barely had time to look at it over the past couple of days what with all the excitement that had been going on. That morning I'd been frantically trying to memorize it over breakfast. I'd felt like I was cramming for a final.

"Lord Lucifer sends his deepest apologies regarding the unfortunate breach of conduct by the previous ambassador," I continued.

Amarantha cut in, her voice dripping icicles. "And what of the unfortunate breach of conduct by the current ambassador?"

11

THE PREPARED SPEECH DRIED UP ON MY TONGUE. I sighed quietly. She couldn't have waited until I was done with the preliminaries before going for the jugular? What about all this formality and courtesy that everyone had told me the faeries loved? Thus far I'd seen little evidence of it.

I decided that my best move was to admit nothing. I hadn't done anything wrong—not on purpose, anyway.

None of the observers were bothering to disguise their curiosity. You could have heard a pin drop in that room.

"What breach of conduct are you speaking of?" I asked, matching frost with frost. I felt Beezle twitch on my shoulder. It was hard to tell if he approved or not. I didn't want to look at him and break eye contact with the queen.

Amarantha's face hardened. "Do not play games with me, foolish girl."

I stepped forward, away from J.B. and Nathaniel.

"Do not speak to me as though I am a child. I am the daughter of Lord Azazel and the granddaughter of Lord Lucifer. I have come here as ambassador to represent their interest and to negotiate with you in good faith. I did not come here to be insulted or spoken to like a servant."

Amarantha stood from her throne and came down the steps to face me. Her beautiful face was suffused with anger. "And I did not negotiate for months with Nathaniel ap Zerachiel in order to have my kingdom invaded, my forest burned to a cinder and my darling pets destroyed by an ambassador speaking with a snake's tongue."

Have I ever mentioned that I have a bad temper, and that it is quick to burn? I stepped closer to Amarantha, so that we were practically nose to nose. My magic surged up, hot and angry, and it crackled across my fingertips. The sound was like a gunshot in the silence.

I felt the change in atmosphere as Amarantha drew her own power around her. Beezle flew backward off my shoulder, apparently sensing that he might be collateral damage if the hair pulling started. Not that I am a hair puller. If it came down to a fight, Queenie would definitely be feeling my fists.

As soon as I had that thought, I made a conscious effort to dial back my anger. My magic receded, still humming just under the surface but less likely to go off spontaneously. Nobody would be happy if I punched out the faerie queen. I modulated my voice. I would not, however, cede ground, so we remained face-to-face.

"Queen Amarantha, I was under the impression that it is generally considered polite to inquire as to the circumstances before making accusations."

She still hadn't drawn down her power. I could feel the electric hum in the air.

"Are you attempting to school me, Ambassador?" she said.

"Only if you need it," I replied.

She seemed to realize that she, too, was on the edge of some precipice and that she needed to step back. If she grew angry enough to kill me (or to try—I wasn't about to stand still and let her do it), who knew how Lucifer might respond? He might decide to bring the power of the courts of the fallen on her head. After all, I wasn't just an ambassador. I was the last direct descendant of Evangeline, the only person Lucifer had ever loved. Surely such an insult could not be allowed to pass.

Maybe that was what Lucifer had intended all along. Maybe he had intended that the negotiations fail. If I was killed, then he could openly make a move for Amarantha's kingdom. At the very least he'd probably considered it as a potential outcome that benefited him. Lucifer, I was discovering, thought about things differently than everyone else. He comprehended dimensions, options and outcomes I would never have even considered.

Amarantha narrowed her eyes at me. The whole room seemed to take a breath and hold it. Then she did something surprising. She stepped back.

"Perhaps this conversation is best continued in my private receiving room."

I stepped back, too, about a centimeter. Just to show that I could compromise. "An excellent idea."

I was keen to get away from the audience. Amarantha would likely be more reasonable away from the staring eyes of her courtiers.

She gestured imperiously to Violet, who quickly came forward to lead the way. There was a door just to the left of the throne and we all filed in behind Violet. I didn't look at J.B. or Nathaniel. I didn't want to see the disapproval that was definitely on Nathaniel's face, and probably on J.B.'s. We'd only been here a half an hour and I'd already managed to bring the negotiations to the brink of total collapse.

Just before entering the receiving room, I noticed five individuals who stood out among the staring crowd. They were all male, dressed in leather, flannel and denim instead of silks and jewels. As we entered the receiving room, Tyrone Wade winked at me. Jude and James both gave me hostile stares. I felt the hairs on the back of my neck stand up. I definitely did not want to run into either of them in the hallway in the middle of the night.

So the wolves were here, too. I wondered if they had discovered who had slaughtered their pack mates. It seemed like a million years ago since I'd fallen out of the sky and discovered the body of the first wolf.

The receiving room was just as plush as I'd expected, with red velvet pillows scattered everywhere and a profusion of gleaming wood. As soon as the door closed behind J.B., Amarantha turned on me.

"Tell me what happened."

I bristled a little at her peremptory tone but decided it was best to just give her what she wanted. The sooner this was resolved, the sooner we could get on with the negotiations and the sooner I could go home. I still had Gabriel burning in the back of my mind, and I needed to figure out what to do about Focalor and Samiel.

As succinctly as I could, I summarized Beezle's kidnap, the hidden portal, our accidental arrival in the outlands, the abandonment of her warriors and my reasons for burning the leviathan and the spider. Amarantha listened with an impassive face. I did not attempt to apologize or make excuses. I simply presented the events as they had happened and waited. She would either accept it or not.

Long minutes passed. I was amazed at Beezle's restraint. He did not make a single smart comment.

"Very well," Amarantha said. "I will verify the presence of this mysterious portal, and have the warriors questioned more closely."

The look in her eye was a little bloodthirsty as she said this, and I thought that the questioning would probably involve pain for the warriors.

She continued. "I accept that wrong has been done to you when they abandoned you in the woods, and in the course of the kidnapping of your gargoyle. I also accept that any offense, if given, has been accidental. However, the fact remains that restitution is owed for the loss of my creatures and my forest."

"What kind of restitution?" I asked warily. I wasn't keen on using Azazel's money, but if Amarantha wanted repayment, I would definitely be sending the bill to Daddy dearest.

She looked at me, and again I could see the careful crafting going on behind her green eyes.

"I wish for you and your party to stay in my court for three days," she said.

Three days? I thought. How would I ever find Gabriel and prevent a demon uprising if I was trapped in Amarantha's court for three days? Plus, I wasn't sure I had enough food to last that long, and I wasn't about to be tricked into drinking or eating anything from Amarantha's kitchen.

"May I ask why you would like us to stay an extra three days?" I asked.

"Perhaps I am interested in you, Ambassador Black," Amarantha said, and showed her teeth. "Perhaps I simply wish to enjoy the company of my son, whom I see so rarely."

As she said this, I realized that this was the first time

she'd acknowledged J.B. since we had entered her court. Not exactly a paragon of motherly love, our Amarantha.

I would have liked to have had a quick consult with Beezle to be sure I wasn't missing anything important—and I was sure that I was. There was no way Amarantha would make such a proposal unless it benefited her first and foremost.

Three days was a long time for me to try to avoid putting my foot in the trap I was sure she as setting for me. On the other hand, I was unlikely to be presented with another form of repayment that would be as relatively easy and cheap as this one.

"Very well," I said. "We will remain in court for three days."

"I could not be more pleased," Amarantha said.

I wished I could say the same.

Amarantha dismissed us shortly after that, saying there was no point in rushing to negotiate, now that our stay had been extended. I hoped she wasn't going to keep giving me the brush-off until it was time to leave. I didn't want to have to rememorize Lucifer's stupid speech every morning.

We were shown to our rooms by more of the silently appearing servants. J.B.'s rooms were in the royal wing, of course, and he left us at the junction of the stairs to go right while we went left. He gave me a little wave but his face was troubled. I wondered if he knew, or suspected, what his mother was up to.

The room was decorated like something from *Amadeus*, of course—frilly and velvety and not very comfortable looking. Beezle stuck out his tongue in distaste while the servant plumped up the pillows and drew down the covers on the bed.

To my chagrin, I discovered that there was a connecting door between my room and Nathaniel's. I made a mental note to put a heavy chair in front of that door.

As soon as the servants were dismissed, Beezle began a flying circuit of the room.

"Looking for bugs?" I asked, putting my clothes away in a closet the size of my entire bedroom at home.

My off-the-rack suits looked sad and wrinkled in such palatial splendor. Even the closets in Amarantha's castle were designed to intimidate.

"Looking for ways to get in," Beezle said. "I know there's a door here somewhere."

After a few moments he stopped and hovered in front of a rather ugly carving of a cherub. The cherub had creepy, staring blue eyes. I'd have to put a sweatshirt over that thing or I would never be able to sleep.

"Here," he said, and pointed to the minute crack in the wall, slender as a fishing line. I would never have found it without him to point it out to me.

"Impressive," I said, and he nodded at the acknowledgment of his superiority. "Now, how to open it?"

"It's probably got something to do with this ugly-ass statue," he said. "Don't you ever pay attention when we watch old horror movies?"

"I may have missed a few things while running back and forth to the kitchen for snacks," I replied dryly.

I put my hand on the cherub and felt carefully around for a button or a lever, anything that might trigger the door to open. When I ran my fingers under the cherub's wing, I found a tiny switch and pushed it. The door swung into a hidden corridor.

"Whaddya think?" I asked Beezle, indicating the corridor.

"It's probably not the smartest idea in the world," he said, putting one claw to his mouth like he was considering the situation. "It might be a breach of protocol to go wandering around the castle uninvited."

"It might also be a breach of protocol to install me in a room where we can be spied upon," I said. "I'm sure Amarantha carefully considered which guest room to put us in."

Beezle clapped his hands together. "An offense for an offense—just the stuff successful negotiations are made of. Let's go. If you could talk your way out of the last mess, I'm sure you can talk your way out of this one."

I didn't need any further encouragement. My curiosity overrode propriety. I wanted to know where the tunnels went. We walked into the surprisingly well-lit corridor. Lamps burned every few feet, and the stone floors were sparkling clean. There wasn't a cobweb in sight. This was not the haunted passage of those old movies that Beezle loved.

Before I swung the door closed I realized we should have some way of knowing which door was mine, and also how to reopen the door from the corridor.

"Beezle, run and grab my lipstick from my makeup bag," I said.

"You mean the lipstick that you spent twenty-five dollars on and never use?" Beezle asked.

"Just get it and keep your comments to yourself," I said.

I examined the exterior of the door while Beezle flew back in the room on his errand. There was a small lever at doorknob height, built flat into the door. There was just enough room under the lever to slide my fingers and pull it out. As I did, I heard a click. Easy-peasy.

Beezle flew back to me and wordlessly handed the lipstick out. I closed the door and then drew a line just above the lever with my lipstick. Hopefully it was small enough to go unseen by anyone walking this way. No matter what I told Beezle, I really didn't think Amarantha would tolerate another offense from me so soon after the last one.

The corridor stretched out in both directions with no defining features or useful signs, like "Watchtower this way" or "Ballroom on the next level." I'd tried to pay attention to where we were taken but the castle had such a profusion of floors and twisting stairs that maintaining any sense of north-south orientation had been impossible.

With no clues to go on, I decided to go right. I remembered vaguely something that I'd read in a historical novel once. The characters had been attempting to negotiate a maze, and one character had said that if you always turned right when possible, you would reach the heart of the maze.

I didn't know if turning right continuously would take me to the heart of the castle, but at least it would make getting back easier. I would just turn left until I found my corridor again.

We'd only gone a few feet when I heard Nathaniel's voice. I stopped for a moment and looked guiltily around before I realized the voice was coming from his room. I crept closer, pressing my ear to the wall. Beezle gave me the big what-the-heck-are-you-doing eyes. I waved him away.

"Yes, of course. This delay won't change anything. No, Lord Azazel is not aware of any of this. He has no inkling."

Interesting. So Nathaniel was sneaking around Azazel's back. But what was he up to?

"Do you take me for an idiot? I can handle her," Nathaniel said angrily. "I said, I can handle her."

Her? Who was he talking about? Me? Amarantha? Or some other player in whatever scheme he was involved in?

"I will speak to you tomorrow," he said firmly. I heard the push-button tone as he clicked off his cell phone.

I waited a few minutes longer but he didn't make any more illicit phone calls and I heard nothing more interesting than the shifting of mattress springs. I yielded to Beezle's insistent gesturing and continued down the corridor. We turned right when we reached the end and only then did we feel it was safe to talk in whispers.

"What in the four hells did you do that for?" Beezle asked. "How do you know Nathaniel doesn't know about the secret doors? You could have been caught."

"I'd be surprised if Nathaniel knows about the doors. He doesn't strike me as observant generally."

"He doesn't strike me as the sort to sneak around on Azazel, either," Beezle retorted. "I didn't think he had the stones."

"I know. He always seems like the world's biggest kiss-ass."

We walked along for a while, turning right when the opportunity presented itself and going down stairs when we found them.

We heard nothing more exciting that the gossip of servants, which seemed to be everywhere. It made sense, I guess, that a castle of this size would need a lot of people to run it.

Amarantha seemed universally revered, which was surprising. Most monarchs would have managed to sow at least some discontent in a one-thousand-plus-year reign. Lady Violet, on the other hand, was despised by pretty much everyone. She "acted above her station," made unnecessary demands and in general behaved as though she were the queen of the castle, not Amarantha.

I managed to avoid detection by the servants by putting

out my wings whenever I heard footsteps approaching. Beezle would hover up near the ceiling out of sight.

My wings were far too large and unwieldy to leave out, though, even folded on my back. A couple of times I'd had to hold my breath as I pressed up against the wall while a faerie passed by. I ran my finger inside the rather snug waistband of my skirt. Maybe Beezle was right. Maybe I did need to take up jogging or something.

We had just about decided that we'd pushed our luck long enough when we heard the wolf howling.

It sounded like it was in horrible pain. I started to run down the corridor in the direction of the sound. We reached a T-junction.

"Where?" I asked, looking left and right.

Beezle flew up behind me, panting with exertion. Talk about someone who needed an exercise program.

"I think it's outside," he panted. "Try to get into one of the main rooms."

I sprinted for the first door that I saw and opened it. Shelves stacked with bread and cheese and hanging meat surrounded us. We were in some kind of larder. I pushed out the door on the other side and surprised several faeries working in the kitchen.

"Outside door?" I asked.

A faerie pointed wordlessly at a heavy oak door on the other side of the kitchen. The wolf's howls grew louder, more anguished, and suddenly the howls of the other wolves rang out inside the castle.

I pushed open the door and emerged into the darkness of full night. The forest that surrounded the castle loomed above the outer walls. I listened for a moment to the sound of howls now growing faint, and turned left. The wolf was dying. I could feel it.

I turned the corner on the castle and was suddenly knocked back by a powerful shock wave. For the third time I was struck by a sense of wrongness, a sense that this was outside the natural order of things. It was the feeling I associated with Ramuell, and I knew the wolf was already dead.

I didn't have time to think or to protect myself as the shock wave hit, and I felt my magic wink out in an instant.

Great. Now I was totally helpless and surrounded by enemies, and the wolf was beyond help. But I could still try to discover the identity of its attacker. I knew one thing for sure—this was the same creature that had killed the other wolves. The shock wave confirmed that.

The darkness made it hard to see, and my lack of magic meant that I couldn't conjure up a ball of flame to light my way. Amarantha had lit the catwalks with torches, but here on the ground everything was swathed in shadow. Beezle puffed and panted behind me. The wolf had long since stopped crying, and the howls of the other wolves had ceased.

I ran forward blindly and tripped, flew a few feet and landed on my face in the dirt. Dirt and other things. Thank goodness my mouth was closed.

I came to my knees and looked around in the faint light. The same scene of carnage that had greeted me twice before was here. The coppery smell of blood filled the air.

"Dammit," I said to Beezle. "How many times are we going to be too late?"

"A question I have asked myself, as well, Madeline Black," a rumbling voice said behind me.

I stood and turned to face Wade, Jude, James and another wolf I didn't know.

"You didn't see anyone, either?" I asked.

"We see you, Agent," James growled.

"You've got to be kidding," I said. "I was trying to help him."

"Peace, James," Wade said with a cautioning hand.

"Why, Wade?" Jude said, angrily pushing forward. He bristled all over with fury. "Three times she has been at the death of a pack member. This time she's covered in blood. What more do you want?"

"Uh, how about some evidence?" I asked.

"I see the evidence all over you," Jude said, and James growled in agreement.

Wolves could see much better than I could in the dark. I'm sure that I appeared pretty incriminating, but I wasn't about to be tried for a crime I didn't commit.

"I was racing to help your pack mate and I tripped in the dark," I said patiently. I didn't have any magic to defend myself and I wasn't about to go hand to hand with a wolf a hundred pounds heavier than me.

"If Madeline Black says that is what happened, then it is so," Wade said.

Jude made a noise of frustration, but he stepped away from me. He had to obey his alpha or challenge him in front of the pack.

I looked at Wade, ignoring Jude. "How was your pack mate separated from the rest of you?"

I knew that members of the pack generally slept as wolves in a large community pile, and the disheveled appearance of the others indicated that they had settled in for the night.

"Ethan said he was feeling restless," Wade said. "Faerie magic is not comfortable for us. Ethan tolerated it less well than others."

"So was he followed outside, or did the killer just take the opportunity that presented itself?" I wondered.

"And was the killer already here under some pretext, or

did he follow us and lie in wait?" Wade said. He turned to speak to the other two. "Collect the remains and search for clues."

He beckoned me closer, and we moved slightly away from the rest of the pack. "Have you any theories, Madeline Black?"

I shook my head. "I can't figure out the killer's motivation. Is someone trying to sabotage your negotiations with Amarantha? If they are, there are more effective ways of doing that. It would be difficult to connect the deaths in Chicago with the faeries seeing as they did not occur in Amarantha's kingdom. Why were your pack mates out alone in the city, anyway?"

"We had come to the city for another purpose. Both times our pack mates were called on their cell phones and left quickly. Neither time did they indicate who had called them or why."

"So they were lured by someone. Do you have enemies that could do this?"

Wade grinned, and it was more the showing of teeth than a pleasant smile. "Our oldest and most determined enemy has long been your grandfather Lucifer."

"Oh," I said, not knowing what to say. I kind of wanted to apologize for my bloodline, but I resisted the urge. "But have you found any evidence that the deaths are related to Lucifer?"

"Sadly, no," Wade replied. "But then, there is no evidence that it isn't Lucifer. There is no evidence of any kind to incriminate anyone. And before you ask, yes, there are other packs with which we have grievances."

"So it could have nothing to do with the fallen or the faeries and have everything to do with a pack argument."

Wade nodded. "Yes, that could be. But if it is pack related, the wolves must be getting magical assistance from another party. Werewolves have the magic to shift from one form to another. We are incredibly strong and heal quickly, but we do not have the ability to spellcast as you and some other creatures do. A wolf attacking another wolf would leave traces of itself behind—in scent, in rent flesh and fur. If another pack is attacking us, then someone is following behind to ensure that no evidence is left behind, and that someone is using magic."

I rubbed my forehead. "Why is it that the more we talk about it, the more complicated it becomes? If there's no evidence, how are we going to find the killer and stop him?"

"Him?" Wade said. "How do you know it is a him?"

I shrugged. "I assumed, I guess. Somehow I tend not to think of women as being this cruel."

And the deaths were cruel. It was one thing to kill—out of need, out of self-defense—but this was not simple murder. The killer had clearly taken a rapacious enjoyment in shredding the victim into pieces.

"If you think that a female is not capable of this, then you have obviously not spent enough time with Amarantha," Wade said.

"Well, that's comforting," I muttered. "Speaking of the queen, are you going to tell her about this? I'm kind of surprised the whole castle isn't out here gaping."

"I am not surprised. Faeries are generally reluctant to involve themselves in situations not to their advantage."

"So there could be a witness somewhere inside the castle, but we'll never know because the faerie wouldn't see the advantage in telling us?"

"That is correct," Wade replied.

"Do you know how much I hate it here?" I muttered.

Wade laughed, a giant belly laugh that boomed through

the courtyard. "Even if you are the granddaughter of Lucifer, I like you, Madeline Black."

I smiled back. It was hard not to like the big burly wolf.

He nodded to me, sobering. "I must assist my pack in the burial of our brother. Until we meet again. *En Taro Adun!*"

He turned and walked away before I had a chance to ask him what on earth "*En Taro Adun*" meant.

Beezle fluttered up. "Have we had enough excitement for one night yet?"

"Oh, yeah," I replied. "Snacks?"

"Only if you brought something good. I'm not eating any of those granola bars."

"Right, because a vitamin might enter your bloodstream and then your whole system would go into shock."

We walked back into the castle through a side door. I was forced to ask one of the servants for directions back to my room. He wordlessly beckoned us to follow him.

After another twisting and turning adventure through the maze that was Amarantha's castle, we came to our room. I was looking forward to swallowing one of Beezle's hated granola bars, showering the gore and dirt off me and collapsing into bed. But as soon as I opened the door, I realized I wasn't going to get my wish anytime soon.

Nathaniel stood in the middle of the room with his arms crossed and a furious look on his face.

"Where in the four hells have you been, and why are you covered in blood?"

12

"UH, I THINK I MIGHT TAKE A FLY OUT TO THE BALCONY I saw down the way," Beezle said. "Back in a little while."

He flew back out the door and pulled it shut behind him. Traitor.

"What are you doing in here?" I snapped back. I was tired, I was filthy, and I was in absolutely no mood for Nathaniel. "I thought I locked that door."

"It is an insult to our future marriage to put a locked door between us."

"It is also an insult to your future wife to assume that her wishes have no bearing if they interfere with yours."

He waved that comment away. "You did not answer my question. Why are you covered in blood? What have you been doing, killing more of Amarantha's pets? I warn you, I will not take it kindly if you do anything further to jeopardize the months of hard work I have committed to reestablishing relations with the faeries."

"Is that all you can think about?" I shouted. "There are bigger things going on here than your advancement in Lucifer's kingdom."

"As my future wife, you should be more invested in my advancement—" he began.

I cut him off. "Enough. Really, enough. You need to stop acting like you can use our engagement as some kind of lever to get me to do what you want. I don't want to marry you, and you talking about it like I'm entering into indentured servitude is not making me feel better about the situation."

He narrowed his eyes at me. "So, you finally admit that you hate me."

I clenched my fists. "Did I say that? No, I said that I don't want to marry you. And why would I? I don't know you. My father forced me into an engagement with you and all you do is tell me how I ought to be acting so that it reflects better on you."

"And all you do is sneer at me and treat me with disrespect. It is clear to everyone that you despise me."

His anger seemed to be growing with each passing moment. I could feel the aura of magic around him pulsing out, pushing against me in fury. There was something unnatural about that power, something that felt not quite like the power he had shown before. My burned-out magic still lay quiet somewhere inside me, and I felt a little afraid. But my own anger overrode that feeling.

"You haven't done very much to try to make me like you."

"Did I not assist you in finding the gargoyle? Did I not

save you from the spider in the forest when you were overcome by poison? Have I not kept the secret of the thrall's disappearance from my lord, as you have asked? You do not know in what jeopardy I have placed myself by this action. Lord Azazel would be in his rights to cast me out of the courts of the fallen, to torture me, to sell me to a demon court in punishment."

I realized that he had put himself in danger for me, and I felt my anger let up a little. I still didn't like him very much, still didn't want to marry him, but it seemed like he was trying. I opened my mouth to apologize, to try to smooth things over, but it was too late.

"And not only do you despise me, but you have shamed me," he said, and his eyes were not exactly Nathaniel's eyes. There was venom, a pulse of malice that, for all his irritating personal habits, I would never associate with Nathaniel. Something was wrong here, something more than Nathaniel's wounded pride. But I was too angry myself to pay attention to that sense of wrongness.

I felt my temper fire up again. "Shamed you how?"

"By loving the thrall," he said.

I felt everything inside me go still. No one could know about that. No one could even suspect that I felt that way about Gabriel. Well, Lucifer knew, but he was keeping that card in his pocket for some reason of his own. But nobody else could know. If they did, Lucifer's hand would be forced and Gabriel's life would be forfeit. It wouldn't even matter that nothing physical had ever happened between us other than a couple of kisses. Even the possibility that a half nephilim might breed with the daughter of Lord Azazel would be enough to send the sword to his neck.

"I don't know what you're talking about," I said, and my voice was all wobbly.

"Liar," he replied, and he stalked toward me. "It is there for anyone with eyes to see."

Was that true? Had I betrayed us? I'd thought I'd done a better job of hiding my feelings.

"I don't know what you're talking about," I said again, and this time my voice was clear and confident. "Gabriel is my bodyguard, nothing more."

Nathaniel gripped my shoulders and squeezed so hard that I cried out. I tried to pull away from him but he held me firmly in place and I felt panic rise up. He was stronger than me, a lot stronger. And I had no magic.

"He may be nothing more than your bodyguard now," Nathaniel hissed. "But that is not what you desire of him. It is there in every look that passes between you. It is there in the way that he stands too close to you. It is there in the way your fingertips brush when you walk side by side. It was there in your eyes when you asked me to help you find him, to help you keep the secret of his disappearance from Azazel. Your heart speaks through your face, Madeline. Your love for that thing is there for all to see, and *my* heart burns in shame when I see it."

His hands clenched tighter. He was going to bruise my shoulders. I tried to calm him, to soothe.

"Nathaniel, I'm sorry you think that. I'm sorry you feel that way." I flapped my hands ineffectually at the ends of my wrists. My arms were locked to my sides. "Nathaniel. Nathaniel, you're hurting me."

His eyes had turned from frost blue to a dark and blazing sapphire. He looked at me but also beyond at something else only he could see. He pulled me tighter, pulled me closer, until our bodies were pressed together and I couldn't escape his embrace. I was horrified to feel his erection brush against my stomach.

"Sorry?" he repeated, and his eyes refocused on mine. They were the eyes of a predator. It was like Nathaniel was gone, replaced by something monstrous. "Sorry? I will make you sorry."

I saw what he intended and I felt cold sweat break out all over my skin. I began to thrash, to scream, but he pressed his lips against mine and swallowed my cry. I couldn't move my arms but I could clamp down on his lower lip, and I did until he cried out and bled.

"You little bitch," he said, and he backhanded me across the face with all his strength.

My ears rang and I saw stars. I think I blacked out for a minute because the next thing I knew he was on top of me, pulling at my bloody clothes.

"No," I said, squirming underneath him, trying to find purchase to punch him, to kick. He had my limbs locked down. "No."

I felt air on my exposed breasts, tasted his blood in my mouth when he pressed another brutal kiss on me. This could not happen.

"No," I yelled this time and with that my sleeping magic awoke.

Just as when I'd been attacked by Samiel in the alley, I let the magic push up and out and through me. Nathaniel was flung from my body and crashed into a dresser on the other side of the room. The mirror shattered into a million pieces and the shards flew off with enough force to embed in his arms and back. I could see the twinkling edges of glass protruding from his neck.

I leapt off the bed, drawing nightfire, and hit him full on in the chest with it before he could think. He cried out in pain and I saw the blast burn through his shirt and through the skin of his chest. Scorched muscle showed underneath. He didn't move.

I stalked toward him, full of fury. He couldn't be dead yet. I wasn't done killing him.

He opened his eyes, and they were bleary. I raised another ball of nightfire on my palm and made to throw.

"Wait," he said, his voice croaky and hoarse.

"Now I know what you are," I said, and my voice did not sound like my own.

I knew that my eyes must be alight with starshine. I could feel the magic inside me burning in a new way and was filled with not only a desire to take revenge, but a desire to hurt. I wanted him to crawl, to be humiliated. I wanted him to feel the helplessness I had felt. And that feeling was so alien, so monstrous, that it made me pause. I dialed it back a little, just enough so that I felt like myself again.

"Now I know what you are," I repeated, and my magic covered me like a cloak, pulsing and angry. "You are a monster. I will never marry you."

He held his hand in front of him as he struggled to his feet, trying to ward off another attack. "Madeline, I don't know what came over me. It wasn't me. You must believe me. It wasn't me. I'm . . ."

"Don't you dare say you're sorry. You're not sorry. You're sorry you didn't succeed."

"No, I did not mean . . ."

"I know what you meant," I said through my teeth. "And what do you think Lord Azazel will say when he discovers that you tried to defile his only daughter?"

Nathaniel went pale as the moon. I saw him tremble all over. "You must not . . . you must . . ."

"I must do what I feel is right," I said. "Your wishes are hardly relevant."

He fell to his knees again, held his hands out in supplication. "You must not tell Lord Azazel. He will kill me."

I narrowed my eyes at him, hating him with every cell in my body. "What makes you think that *I* won't kill you?"

His hands fell to his sides. "You are right. I have behaved unforgivably. You are well within your rights to end my life."

I had never seen him like this—his will broken, his body injured. Despite what he had done to me, what he had meant to do to me, I felt a stirring of pity. I knew that I shouldn't. I was sure now that Nathaniel would never value anything above his own pride, his own advancement. I knew I didn't want to marry him before—now I knew that I never could. I could never be of so little value to my husband.

"Go," I said. "Our engagement is over. I will break it to Azazel."

"Will you tell him what has occurred here?"

"I will if I have to," I said.

His face shifted and he looked suddenly crafty for a moment—and I again had the sensation that another person was looking through his eyes. "It would be my word against yours, in any case."

I felt my magic rise up again, my anger peaking once more. "Do not attempt to threaten me."

He cowered back, the crafty light in his eyes winking out, and dropped his head. "You are right. I am sorry. You are right."

"And it wouldn't be her word against yours anyway," Beezle said from the doorway. "I am a witness, and Azazel knows that I must speak the truth. So you'd be fucked for sure if she decided Azazel needed to know."

I hadn't heard Beezle reenter. He hovered near the door, his small face full of thunder.

"Get out of here and do not even breathe in my direction for the next three days," I said.

Nathaniel stood unsteadily, his right hand covering the exposed muscle in his chest. He staggered to the connecting door without a word and stumbled through.

I watched him, my body full of tension and magic, until the door closed. Then I looked at Beezle.

"When did you get here?" I asked.

"Right after you blasted that thrice-bedamned bastard into the mirror," he said.

Beezle hardly ever swore. Neither did I, for that matter. That, more than anything, told me how upset he was. We looked at each other in silence.

"I shouldn't have left," he said. "I didn't think he would try something like that."

I shrugged. "I didn't either."

"We probably should have suspected after we overheard him on the phone," Beezle said.

"Right. Sneaking around behind Azazel," I replied.

"If he could do that, he could do anything," Beezle said.

"Yes," I said faintly.

He flew to me, hovered in front of me, put his tiny claws on my cheeks. "It's okay to cry."

"Okay," I said, and I did.

After a good cry, and a thorough washing in the shower in which I scrubbed everywhere Nathaniel touched at least a thousand times, I curled up in bed with the blankets over me and my eyes wide open. Try as I might, I couldn't sleep a bit. Beezle didn't sleep either, maintaining a watch over the connecting door despite the fact that we'd hooked a chair under the doorknob.

When the first rays of dawn trickled in through the window, I sat up in bed and threw the blankets off, done with the pretense of trying to sleep.

"Breakfast?" Beezle asked, stretching.

"I'm not hungry," I said.

I didn't want food. I wanted Gabriel. If he had been here, Nathaniel never would have even tried to hurt me. If Gabriel had been here, I would never have been alone with Nathaniel in the first place.

But you took care of yourself, didn't you? I thought. Well, yes, I had. When it came down to it, I didn't need to cower behind a big, strong man. But it would be nice to have a partner to lean on, and that was what Gabriel was to me. When he was with me, I felt all the broken, empty parts of me were filled, and just at that moment it seemed like there were more broken and empty parts than usual.

I walked to the window, looked down at the hustle and bustle in the courtyard. It appeared that more parties were arriving at Amarantha's court. Several black limousines were lined up near the front door.

I wondered if Wade had told Amarantha what had happened last night, and I wondered where Gabriel was now, if he was safe, if I would ever be able to find him.

I noticed J.B. walking arm in arm with Violet as they greeted the new arrivals. I felt that little flutter in my chest that I had felt the day before, the one that had felt like jealousy, and I knew that it was unfair. If I wasn't going to date J.B., then I couldn't be upset if he chose someone else.

But really, the catty part of me whispered, *couldn't he have chosen someone better than Violet?* I guess she was okay if you wanted a great body and a snotty personality, but I'd always thought J.B. had more depth than that.

"And really, don't you have enough man issues without adding J.B. to the mix?" I mumbled to myself.

"What was that?" Beezle said. "I'm an old gargoyle. I can't hear you."

I turned to answer him and found him digging in the carry-on bag full of snacks that I'd brought. Empty wrappers and banana peels were strewn on the floor. In the few moments that I'd been at the window he had devoured more than half the food I'd brought.

"Beezle!" I shouted, and he looked up at me guiltily. "That food needs to last three days!"

"I can't help it," he whined. "You know I'm a nervous eater. And this stuff isn't exactly nutrient dense, you know. Not like a slice of cake, say, or a doughnut."

"I think you need to reexamine the definition of 'nutrient,'" I said. "I packed that stuff because it *was* nutrient dense."

"Yes, but where is the fat and the sugar? When did you decide to get on a health kick?"

I rolled my eyes and turned away to dress. I didn't want to spend time explaining to Beezle that healthy foods were easier to pack and that we shouldn't be eating so many doughnuts anyway. It didn't matter if he ate the whole sack of food in any case. I wasn't sure I would ever feel like eating again.

Whenever I thought of what had happened the night before, a ball of shame burned in my stomach. I knew that it was Nathaniel who should feel ashamed, and that I had done nothing wrong. But I felt humiliated and helpless, even though I had defended myself.

I never thought it would happen to me. Maybe because

I'd spent so much time sheltered from other people. Maybe because I'd thought Nathaniel would always respect Azazel even if he didn't respect me. I guess everyone thinks it will never happen to them.

I pulled on one of my suits—a black pin-striped one that reminded me of Dana Scully. All I needed was a pair of super-high heels and a red bob, but all I had was black flats and my own messy mop. I pinned my hair in something resembling an updo, and slapped makeup on my face like armor.

My mouth and cheek were bruised where Nathaniel had hit me. I did my best with the cover-up but everyone was going to know I had been hit.

Beezle fluttered up to my shoulder and landed there. He squeezed his claws comfortingly. "No one has to know."

"They'll know something happened," I replied.

"Just glare if anyone tries to ask. You are royalty, after all. You don't have to answer questions if you don't want to."

I practiced my best haughty do-not-speak-to-me-you-peasant look in the mirror. It might put off strangers, but I shuddered to think what J.B. would say when he saw me.

Then I took a deep breath and went out of the room, where I promptly managed to get lost.

After much rushing around hallways listening to Beezle's useless directions and not seeing anyone to help me, I spotted Jude coming out of a guest room. Great. My least favorite wolf. But at least he would be able to point me toward the throne room—I hoped.

"Jude!" I called, jogging to catch up with him. Beezle flew behind me.

He continued walking down the hall like he hadn't heard.

"Jude!" I cried, more insistently.

It seemed like he walked a little faster.

"Are you kidding me?" I muttered. "Are you seriously going to pretend that you don't hear me?"

I sped up until I caught up to him and then tapped his shoulder. I lost Beezle, who panted several feet behind me. Jude turned on me with a snarl.

"What is it, spawn of Lucifer?"

I backed up a step. His fangs were showing. It was very off-putting to see a wolf's fangs in a human's mouth.

"Okay," I said, holding my hands up. "First off, I'm not precisely Lucifer's spawn."

"Intervening generations do not change the fact that you are of his blood," Jude growled.

"Okay, whatever," I said. I wasn't about to get embroiled in genetic technicalities with Jude, who clearly wanted to be anywhere that wasn't near me. "Listen, can you tell me how to get to the throne room? I seem to have made a wrong turn somewhere."

He smirked at me. "All the powers of the devil don't come with a compass?"

"Fine, don't help me," I said, pushing past him. Obviously Jude had some issues that precluded the possibility of his acting like a civilized human being.

"Wait a second," he said, and grabbed my shoulder roughly.

Something flashed through my head—Nathaniel holding me in place by my shoulders. I turned on Jude with a yell and knocked his hand from me. My breath came hard and my hands were curled into fists.

He stepped back a little and held up his arms to show he wasn't dangerous. I could see him examining my face closely and I felt a wave of embarrassment redden my cheeks.

"Who hit you?" he growled.

"Nobody. I fell last night, remember?" I looked down. I couldn't believe I was lying, making excuses.

He put his hand under my chin, more gently than I thought him capable, and forced my face up to his.

"Somebody hit you," he said. "I can smell a lie."

"Yeah, well," I said, getting some of my gumption back. "I blasted him across the room, so he paid for it."

"Good," Jude said shortly, and dropped his hand away. "Follow me. I'm going to the throne room anyway."

He started down the hallway again. I trotted after him, which was necessary because he was quite a bit taller than me and it took me five steps for every one of his.

He didn't say anything else, and I was okay with that. I didn't know what to make of that moment in the hallway, and I'm sure he didn't either. He was probably already regretting being nice to a descendant of Lucifer. Beezle had caught up with us and settled on my shoulder, letting me do the heavy lifting.

Several minutes later we were at a side entrance to the throne room. Apparently this was the way you came in when you weren't being formally announced. There were several knots of courtiers already assembled in little cliques around the room.

Amarantha was receiving the various parties that had arrived that morning. There were a couple of different faerie factions from other parts of the country coming in. She looked completely in her element, and I wondered how long she'd practiced that look of benevolent tolerance before she'd perfected it.

Jude took off for the small party of wolves on the opposite side of the room and I looked around for J.B. Wade saw me and gave me a friendly wave, but his brows were furrowed as he consulted with the other wolves.

None of the other courtiers seemed inclined to invite me into their group. I stood awkwardly off to the side, looking hopefully around for someone who would want to talk to me. It probably didn't help that Beezle had fallen asleep on my shoulder and he was snoring loud enough to wake the dead.

I felt a tap on the shoulder that wasn't hosting a fat, lazy gargoyle and a second later J.B. was in front of me. I took Beezle off my shoulder because my right ear was deaf and stuffed him in one of the patch pockets on the front of my suit. His arms and head hung over the seam of the pocket, but he kept snoring. I was getting a little worried about Beezle.

I wasn't exactly sure how old he was, but he definitely seemed to be slowing down lately. What would I do if he turned to stone?

"You look like Molly Ringwald in that movie where she shows up at the prom without a date," J.B. said.

"Does that make you my Andrew McCarthy?" I asked.

"Only if you promise not to call me Blaine," he replied, and then his face creased in anger. I knew he'd seen the shadow of the bruise through my makeup. "What happened to you?"

"Can we not talk about it?" I asked. I really wasn't up for telling the whole story now, and my lies were so pathetically feeble that J.B. would see right through them.

He grabbed my arm and pulled me over to the side of the room, away from nosy courtiers.

"No, I really would like to talk about it, because there's only one thing that could make a bruise like that. A fist."

I sighed. J.B.'s testosterone was up. The last thing I needed was him going after Nathaniel. I didn't even want to think about what kinds of problems that would cause between the courts of the faerie and the fallen.

"Okay, you win. I got hit, but I hit him back and now it's all over so you don't need to ride to my rescue," I said quickly and quietly. "I was in a lot more danger when I faced Ramuell."

"Just tell me who did it," J.B. said grimly.

"No," I said. "I don't want you to get involved in this."

"For chrissakes. When the hell are you going to trust me?" he said, rubbing his hands through his hair in frustration.

I looked at him in surprise. "I do trust you. You're probably the closest friend I have after Beezle."

There was speculation in his green eyes. "Really? Closer than Gabriel?"

"Gabriel is my bodyguard," I said stiffly.

J.B. snorted. "He wants something to do with your body, but it ain't guarding that he's thinking about."

That was the second time in less than twelve hours that my relationship with Gabriel had been questioned. Apparently, we had done a super-crappy job of trying to keep things secret. What made it even worse was that *nothing* had really happened between us. There was just a lot of longing and the restless nights that go with it.

And this was yet another topic that I was not keen to discuss in a room full of avidly watching courtiers.

"Did Wade tell your mom about the wolf killing last night?" I asked.

"Yes, and she's not happy about it," he said with a small smile. He seemed to enjoy his mother's annoyance.

"Why not?" I asked. "I mean, beyond the obvious."

"It's a terrible insult to the wolves that this occurred in Amarantha's own courtyard. It indicates a breach of security and violates a ton of faerie rules involving etiquette and the safety of guests."

"So she's pissed because now they have more leverage to negotiate for that land that they want. They've been insulted and she has to repay them," I guessed.

"Uh-huh," he said. "She's in a real snit about it."

"Well, if she's anything like my father, then it would be good for her to not get her way now and then."

"I think so, too . . ." he said, and trailed off.

He stared at something over the heads of the courtiers. The room had gone completely silent except for the swishing of fabric as everyone turned to look at the main entrance to the court.

I stood on my tiptoes and tried to see. Unfortunately that only made me five foot two instead of five foot. Considering that most of the faeries were built on the tall and lean scale this meant that all I saw were a lot of shoulder blades.

"What's going on?" I asked.

"Shh," J.B. said.

The faerie toady who stood by the door announced the arrivals. "Lord Focalor of the kingdom of the fallen, escorted by Antares ap Azazel and sundry demons, and bearing a gift for Queen Amarantha."

Antares. Focalor. What in the four hells were they doing *here*?

The crowd parted as they approached the throne. I could see Antares, and the demon that had been in my vision, the one that had negotiated with Samiel. So my guess was correct—he was Focalor.

A crowd of smaller demons followed behind Focalor and Antares. Antares held a leash in his hands attached to a figure who walked between my half brother and his lord.

His back was covered in lash marks, he was filthy, his black wings drooped, and his hands were bound behind his back. But his head was high and his dark eyes burned with anger.

It was Gabriel.

13

THE ROOM BROKE OUT IN FURIOUS MUTTERS. MOST OF the faeries seemed shocked that Focalor had not only entered Amarantha's court under his own banner and not Lucifer's, but that he'd done Amarantha the insult of bringing lesser demons with him. I knew all of this was important. I knew that it probably meant that Focalor was moving openly against Lucifer. But I only had eyes for one person.

"Gabriel," I whispered, and I started toward him.

"Don't," J.B. said, and he grabbed my hand and pulled me back.

"Why not?" I said angrily under my breath. "I'm within my rights to take him back. Gabriel is my bodyguard."

"But he came here with Focalor's party. You would be insulting Amarantha if you tried to take him from the demons in front of the entire court."

"Do you think I care about insulting the queen?" I hissed. "Do you see him? Do you see what they've done to him?"

J.B. squeezed my hand. "I see. I know. Don't worry. We'll get him back. But let's find out what they want before we go in all guns blazing."

Focalor had approached the throne. Antares stood a few feet back with Gabriel. I could see the metal collar they had put around his neck. It was lined with spikes that protruded from it every few inches and Antares was obviously taking pleasure in yanking on the leash so that Gabriel's flesh would bleed anew.

The little knot of demons stood farther back in the center of the room, and all the faeries were taking care not to brush up against them accidentally. The courtiers had pressed back against the walls and cleared an area of several feet around the demons.

Amarantha appeared to be disgusted by the whole proceeding. Violet, standing at the queen's right hand as always, looked like she was either going to puke or faint. I couldn't blame her. The stench of the demons, that sulfuric cloud that always seemed to follow them, was slowly filling the throne room. The servants were attempting to discreetly open the gigantic windows that lined one side of the room, but the courtiers pressed back so far that it was difficult for the servants to do their jobs.

I, on the other hand, pushed forward so that I was in front of the crowd, close to the throne and with a clear view. Antares caught my eye and winked menacingly. I felt magic crackle over my fingers and suppressed the urge to blast him into kingdom come. I was sure that would violate some desperately important accord of the faerie court, and the only thing I wanted right now was to get Gabriel back.

If I had to control my temper for a few minutes, then so be it. But Antares was going to pay for this, sooner or later.

Focalor bowed low to Amarantha. It was the kind of bow that seemed correct but there was something disrespectful about it all the same. Which he probably was.

"Queen Amarantha, most beautiful light of the faerie court," Focalor began, and his voice oozed with the false compliments.

"Lord Focalor," Amarantha replied, and her voice was polite although her teeth were gritted. "How dare you come to my court under your own banner, and sully this place with these low creatures?"

She gestured to the demons, who were flicking their tongues and growling and oozing all over the place.

Focalor bowed his head. "Forgive me, my lady. I was under the impression that it was customary for a lord to be escorted by his retinue. Do not your own accords state that hospitality shall be given even unto the escorts of a guest in your court?"

He smiled, and I wondered how Amarantha would get out of this one.

"You have not been invited, nor have you been accepted; therefore you are not yet a guest of my court," she replied. "If you have come to bargain with me, then your *retinue* must remove to the courtyard."

Focalor narrowed his eyes. I saw Amarantha make a small movement of her index finger. The servants who had been hovering unobtrusively in the background moved swiftly to the front of the crowd and stood at parade rest. Ah. So the servants were also warriors, and Amarantha wanted them on hand in case things got ugly fast.

For a moment it seemed her paranoia was justified. Focalor looked like he was ready to loose his demons on the courtiers rather than submit to Amarantha's will. I readied my magic. Next to me I saw J.B. draw a long wooden rod from his pocket. I had seen him use this once before. Apparently it gave him some extra powers.

Then Focalor smiled his hideous smile, and said, "As you wish."

The demons went snarling out of the room, followed by a couple of warriors to make sure that they went the right way. Antares and Gabriel stayed. I tried to catch Gabriel's eye, but he stared stoically ahead, seeing nothing.

"My lady, I have come to you to establish relations between our courts," Focalor said.

"We already have in this court a representative of Lord Lucifer," Amarantha replied. "Lady Madeline Black ap Azazel. It is not necessary for your lord to send more than one ambassador at a time."

Focalor showed his pointed teeth. I remembered Beezle telling me after my vision of the Forbidden Lands that Focalor was one of the fallen, not a demon, and I wondered why he didn't look angelic like the other fallen. What had he done that had twisted his appearance so thoroughly?

"I have not come as a representative of Lucifer. I have come to establish relations with my own court and under my own banner as an independent entity."

There was an intake of breath in the room, and several heads craned around to stare at me. So this was it. Focalor was moving against Lucifer publicly. What power was he holding that made him think he could succeed?

I knew that I couldn't let Focalor's statement pass without comment. I was there as Lucifer's representative.

I stepped forward, heard J.B. whisper, "Carefully."

Beezle still snored away in my front patch pocket. His arms hung over the side and his head drooped. Unbelievable.

I'm sure that I looked really authoritative with a snoozing gargoyle as an accessory. But I marched up to the throne and stood within a foot of Focalor, even though the stench of him turned my stomach. I didn't try to look at Gabriel this time. I didn't want everyone in the room to see the desperate need that would surely be on my face. I was learning that I didn't hide my emotions well.

"Lady Amarantha, if I may speak?" I asked, and she nodded. I directed my comments to Focalor. I tried to make an effort to sound all formal and ambassador-y. "I believe Lord Lucifer would be somewhat surprised to discover that you are, as you say, an 'independent entity.' The laws which have bound you these thousands of years have not recently been altered, have they?"

"The laws which have bound me have begun to chafe," Focalor replied.

"So put some cream on it and deal," I replied, dropping the formality. I just didn't have great people skills. I wondered again why Lucifer had chosen me. "You know, I know and everybody in this room knows that what you're doing right now is sedition."

Focalor bowed in acknowledgment. "If that is what my lady chooses to call it."

"I call you a traitor to Lucifer's court," I said.

Focalor stepped closer to me, and I glared up at him. I realllllllly hated that I was so short. I could never look eye to eye with anyone. The heat and stink coming off his body was intense and I tried to breathe through my mouth.

"That is a strong word, Lady Madeline. Be careful. Words can get you into trouble."

"Trouble is a word you'd better get used to, because Lucifer is going to bring the freaking thunder down on your ass," I snapped. "I'm not going to stand here and exchange smart comments for the rest of the day. If you have even an iota of intelligence, you'll take your little demon toys and my worthless half brother and go home. But you can leave Gabriel. He is my father's thrall and you have done Azazel an insult by taking him. If you leave now, I will speak to Lucifer on your behalf. Perhaps he'll be lenient since no harm has yet been done."

"I am not afraid of Lucifer or Azazel," Focalor hissed. "I have access to powers that they cannot comprehend. Lucifer will no longer reign supreme on this Earth. And I do not have to accept the insults of Azazel's whelp."

There were several shocked intakes of breath.

"You should remember," I said, and I felt my magic moving through me, eager for the fight, "that I am not only Azazel's daughter. I am Lucifer's granddaughter, and the power of the Morningstar flows through me. What you have done is tantamount to declaring war on my grandfather's kingdom. Whatever powers you think you have, they won't do you any good when I pull your heartstone from your chest."

That was kind of an icky and demony threat coming from me, but I wanted to make sure that Focalor knew that I meant business. I also knew that there was this rule and that rule and the other rule about harming other members of the courts of the fallen, but I thought Lucifer might give me a pass if I averted a massive war by killing Focalor. I'd probably get stuck doing another shitty favor for old Granddad, though.

"Enough," Amarantha thundered.

We both turned to look at her. I'd kind of forgotten that we were standing in her court, actually. I was all wrapped up in trying to figure out how to take Focalor down before he slashed my throat open with his claws.

"Whatever the arguments between the courts of the

fallen, *my* court is not the place to air your grievances. You have both done me a grave insult by bringing this here."

"He started it," I muttered.

"Lord Focalor, in exchange for this insult, I demand that you leave Lord Azazel's thrall with me."

I started to protest, but Focalor cut me off.

"That suits me very well, my lady, as I had intended to gift the thrall to you in any case."

What? What purpose could Focalor possibly have in giving Gabriel to Amarantha? Well, besides the obvious purpose of pissing off Azazel.

Amarantha looked deeply pleased. There was something else going on here besides Focalor openly declaring war on Lucifer.

"That is an exceptional gift, my lord Focalor," Amarantha purred. Suddenly all of Focalor's insults were forgotten. "Violet, take the thrall to my chambers."

I looked at Gabriel, who still wore a stony expression; at Amarantha, who could barely disguise her glee; and at Focalor, who gave me a smug smirk. I didn't bother looking at Antares. There was no doubt that he was thrilled to pieces at pulling one over on me.

"You can't accept Gabriel as a gift," I said, trying to control my temper. I was not in Amarantha's good books at the moment. "He's not Focalor's to give. Gabriel is Azazel's thrall and in Azazel's absence I speak for him."

"It seems to me," Amarantha said silkily, "that you should have taken better care of your father's thrall in the first place. The thrall is in Focalor's possession, not yours. Therefore you have no claims over him."

"Thank you for accepting my gift, lady," Focalor said.

"In exchange for this generosity, you may remain as a guest of my court," Amarantha said. "However, due to the delicate nature of my courtiers, your demons must remain outside."

"Understood, my lady," Focalor said.

Violet stepped forward to take Gabriel's leash from Antares. Amarantha stood from her throne. She practically hummed with anticipation.

Two of Amarantha's warriors/servants came to Focalor's side and escorted the fallen lord and Antares from the throne room, presumably to show them to their quarters.

This was ridiculous. I was going to start shouting and blasting everything in the throne room in a minute. Amarantha could not possibly be accepting Focalor's claims of independence from Lucifer. She could not possibly be taking Gabriel from me.

Amarantha turned to enter her receiving room. I started after her, but felt a hand on my shoulder.

I turned to shout at the person holding me and saw that it was Wade.

"Don't," he said quietly. "Don't give her more ammunition to hurt you. If you want your bodyguard back, think before you act."

To my horror I felt tears filling my eyes. Violet led Gabriel into the receiving room behind Amarantha.

"Don't let them see you cry," Wade said.

"Yes," I said, and I blinked until I felt the tears receding.

I would not cry in front of Antares and Focalor. I would not give them the satisfaction of knowing how much they had hurt me.

"Good girl," Wade said. "Now, come away. I need to speak with you."

Everyone in the room was staring at us. The other wolves gathered around me. J.B. joined them.

"Come away," Wade repeated.

He took my arm and I let him. I wasn't sure I could walk without support. The rush of adrenaline had left me and I felt shaky. I marched out of the throne room with my head held high, the werewolves flanking me like a guard of honor. As soon as the throne room doors closed behind me, we heard the explosion of chatter.

"So glad to know that I'm good entertainment," I said.

"We must find a place where we cannot be overheard," Wade said, looking to J.B.

"The east tower," J.B. replied. "My mother designed it specifically for privacy. No one has the key except members of the family."

J.B. led us through the maze of Amarantha's castle. I barely registered where I was putting my feet. What was Amarantha going to do with Gabriel? How was I going to get him back?

Gabriel. I needed Gabriel. Amarantha had Gabriel. These thoughts chased around my head to the exclusion of everything else.

Several minutes later we climbed a series of spiral stone steps and entered the east tower. The room was designed for comfort rather than show. There was a large fireplace, several soft rugs and lots of well-stuffed furniture. Pillows were scattered everywhere and there was lots of gleaming warm wood. Overall the effect was a lot homier than the rest of the castle.

Wade led me to armchair and set me down in it like a child. I looked up at him blearily.

"What are we doing here?" I asked.

"We have important matters to discuss and it is imperative we not be overheard. Do you know why your mother is so pleased by Focalor's gift?" Wade asked J.B.

J.B. shook his head. "She did look like the cat that swallowed the cream, though, didn't she?"

Wade's face was unusually grave. "Amarantha has long desired some kind of leverage over Lucifer. Focalor's gift has given her that means."

The urgency in Wade's voice was finally getting through to me. "I don't see how owning Gabriel would tilt the balance of power much in her favor."

"Owning him, no. But you are not thinking as Amarantha thinks. Everyone knows how Lucifer is fanatically devoted to preserving his bloodline. It is one of his only weaknesses."

Suddenly what Wade was saying made an awful kind of sense. Images of Gabriel and Amarantha tangled together flashed through my head, and I felt sick. "You mean she wants Gabriel for some kind of stud?"

Wade nodded. "Additionally, she would have access to more of the Morningstar's powers through her child."

"Why the hell are all these immortals so obsessed with bloodlines?" I said angrily. "It's not as if any of them act like Parent of the Year. They only want children to use for the consolidation of their own power."

"How did you come by this information?" J.B. asked. His voice sounded funny. When I looked at him, I saw he'd gone a little pale.

"Wade does not need to answer to you," Jude growled, and James and the other wolf added their own grumbles for good measure.

I had not really noticed the other wolf before except as an anonymous member of the pack. Jude always attracted so much of my attention that I was barely aware of the others. I focused on him for the first time now.

He was large and burly like Jude and Wade and wore the wolf uniform of flannel, leather and denim. He was older and blond with streaks of silver in his ponytail. The coloring was unusual and I thought he probably made an exceptionally handsome wolf.

James was staring at me intently, as usual. His silver blue eyes seemed strangely familiar all of a sudden, like he was related to someone I knew. And just as before, they radiated intense dislike. Maybe I had done him or a family member some wrong in the past and that was why he couldn't stand me.

"Do I know you from somewhere?" I asked. It was going to nag at me until I figured it out.

He looked away from me, as if he'd realized he was staring. "No. I am a recent member of Wade's pack."

I looked at Wade questioningly. He shrugged. "James was a solitary wolf for a time just after his maturity. We often have members join us this way."

"Okay," I said, but I still stared at James. There was something about him . . .

"Can we get back on track, please?" J.B. said, annoyed. "I want to know how you came by such privileged information. I know my mother does not disclose her plans to all and sundry, and she certainly wouldn't be disclosing them to you when she's spent so much time trying to thwart you at every turn."

"I cannot reveal the source of my information," Wade said serenely, but there was a note of finality in his voice. "The important fact here is not where I heard this, but that Amarantha has achieved her desire. She has been given a thrall from Lucifer's bloodline. He could be impregnating her even as we speak."

This time I couldn't stop the little cry of distress that left me. Everyone looked at me.

Okay, fine. I really did a crap job of hiding my feelings. I rubbed my forehead. Did I need this additional problem of trying to stop Amarantha from bearing a child of Lucifer's bloodline even if I did manage to extract Gabriel from her? How many more intrigues would present themselves before all of this was over? There was a wolf-killer running around loose, and war had been declared on Lucifer's kingdom. Samiel was still hanging around in the background somewhere and he definitely wanted my head. And somehow I was supposed to salvage this mess with Amarantha and try to get her to reestablish relations with Lucifer.

Priorities must be made. First thing first—there was no way I would be able to live with the idea that Gabriel had made a child with Amarantha. Never mind the politics. This was personal.

"How can I get Gabriel away from the queen?" I asked J.B.

"If she wants a child of Lucifer's blood that badly, there's probably nothing you can do," he said grimly. "At least until she's had her way."

"That is not a productive thought," I said. Maybe I could trade favors with the wolves. If they would help me with this, I could help them get what they wanted from the queen. "What about your negotiations with her for the land that you want? Did you manage to get her to concede?"

Wade shook his head. "Despite the insult of having a member of our pack killed within sight of her castle she still has not given us what we want."

"And don't expect her to anytime soon, even if she knows that she ought to," J.B. said. "My mother could give a mountain lessons in stubbornness."

"So there really isn't an opening there," I said. "Although maybe if I came forward as an additional witness . . ."

"But she's pissed at you for threatening Focalor in front of everyone," J.B. reminded me. "Your veracity as a witness would be lessened."

"Right," I said. "So I've got no leverage."

"Other than the fact that you are of Lucifer's bloodline," a little voice growled.

I looked down to see that Beezle had finally woken up and was struggling out of my pocket. The two wolves who had not met Beezle before looked shocked that the inanimate object in my jacket was talking.

"So nice of you to join us," I said.

"You think that just because I'm asleep I can't hear what's going on?" he said, finally managing to extract his squat lower half from my pocket. "I'm a gargoyle. We can hear everything, even when we're stone."

"It's not the sleeping that would impair your hearing. It's the snoring," I said sweetly.

"Fine, if you're going to be that way, then I won't tell you my brilliant plan."

I rolled my eyes. "So sorry, Beezle. Now spill."

He hesitated for a moment, like he was going to make me apologize further. But Beezle's desire to have his intelligence admired from all angles overrode his injured pride.

"Amarantha wants leverage over Lucifer, right? That's why she wants a child of his bloodline," Beezle said.

"Yes. Although I'm not sure that wouldn't backfire on her," I said thoughtfully. "The two courts would be tied together irrevocably."

"Right," Beezle said. "So it's your job to convince her that having Gabriel's kid would put her at a disadvantage, and then offer your services to her instead."

"Services?" I said. "Not the kind of services she wants Gabriel to provide?"

"Get your mind out of the gutter. No, you offer yourself as a kind of soldier when she wants backup."

I could see a lot of problems with this plan. "First of all,

I'm not a mercenary. Second of all, Lucifer probably would not be too happy if I allied myself with Amarantha, even temporarily. Third of all, having an extra hammer around to wield is nothing compared to having a tie of blood, even if that hammer is one of Lucifer's."

Beezle crossed his arms grumpily. "So what's your brilliant plan, then?"

"To do whatever it takes to get Gabriel back."

Wade looked at me speculatively. "Be careful. You wouldn't want Amarantha to know that. She is excellent at taunting you with what you most desire."

"And she'll make you bleed for it in the process," J.B. added.

A little pain was nothing if it meant getting Gabriel away from the queen's clutches.

Amarantha wasn't pleased with me at the moment, but surely she wouldn't refuse an audience with her son.

"J.B., do you think you could get me in to see your mom?"

He looked troubled. "If that's what you really want."

What I really wanted was to be at home again with Gabriel and Beezle and all of this court nonsense forgotten.

"That's what I really want."

Even if I had to bleed to get it.

14

THE WOLVES CLEARED OUT WHEN J.B. AND I LEFT FOR
Amarantha's rooms. It would look too much like we were
ganging up on the queen if we all went. Also, I was hoping
that in the privacy of her rooms and away from her courtiers, she would be more reasonable.

Although I wasn't holding out a ton of hope.

"Where's Nathaniel this morning?" J.B. asked casually
as he led me toward the wing of the castle that held the family rooms.

"Probably licking his wounds," Beezle sniggered.

I glared at Beezle, who was perched on my shoulder again.

"So he's the one who hit you," J.B. said. "I thought so."

"Nobody said that."

"You don't have to."

"I took care of it, okay? So there's no need to go all
manly about it," I said.

J.B. looked like he wanted to argue, but then closed his mouth. "Fine. I respect your ability to take care of yourself."

I looked at him, shocked. I was so accustomed to everyone treating me like a helpless idiot that it was both surprising and refreshing to hear J.B. acknowledge that I was neither.

"You did survive Ramuell on your own, after all," he said.

"She did not," Beezle argued. "She got her human heart torn out."

"Am I here or what?" I said crossly. "That constitutes survival."

"The queen's private chambers are at the top of this flight of stairs," J.B. said. "I've sent a message ahead for Violet to expect to receive us."

"And Violet would do just anything for you, *Jonquil*," I said.

He looked at me mildly despite the provocation. "If you're going to go all gooey-eyed whenever Gabriel is in the room, then you have no right to act jealous if I'm with another woman."

I glanced down at the floor, properly chastised. "Point taken."

"But I'd still prefer you to anyone in the world."

I looked up, pleased and confused, which was the way I often felt around J.B. I smiled, but we had reached the top of the stairs. J.B. knocked on the door and Violet let us in, giving me a sideways glare.

"I did not expect Ambassador Black to accompany you," she cooed.

"She needs to have a word with my mother," J.B. said. "I thought I could speak with you in private while they did that."

Violet glowed with pleasure at the thought of some

private conversation with the prince. She left us in the receiving room, which looked a lot like Amarantha's receiving room downstairs, and went into an inner chamber to consult with the queen.

I couldn't tell if J.B. was playing it up so that I could get my audience with the queen or playing it up for his own sake, but as he'd pointed out, I'd no right to be jealous. Even if I was. A really tiny bit.

I wasn't sure what my plan of action was, but a few moments later Violet returned and indicated with a curt nod of her head that I was to enter.

"The gargoyle, however, must stay."

"Beezle comes with me everywhere," I said, surprised. Amarantha had never seen Beezle as a threat before.

"The gargoyle must stay," Violet repeated. "Or you may forfeit your audience with the queen."

Digging my heels in about Beezle didn't seem the smartest way to begin, so I reluctantly let him fly off my shoulder to land on the fireplace mantel. He didn't say anything, but his face had a scrunched-up, worried look.

I entered the inner chamber.

Amarantha had obviously arranged a little display for my discomfort. She was wearing nothing but a diaphanous negligee that left zero to the imagination and she had draped her centerfold body over a red velvet chaise. Her left hand picked at a small plate of fruit while her right held a black satin leash attached to Gabriel's neck.

She had arranged him on the floor like a dog at her feet. He had been washed, and oiled, and the black feathers of his wings shone with gloss. She had even put him in a loincloth. He looked up at me when I entered but then looked away, like he was embarrassed to have me see him that way.

The overall effect was so cheesy, so *obvious*, that I

would have laughed had it not been Gabriel attached to the leash. As it was, I had a hard time keeping my legs steady. Until I saw the smug look of satisfaction on Amarantha's face. Then I was overwhelmed by a burning need to smack her six ways from Sunday.

"Yes, Ambassador Black?" she purred, and popped a grape in her mouth. I saw her pull the leash a little tighter, as if assuring herself that Gabriel was still hers.

I considered and discarded several plans of action, and then decided it was best to act like myself. I never did well when I tried to play the formality game.

"You know why I'm here," I said. "Gabriel is not yours to own, and I want him returned to the court of Azazel."

"I do not think you are in a position to make demands, Ambassador Black. You have insulted me by threatening a guest in my court with bodily harm."

She stroked her painted nails through Gabriel's hair. I was mesmerized by the sight, and a little nauseated. When I looked up again, I saw that she had been watching my face, and that made me angry.

"Look, your skin show might impress other people, but mostly I think it just shows how little class you have. It's very difficult to take you seriously as royalty when you're dressed like a stripper."

Her eyes flashed and she stood up from the chaise. Christ, she was even wearing teeter-totter strappy heels. All she needed was a pole and a few dollar bills.

"Now you insult me to my face," she said, and as she stalked toward me she pulled on Gabriel's leash. He crawled forward at her heels, his head down. "I will be happy to inform Lord Lucifer that his granddaughter is obviously not interested in reestablishing relations between our courts."

"Don't try to threaten me with Lucifer," I said. "Especially since you're the one who wants your relationship to be a lot closer than it is now."

She narrowed her eyes at me, and I wondered if it was prudent to mention that I was informed of her baby plan. Then again, it was a lever, and I didn't have too many of those.

"What are you speaking of?" she hissed.

I smiled. "I am the Morningstar's granddaughter. I know more than you think."

I could see the neurons firing behind her eyes as she rapidly calculated how much I could possibly know. She tried for bravado.

"I do not know to what you are referring," she said haughtily.

"Yep, you want to be a lot closer with Lucifer." I tapped her on the tummy, just to make sure she knew that I knew.

Her teeth ground together as she realized I was onto her. I was sure she didn't want word of this getting back to Lucifer before the bun was in the oven. The whole point of a secret plan is to surprise your enemies.

"I cannot give up the thrall," she said, trying a different tack. "He was a gift from Lord Focalor and it would be an insult to him to return such a gift."

"You could regift," I suggested. "And by the way, don't think you're not playing with fire with Focalor. Lucifer is definitely not going to be happy with you for negotiating with one of his underlings."

"Then Lord Lucifer should keep better tabs on his own kingdom," Amarantha shot back. "What I do in my own court is my business."

"Unless you're rather stupidly being maneuvered into getting between Focalor and Lucifer. In which case your kingdom will probably burn to the ground while they work out their differences," I said.

From the look on her face I would say that this hadn't occurred to her.

"Look," I said urgently, trying to take advantage while she seemed unsure. "Give me Gabriel and we'll go—me, Nathaniel, everyone. Tell Focalor that you need to consider carefully before you cross Lucifer, but leave the door open for future relations. Then he'll take his toys and go home, too, and you'll be out of it. In the meantime, I'll get Lucifer on the problem and hopefully this little rebellion will be squashed before it goes anywhere."

"And what if it is not, as you say, 'squashed'?" she asked slowly.

"You'll still be out of the conflict by sending everyone away from your court and not openly allying yourself with one faction. If you still want to renegotiate a treaty between Lucifer's court and yours, I can always come back after the smoke has cleared."

I watched her, trying not to betray my hope. Maybe she would buy it. Maybe all of this could be fixed with logic and very little bloodshed. Maybe we would all just be able to go home.

Then she shook her head. "I agree with you in principle, and perhaps I will take your advice regarding Focalor. But I still do not wish to give up the thrall."

"Amarantha," I said, and she looked mildly offended that I was speaking to her as an equal. But I'm not big on titles, and I wanted her to feel like I was her confidant. "If you don't give up Gabriel, then it's tantamount to accepting Focalor as your ally. You're insulting Azazel, and Lucifer won't be able to tolerate it. He will be forced to include your court when he goes after Focalor."

"By then he may have other motivation to spare us," she said stubbornly.

Fine. I would say it right out even if she wouldn't. "You're only going to piss Lucifer off if you have Gabriel's baby."

"Everyone knows Lord Lucifer is irrational about his bloodline," she said. "That will protect me."

"No, it will protect the *baby*," I said, speaking slowly so that she would understand. "What makes you think that Lucifer won't kill you the second the child is born and then take that child to his own court to live?"

For the second time Amarantha looked unsure. "He would have the wrath of all the faerie courts on his head if he did such a thing."

"Not if he argued that you had insulted him in the first place by using his grandson as a stud. Not if he was able to convince the other courts that the insult could only be paid with your life. If you've done any reading over the last thousand years, then you know that Lucifer's powers of persuasion are quite, well, persuasive."

I could see all my arguments playing around in her head, and I could see just as clearly that I would fail. Amarantha was used to getting her own way, and damn the consequences.

Then something shifted in her face, and she gave me a crafty look.

"There may be a way for all of us to save face in this," she said.

"And what is that?" I asked warily. I felt a dribble of cold sweat trickle down my spine. She looked way too pleased with herself all of a sudden.

"There could be a competition between yourself and a representative of Focalor's camp, with the thrall as the prize."

"What kind of a competition?" If it was a hand-to-hand combat situation, I was probably screwed, because Antares would definitely volunteer for sister-beating duty and he had already proven that he was stronger than me.

"A test of strength and wit and cunning. If you win, I will return the thrall to you and formally reestablish relations with Lord Lucifer. If Focalor's representative wins, then I will accept the thrall as my gift and establish ties with his court. This seems to me a fair way to settle the argument between the two of you without becoming embroiled in the conflict."

"Except that if you side with Focalor for any reason, Lucifer will not take it kindly. I'd advise you to think on that—again," I said.

"It seems to me that you are frightened to face Focalor. If Lucifer's court is so strong, then surely my little test will be nothing for you, and you will be on your way home with your thrall in hand tomorrow," Amarantha said.

I knew she was goading me. I'm not stupid. And I also knew that I was going to undertake her test no matter what. I wouldn't be able to live with myself if I didn't at least try to get Gabriel back.

"I'd like some more specifics on this test before I agree," I said.

"As I said, a competition of strength and wit and cunning—the Maze."

Gabriel looked up suddenly and jerked on his leash. "Madeline, no, you must not."

"Silence," Amarantha hissed.

He stood abruptly, yanking the leash from her hands. Amarantha looked furious. He put his hands on my shoulders and gazed intently into my eyes. I reached up and covered his hands with mine.

"You must not do this. The Maze is too dangerous."

"I said, silence, thrall!" Amarantha shouted. She stalked back to her chaise and pulled out a short wooden rod of the same type that J.B. carried and pointed it at Gabriel.

"No!" I cried as she shot him with a bolt of magic from the rod.

He fell to the floor, writhing in pain. I noticed for the first time that he wore two slim silver bracelets around each wrist. The bracelets crackled with power. So they were some kind of binding, then—to keep his abilities suppressed, I assumed, and to keep him under control when he acted up.

I gave Amarantha a furious glare. "He's not yours to treat like a dog."

"He is mine for now, and mine to treat as I wish. Are you willing to participate in my competition, and win him back?"

I was sure the Maze would be dangerous. I was sure that she didn't care if I lived or died, and that my death might be preferable in the long run. I was also sure that while I was risking my life she'd be trying to get Gabriel's baby anyway, so that no matter the outcome of the contest she'd still have her child of Lucifer's bloodline.

"Of course," I replied.

"No!" Gabriel shouted from the floor. He turned to Amarantha. "You cannot let her go there. She is human; she will never survive."

Amarantha's only reply was to blast him again.

"You have accepted my offer. It is done."

I looked at Amarantha. "Let me know if Focalor agrees."

She nodded, her eyes filled with glee. She definitely expected me to get pasted.

I glanced at Gabriel. "I will come back for you."

He shook his head, and I could see he was already grieving for me.

"I will come back for you," I said again, and then I turned on my heel and walked out.

It probably goes without saying that J.B. and Beezle were not happy with my decision. J.B. followed me back to my room with a clenched jaw and Beezle spent the whole time saying things like, "Who's going to take care of me when you're dead?" and "Is that fool really worth your life?"

J.B. slammed my bedroom door shut behind us. "Are you out of your mind?"

I crossed the room and dug in my pack for a granola bar. I was suddenly ravenously hungry. I unwrapped the bar and chomped it down in a few bites, then dug around looking for something else to eat. Unfortunately, Beezle hadn't left much behind after his nervous binge this morning.

"Did you hear me?" J.B. asked.

"I know exactly what I'm doing," I replied, sitting on the bed.

"I don't think that you do. You have no idea what's in the Maze," he said grimly, running his hands over his head. Whenever he got nervous or upset, he would tug on his hair. He was starting to get that bedhead-y look, and that told me more than his tone that he was really unhappy.

"Why is it that nobody has any confidence in my ability to survive this thing?" I said. "You told me just this morning that you believed I could handle myself because I beat Ramuell."

"Ramuell was nothing compared to the Maze."

I thought about that for a minute. "Okay. So tell me what I'm facing here."

"I can't. It's different for everyone," he said.

"How can that be?"

"The Maze is enchanted. Each person who enters must face their worst nightmares, their most horrible monsters. And the worst your psyche can dredge up is far more damaging than anything that Amarantha can devise. No one, and let me emphasize this, *no one* in over a thousand years has survived the Maze."

"Oh." This was not good.

"Right. Oh." J.B.'s fists buried in his hair.

"The best we can hope for is that you will return alive but insane," Beezle said.

"Well, on the upside, this means that Antares will probably get eaten by something," I said. "Because I know that if there's a competition between myself and a representative from Focalor's court, he will be jumping up and down to volunteer."

"Yes, but would Focalor be willing to waste one of his best lieutenants on a suicide mission?" Beezle said. "I know that if Lucifer or Azazel was here, he would not let you do this."

"Lucky for me neither of them are here," I said dryly. "Look, I'll just clear my mind or whatever and get through it. I'm not powerless."

"It's not a matter of clearing your mind. Do you think this is some simple enchantment that will skim the surface of your brain? The Maze is a living thing, a creature of immense power. It can see into every nook and cranny. It will find horrors that you never even were aware of deep inside you," J.B. said.

Now I was starting to get scared. But I wasn't going to tell them that.

"I have to do it," I said.

J.B. grabbed my shoulders. His face was desperate. "Doesn't it mean anything to you that you're going to die for someone who can never love you? Doesn't it mean anything to you that I am standing right here and that *I* need you?"

He'd been so good-natured when I'd turned him down that I hadn't realized he felt this way. I hadn't thought that there was more to it than a flirtatious attraction.

I shook my head and swallowed the tears that I felt

burning in my throat. "I'm sorry, J.B. I'm more sorry than I can say. I never wanted to hurt you."

His hands fell away, his shoulders slumped. "That's what girls always say when they don't want you."

"I guess being the children of immortals doesn't exempt us from stupid human clichés," I said, trying to smile.

He gave a hollow laugh. "That will be a real comfort to me when they bring back your body."

I took his hands and stood up, my eyes on his. "You believed in me before. Believe in me now. I will come back."

"In how many pieces?" Beezle said.

"One," I said. "I promise."

"You can't make that promise," J.B. said.

I smiled. "I'm Lucifer's granddaughter. Promises are a family specialty."

J.B. left, and Beezle went with him.

"I can't stay here and watch you tick down the moments until your inevitable death," he said.

"Give me a break, Beezle," I said, hurt that he didn't believe in me, that he didn't want to stay with me. "I figured you'd want to make gloomy pronouncements until it's time to go. It helps me get psyched up."

He shook his head, his face unusually grave. "Not this time."

And that more than anything terrified me. If Beezle couldn't crack wise about the Maze, then maybe there really was something to be scared of.

Maybe it really was worse than Ramuell. I hadn't thought that was possible.

I scrounged up a small bag of almonds that Beezle had somehow overlooked, drank some bottled water, and changed into my regular, non-ambassador clothes. I'd packed my favorite blue jeans and a long-sleeved black tee plus my black Converse sneakers. I took down my stupid updo and carefully braided my hair into one long plait that ended in the middle of my back. Then I wrapped the plait around my head so I looked a lot like Princess Leia, but at least my hair was out of the way and couldn't be used as a weapon by anything scary that I might meet in the Maze.

I looked at myself in the mirror. This was as good as it was going to get. I was ready for battle.

"It would be nice to have a machete or something, though," I muttered to my reflection.

"Would a sword do?" a voice said from the connecting doorway.

I whirled around. Nathaniel stood in the doorway watching me. He clutched one arm around his middle where I had burned him. I saw white bandages showing under his unbuttoned dress shirt. His face was pale and he looked like he was in horrific pain.

"You look terrible," I said with a total lack of sympathy. "Why haven't you healed yourself?"

"It seems," he said, struggling a bit with the effort of speaking, "that the spell you used on me cannot be healed in the usual way. I must wait for my body to reknit itself."

"You know it's no less than you deserve," I said.

He nodded. "I am well aware that my behavior was reprehensible. But there was something . . . You must believe that I did not feel like myself."

"You felt like a rapist?"

"No," he said slowly. "More like I was under the influence of a power not my own."

I didn't want to give credence to this. Nathaniel had

hurt me. But I had a flash of remembrance, the feeling I'd had of something alien looking out from Nathaniel's eyes.

"What power could have overcome you?" I asked. "You're not the weakest of Azazel's court."

Nathaniel's eyes flashed. "Whose castle do we presently reside in?"

"Amarantha? Why?"

"Perhaps she wanted to drive a wedge between us. Perhaps she wanted to destabilize your base of power in her court."

"Well, she succeeded," I muttered. I crossed my arms, then let them fall at my sides again. I wasn't going to hide from him. "Was there something you wanted?"

"The gargoyle told me that you are to enter the Maze."

I was surprised. I didn't think Beezle would have left me only to talk to Nathaniel, who was not one of his favorite people at the best of times.

"What's it to you?" I said.

"I would rather you returned from the Maze alive than dead," Nathaniel said. "I have come to give you a gift."

He stepped out of the doorway, and it was then that I saw the sword he carried in his free hand.

It was about four feet long, and the metal was silver in color, but it gleamed like no metal I had seen before. The blade was carved with a series of strange sigils that glittered in the lamplight. The cross guard and grip were black as obsidian but shone with a strange light in their depths. A serpent was carved around the hilt. Its black eyes seemed to see me, weigh me, judge me in a moment.

I knew that I was looking at something that was not of this earth.

"It is the sword of my father, the angel Zerachiel,"

Nathaniel said. "He had dominion over the earth at one time. Lucifer gifted him with this sword many millennia ago."

I reached out to touch the strange blade, but then drew my hand away. "Why would you give this to me?"

He looked away from my questioning gaze. "I had hoped to give it to our son one day. Since that future is no longer to be, I wish you to use the sword to survive the Maze. It was forged by Lucifer's own hand, and it has powers of its own. The sword would be pleased to be held by Lucifer's blood again."

I still hesitated, and Nathaniel read my hesitation correctly.

"It is a gift freely given. There will be no price to pay. I ask only that, if you return from the Maze, you think better of me. You cannot know how I regret what occurred last night," he said.

I didn't think I'd be thinking any better of his character anytime soon, and it was difficult for me to reconcile his apparent regret with the terror and helplessness I'd felt. Even if there was a strong possibility that he had been under a spell, the memory would stay with me forever.

But I appreciated any help I could get surviving the Maze, even if I didn't know the first thing about swordplay. I just hoped that I wouldn't cut off one of my own limbs accidentally.

"Thank you," I said, and I reached for the sword.

As soon as the hilt met my palm, I felt something deep inside me sing out with joy. The snake seemed to writhe against my skin, and the blade noticeably gleamed brighter.

"It recognizes you," Nathaniel said softly. "It has been waiting for you."

There was a power surging in my blood, a power that

had been buried so deep that only the sword could have drawn it from me. I looked up, and Nathaniel gasped.

"Your eyes," he said.

I turned my head toward the mirror, and instead of the field of stars that manifested when I wielded my magic, I saw the burning heart of the sun, the light of the Morningstar.

"I think that when Focalor sees you, he will think twice about crossing Lord Lucifer," Nathaniel said.

"Never mind Lucifer," I said, and the new power inside me called out for battle. "He'd better worry about crossing me."

15

NATHANIEL FITTED ME UP WITH A SCABBARD THAT slung across my body so that I could carry the sword on my back. Despite my growing suspicion that someone had been controlling Nathaniel during his attack, it was difficult to stand still while he touched me. Whether by his own power or another's he was the one who had put his hands on me with the intent to harm.

When he was done—with a lot of apologies on his part and a lot of indrawn breaths on mine—he made me practice my draw.

"Better swordsmen than you have cut their own necks drawing their swords this way," he said. "But you are so small that you would not comfortably be able to carry the blade at your waist."

Despite my total lack of experience the sword leapt to my hand easily and smoothly every time.

Nathaniel stood back, satisfied. "It is coming to your call. That is good. It will help you when you face the unknown."

There was a knock at the door, and I opened it. A servant stood there.

"Queen Amarantha requires your presence in the throne room, Ambassador Black."

I glanced back at Nathaniel. "Showtime. Are you coming?"

He shook his head. He looked tired, and sad, and in pain, and I didn't know how to feel about that. "Go with the grace of the Morningstar."

I nodded, and then followed the servant to the throne room.

I tried not to think about what was going to happen. Nathaniel's gift had given me a little more confidence, but the odds still did not look good. The fact that no one had ever survived the Maze was something I tried not to think about.

The courtiers were assembled when I entered the throne room. The wolves stood near Amarantha's throne at the front of the crowd. Wade looked deeply troubled, Jude frowned like he wasn't sure about how to feel, and James . . . There was a strange, almost bloodthirsty, light in his eyes.

I didn't have time to wonder about the wolves' feelings. I had my own skin to worry about.

I crossed the room, and as I passed the courtiers they whispered.

"Did you see her eyes?"

"Where did she get that sword?"

Focalor and Antares stood in front of Amarantha's throne and they both turned to watch me approach. When Focalor saw my eyes, his jaw clenched, and I thought I saw a flash of fear in his demon eyes. Antares was too stupid to be worried about any threat from me. He looked pathetically eager.

I saw J.B. and Beezle standing a little to the side. Beezle rested on J.B.'s shoulder and I felt a strange pang of hurt. Beezle never did that with anybody but me. J.B. looked like he was going to be sick.

Amarantha clapped her hands together in satisfaction when she saw me. I was happy to see that she had put on something more substantial than the lingerie model getup she'd had on earlier, although the dress's low cut still didn't leave a lot to the imagination. Subtle, thy name is not Amarantha.

Gabriel was nowhere to be seen. I wondered if he was being punished for defying Amarantha earlier, or if she just didn't want him anywhere near me before I went into the Maze.

"Ambassador Black, you will be pleased to hear that Lord Focalor has agreed to participate in the challenge of the Maze. His representative Antares will be entering the Maze with you."

"Big surprise," I muttered.

"The terms are as follows," Amarantha continued. "Ambassador Black will enter from the east side of the Maze. Antares ap Azazel will enter from the west side at precisely the same time. The thrall Gabriel ap Ramuell is held at the center of the maze. Whoever reaches the thrall first will take him as their prize. Once you have successfully returned with your prize, I will commence negotiations with the winning court. Are these terms acceptable to you both?"

Focalor nodded. "I look forward to negotiating a treaty with you, my lady."

So Focalor seemed to have gotten his confidence back. Apparently a little power of Lucifer manifesting inside me wasn't enough to worry him.

"Are the terms acceptable to you, Ambassador Black?" Amarantha said.

"I have one term of my own," I said.

Out of the corner of my eye I saw J.B. close his eyes in frustration. Well, I wasn't going to get anything without asking for it, and even if I managed to get out of the Maze alive and with Gabriel, there was still the Focalor problem to deal with. The least I could do was to make this contest about more than Gabriel. If I could stop the demon uprising, then it was worth any amount of pain I might endure.

I turned to Focalor, who quirked his eyebrows at me, as if to say, "I'm listening."

"If I find Gabriel before Antares and make it back here first, you drop your grievance against Lucifer."

Focalor narrowed his eyes. "My grievance with Lucifer is long-standing and far-reaching. Why should I sacrifice my legitimate claim against him?"

"If a representative of your court is defeated by a representative of his—or vice versa—is that not enough to satisfy the laws of the kingdom without further bloodshed?"

Focalor showed his teeth to me. "You are implying that further bloodshed is something I wish to avoid."

"Do you agree or not?" I said impatiently. "You seem to think I'm going to lose anyway so why not consent? If Antares comes back first, you get to be as mad at Lucifer as you want to be."

He looked thoughtful. "But what if you come back first, as unlikely a possibility as that may be?"

"Then you go back to your court, apologize to Lucifer and hope like hell he doesn't smite you off the face of the earth."

"That is not a very appealing option," Focalor said.

"Just stop dithering and be a man about it," I said,

impatient to get into the Maze. I wanted to get this over with. "Yes or no?"

Focalor took a moment longer, seeming to weigh all the options. I could see him calculating the long odds that I would actually survive the Maze.

"Very well," he said.

"You have witnessed it, Queen Amarantha," I said formally. "If I defeat his representative in the Maze, then Focalor will drop his grievance against Lucifer and return to the fold."

Like Amarantha, Focalor would agree to anything because he didn't think I actually had a chance. Then again, Beezle didn't think I had a chance either. He was usually my biggest cheerleader, so maybe they were right and I was wrong.

Amarantha nodded. "And you agree to all terms as well?"

"Yes," I said.

"Then let us proceed," she said, and signaled to Violet. "You may follow Lady Violet to the entrance, Ambassador. Antares ap Azazel, you may follow Narke."

One of the forest warriors stepped forward to take Antares out a side entrance. Violet indicated that I should follow her out of the main doors.

I looked at Beezle and J.B., but they both looked away from me. All right, that hurt a lot. The least they could do was say good-bye if they thought I was going to die.

I turned my back on the throne, and followed Violet to my doom.

Violet led me through the courtyard and out into the forest without a word. She found a path among the thick and low-hanging branches that I couldn't have seen with a microscope. She didn't try to make conversation and I was too busy trying not to hyperventilate to act polite.

After about twenty minutes of hard walking, we suddenly emerged into a clearing, and in front of us was the Maze.

A massive wall of stone rose in front of us, blocking out the weak early-winter sun. I realized I'd forgotten a coat and that it was maybe forty degrees outside.

The wall was covered in strange grayish green vines with enormous leaves. As I looked, the vines shifted like snakes across the surface of the wall. J.B. was right. The Maze was a living thing, and a faint pulse of energy came off it as we stood there: the questing tentacle of a blind animal.

The pulse moved through me from the tips of my sneakers to the crown of my head, and I shivered uncomfortably. I felt exposed, like my chest had been peeled back to show my beating heart.

A moment later an opening appeared in the wall of the Maze. The interior was dark and shifting, and I could see nothing beyond the doorway.

I stepped forward. "Okay, I guess this is my stop."

Violet didn't answer. I looked around and saw that she had already disappeared back into the forest.

J.B. could do a lot better than her. Seriously.

"And I'm going to tell him so when I get back," I said.

Then I took a deep breath, thought of Gabriel, and stepped into the Maze.

The door closed behind me, leaving me stranded in pitch-darkness. Even the top of the Maze was covered.

I summoned a small blue ball of nightfire to light my way with my left hand, and pulled the sword from its scabbard with my right. The snake beneath my palm nudged my skin, like the comfortable press of a dog's nose. It felt almost as if I had a friend with me.

I held the nightfire out ahead of me and checked both directions. There was no obvious difference between the two, so I decided to use my medieval maze trick again and choose right whenever possible.

I started to move forward with the ball of light ahead of me. My breath came in harsh pants and it sounded unnaturally loud in this enclosed space. My light cast a pitiful circle. The dark seemed to press all around me, brushing over my shoulders, swiping fingertips over my neck.

"Don't be afraid," I told myself, and my voice echoed down the hall, wavery and very, very frightened.

I could have faced anything if only there had been a little more light. The total darkness was getting to me and I'd only been in the Maze a few moments. How long was this thing? How far would I have to go? It couldn't be short or else there would be no challenge. The sword in my hand gave me a friendly little nudge again, and I deliberately tried to calm my breathing. There was no point in freaking out when I hadn't even faced anything yet.

I tried not to think about Antares and how far he might have gotten already. Did demons even have nightmares? What could he possibly be afraid of that would impede his journey to the center of the Maze?

The tunnel ended in a T-junction and I turned right. I didn't have a better plan. I wished Beezle was there to tell me I was acting like a dummy. I tried not to think about how much it hurt that he hadn't even said good-bye to me. It had always been me and Beezle. I'd had Beezle with me longer than I'd had my mother.

After walking for several minutes I started to feel like

the Maze was trying to lull me into a false sense of security. I hadn't had to deal with anything worse than the pressing darkness, and as long as I didn't think about it too hard I was able to handle it. The companionable feeling of the sword helped.

Then the spider came looming out of the darkness.

There was no warning as there had been in the forest, no hiss and click of its pincers, no heavy thud on the ground. There was only a spark of red eyes and the silent scream of its open mouth as it descended on me. I saw a flash of its hairy legs a second before it landed on me and I fell to the floor, rolling away from its grasp. The nightfire in my hand winked out.

I came to my knees and slashed blindly into the darkness with the sword. The blade connected with something solid and I felt it slice cleanly through chitin and flesh. The spider screamed and the blast of its breath stank of blood and rotten meat.

I jumped to my feet and ran down the corridor away from the spider. I could hear it behind me now, stumbling and crashing against the narrow walls—thump, thump, thump, thump, thump, thump, thump. Only seven thumps. I'd slashed off one of its legs.

If I lit another ball of nightfire, the spider would easily find me. I was sure its eyesight was better in the darkness than mine but I wasn't about to give it an advantage by lighting myself up like a neon sign. I gripped the sword in one hand and waved my other hand in front of me so that I wouldn't run into a wall.

My free hand scraped stone and vine. The spider was still several feet behind me, struggling in the tight confines of the Maze. I sincerely hoped it would get stuck.

I turned right, and as I did the sounds behind me went silent. Had the spider given up, or had the Maze taken it back? Should I dare the light?

After a moment of dithering I decided it was better to risk the light and know for sure what was going on. I conjured nightfire and cautiously peeked around the corner.

That was when the spider struck me from behind.

I had a moment to think, *Oh, that's not fair*, and then the spider closed its pincers around my right leg. I screamed as its jaws pierced my flesh and it shook me around, slamming me against the sides of the corridor.

The sword warmed under my palm until it felt almost too hot to hold. I was abruptly aware that the corridor was lit up like the sun and the light was coming from the sword. The spider screeched and dropped me to the ground, scuttling backward.

I rolled over to see it receding down the hallway as quickly as its enormous body would allow. I wasn't about to let it get away and sneak up on me again. I staggered to my feet, blood pouring from the wound on my right leg, and felt that leg buckle and give way underneath me.

The heat of the sword was searing my skin. I was part-human; my body wasn't made to wield the sun. But I held on to the grip as tight as I could and raised the sword high. The spider flinched away from the light, its seven legs flailing in agony.

I summoned my power and my will and pushed it through my heartstone. This was the magic that had destroyed Ramuell, and I let it flow through me.

The spell hit the spider full on in its ugly face, and I had the immense satisfaction of seeing it burn molecule by molecule until it was gone.

I leaned against the wall, panting and covered in sweat.

Blood from my leg dripped onto the floor, making my sneakers slide around. I sank to the ground because it was easier than scrabbling for purchase in my own gore.

The sword was still lit up like Vegas at night. I looked at it. "You could have done this earlier, you know, when I was freaking out about the dark."

A little pulse answered me, as if to say, "I didn't know you wanted me to."

I examined the wounds underneath the ragged remains of my right pant leg. The cuts were almost perfectly round but tattered at the edges, where the spider's serrated pincers had cut the skin. Blood flowed sluggishly, which was good because it meant I wouldn't bleed out anytime soon. But I wasn't exactly carrying a first aid kit with me.

The sword winked at me, and somehow I knew what it was telling me. I pressed the blade to the wound on one side of my leg, and then I screamed, because it hurt like hell. But when I pulled the sword away the wound was cauterized. The other side was harder to do. It's hard not to flinch when you know what's coming.

"When Gabriel heals me, it's a lot nicer than this," I muttered. "There's usually kissing involved."

The sword would have shrugged its shoulders if it had any.

"Now I'm anthropomorphizing a weapon," I said. "If I keep this up, I'll be talking to my buttons before it's all over."

I pushed wearily to my feet and tested my leg. It hurt like hell, and the muscles were still torn even though the wound was closed. But I was sure the Maze had more surprises for me, and that I wasn't even close to the end. I limped forward.

At least this time the sword provided light for me, so I was able to see the demons when they attacked.

They came crawling down the walls and the ceiling, a horde of seeking tentacles and flickering tongues and razor-tipped claws. Some of them were small, some large; some squished and some walked. They were covered in boils and lash marks and burn scars. Some of them hissed, some of them drooled, some of them gnashed blackened teeth. All of them had their slitted yellow eyes focused on me.

There were so many of them I didn't have time to think about what I needed to do. I just started blasting away with my magic with one hand and hacking away with my sword with the other. Demon blood splattered my hands and demon saliva burned my arms. Heads rolled beneath my feet and clawed hands grasped at my ankles. I kicked out, slashed down, parried up, poured my magic out in a steady stream like a machine gun without the safety on. My sword hand worked without my knowledge or skill, led by the will of Lucifer long ago embedded in its crafting.

I don't know how long I fought the demons, or how many I killed. I only know that after what seemed like hundreds of corpses were piled in the corridor behind me the attack abruptly petered out and I was alone again.

I limped away from the stench of dead demons, my right leg dragging behind me. I tried to call my wings but they wouldn't come for me. So the Maze would let me have my magic, but only to a degree. I guessed my wings would make things too easy. I hoped the Maze gave Antares a similar disadvantage.

I managed to make it down a few corridors unmolested. Once I was sure I was well away from the site of the demon battle, I stopped and took stock of my injuries.

My long-sleeved tee had been burned in several places on my arms from demon saliva. Long shiny welts on my arms and hands peeked from underneath the torn cotton.

One demon had managed to get a good hold on my left leg and tear the denim at the knee. It had also left a long shallow cut that had mostly clotted up.

The ragged pieces of my clothing were now more annoying than protective, so I ripped the sleeves out of the shirt at the armholes and used the sword to turn the jeans into cutoffs. I looked sadly at my favorite sneakers, which were so covered in demon gore that I would probably have to throw them away. If, that was, I actually survived.

My sword arm felt sore and the sword itself weighed a ton now that the adrenaline of battle was spent. I was afraid to put it in the scabbard since the Maze seemed to like surprising me, but it was hard to carry at the ready. I limped along with the sword hanging loosely at my side, the tip just barely clearing the floor.

I was starting to feel tired and a little delirious. I hadn't had anything to eat except a granola bar and a few almonds in more than twenty-four hours, and I'd spent a lot of that time under extreme stress. I just wanted to close my eyes for a while and rest. If I could sleep a little, I would feel better.

But the Maze sensed weakness, and that was when Antares rounded the corner.

"Still alive, little sister?" Antares hissed.

He looked completely unharmed by the antics of the Maze. *Unfair,* I thought for the second time since I'd entered Amarantha's sadistic toy. Why should he be raring and ready to go when I was ready to fall flat on my face?

It would never do to show weakness to Antares even if I was at a low point. "Are you lost, *little* brother?" I said, and held the sword up and ready to attack. "I was sure you would have run home crying to Focalor by now."

Antares just smiled at me, and moved closer. I called for my magic, but there was nothing there. This wasn't the feeling that I had when I had overworked myself and used too much power at once. Despite the continuous stream of demons I hadn't felt my magic growing weak.

This was different. It was like the magic just wasn't inside me, like it had never been inside me. But that was impossible. Even without the new powers awakened by Lucifer's sword, I still had my Agent magic.

Then I understood. The Maze had taken my power from me. J.B. had said that the Maze would find my worst nightmares, and being powerless in the face of Antares definitely qualified.

"Looking for something, sister?" Antares taunted, and it was then that I realized something else. This wasn't the real Antares. This was a manifestation of the Maze drawn from my own mind.

"Yeah, your head on a plate," I snapped back. Even when I was exhausted and injured, my mouth ran away from me.

"Come and get it, then," Antares crooned, and crooked one clawed finger at me.

I rushed at him with my sword up and held in both hands. I don't know what I was planning to do but Antares kicked my legs out from beneath me before I even got close. I landed hard on the back of my head and saw stars spinning above me.

Antares yanked Lucifer's sword from my hand and tossed it away. It still lit the corridor, but its brightness dimmed a bit once it was away from me. I tried to stand and get away but Antares kicked me in the stomach.

It was like the first time I had met him, before I knew he was a demon, before I knew he was my brother or that I was Azazel's daughter. He had beaten me within an inch of my life and the only thing that had saved me had been Gabriel's magic.

But Gabriel wasn't here now, and I was just as powerless as I had been the first time. I held my hands up, trying to protect myself from Antares's vicious kicks, but I was so tired and hurt that all I could do was roll feebly away. He kicked me in the ribs again, and I coughed, tasting blood in my mouth.

He's going to kill me, I thought.

I rolled to my stomach, tried to inch away in a crawl. Antares laughed behind me.

"What do you think of your beloved heir now, Father?" he asked.

I raised my head and saw through blurry eyes that two other figures stood farther down the corridor. I blinked to focus and saw the frowning faces of my mother and father.

"I should not have put so much stock in her," Azazel replied. "I should have chosen you, my son."

Antares laughed, grabbed me by the back of my shirt and turned me over. He punched me in the face and I heard my nose crack. Blood rushed out in a torrent.

"I'm sorry that I bore you such a weak daughter," Katherine said to Azazel.

"Mom?" I said weakly. "Mom, help me."

"Help you?" Katherine scoffed. "I should have never had you in the first place. If not for you, I could have spent a lifetime with Azazel."

I knew it wasn't my mother. My mother was dead. It was the Maze, trying to break my will. But it still hurt to hear something with my mother's face and my mother's voice say such things.

"No one is going to help you, little girl," Antares said, and he held his claws above my throat for the strike.

"Help me," I said, and I held out my hand.

Lucifer's sword was in my palm before Antares could

blink. I swung the blade without thinking and his head separated cleanly from his shoulders.

I fell to the ground as Antares's grip loosened in death. I turned to my stomach, choking on my own blood. I coughed out the mess backing up in my throat and felt oxygen entering my brain again.

I lay on the floor, the cool stone of the Maze pressing against my swelling face. If every part of my body had hurt before, it felt three times as bad now. If Antares hadn't broken any ribs, it would be a miracle.

There was a little pulse in my hand from the sword.

"I'm getting up," I said.

It pulsed again when I didn't move.

"I'm getting up," I repeated, and this time I pushed myself up to my hands and knees. It was hard to breathe. Yup, I was pretty sure Antares had broken a rib.

A little match flame burst to life inside me again. The Maze had given me my magic back. Gee, thanks for nothing.

The sword pulsed again, this time more urgently.

"What now?" I said wearily, and used the wall to help me stand.

I was still there, eyes at half-mast, the sword furiously pulsing at me, when Ramuell entered the corridor.

16

I LAUGHED, AND I SOUNDED A LITTLE CRAZY. "OF
course it would be you."

Ramuell grinned at me. His teeth looked sharper than
they had before I'd killed him.

"Not broken yet, little Agent?" Ramuell asked, and
somehow I knew it was the voice of the Maze talking
through him.

I stood away from the wall and held out my arms, showing the Maze my injuries. "Bruised but not broken."

"I have defeated more powerful beings than you in my
time," the Maze said in Ramuell's voice.

I narrowed my eyes. "And beings more powerful than
you have underestimated me before."

The Maze laughed, a long and sinister chuckle. "We
shall see. I am not about to be laid low by a mere human."

The sword pulsed, and the magic inside me surged up in

answer to its call. I smiled at Ramuell, and echoed the taunt Antares had made at me.

"Come and get me, then," I said.

Ramuell laughed again, and as he laughed the form of the nephilim slowly disappeared. "Oh, I will, little Agent. I will."

I waited, braced, but Ramuell's form didn't reappear. "Just an errand boy, then."

I started forward, trying not to think about how much every part of me howled in pain. I wished Gabriel had taught me how to heal myself the way the angels did. Of course, the Maze would probably have taken that ability from me anyway, so there was no point in wishing for it.

"If wishes were horses, beggars would ride," I said. My mom used to say that. It was one of those phrases that made sense if you thought about it, but sounded kind of weird to say.

"Okay, now you're rambling," I said aloud.

The silence of the Maze was getting to me. I never realized how much I depended on the constant stream of chatter emitting from Beezle. As friendly a companion as the sword was, it definitely lacked something in the conversation department. It had been kind of a relief to exchange villain/hero wisecracks with Antares and Ramuell.

I walked for a long while, my feet dragging, my free arm wrapped around my broken rib. The sword emitted a steady glow of sunlight so that no surprises could pop out of the darkness. I turned right whenever I could and hoped that I was getting closer to the center, and Gabriel.

I didn't hear him approach. All of a sudden I rounded a corner, and Nathaniel stood there, looking implacable. My magic winked out again, and I felt a surge of panic. All I had was the sword.

Then the sword betrayed me.

Nathaniel held out his hand and the sword struggled out of my grip and into his.

"I believe this belongs to me," he said. "And so do you."

He stalked toward me, and I froze, recognizing the look of intent on his face. I held out my hands, but I had no sword and no magic. This time he was relentless, and I really was powerless to stop him.

When he finished and stood up, I felt like something in my soul was broken forever.

"Get dressed," he said.

I pulled on the ragged remains of my clothes, tears I couldn't stop falling from my eyes. He reached for my wrists and clamped a pair of handcuffs over them.

"You belong to me now," he said and pulled me to my feet.

Gabriel stood before us, a look of contempt in his eyes. He was disgusted by me, and I knew he had seen what Nathaniel had done.

"Gabriel," I said, and reached toward him, my hands bound together. "Gabriel, help."

He spit in my face, and then he turned and walked away. Amarantha waited for him and he entered her embrace willingly.

I howled in pain and in anguish, all the shattered pieces inside me splintering into shards. "Gabriel, Gabriel, no! Gabriel, DON'T LEAVE ME!"

Nathaniel jerked at my handcuffs, pulling me like an animal. "You are mine, now and forever."

Gabriel disappeared around the corner. The light of the sword seemed to dim, and the light of my heart sputtered and died.

I heard a long, sinister chuckle. Ramuell stood where Nathaniel had been.

"Had enough yet, little Agent?"

Had enough. Yes, I'd had enough. Had enough of always being the helpless one, the powerless one. Had enough of being human in an alien world, had enough of seeing the only man I'd ever wanted walk away from me.

Gabriel wouldn't walk away from you, a little voice in my head said.

He did. He always does.

No, he wouldn't walk away if you needed him. He wouldn't leave you to Nathaniel, to danger. He would never go to Amarantha.

He wouldn't leave me. That's what I told Beezle. He wouldn't leave me.

"He wouldn't leave me," I said aloud, and I flexed my wrists. The handcuffs broke and fell away. The sword returned to my hand.

As I looked into Nathaniel's surprised face, I swung the sword that the real Nathaniel had given me. I can't say that I didn't feel a ton of satisfaction in watching his head roll way down the corridor, even if it was only a puppet of the Maze. I felt my magic surge up inside me once more as I gazed into the eyes of the foe I had vanquished once before.

I had defeated Nathaniel. I had killed Ramuell. I had *survived*. I wasn't powerless.

The Maze-Ramuell looked surprised as I stalked forward. The nephilim took a step backward away from me, and I knew then that the Maze would never beat me.

"You will not break me," I said, my anger giving me strength, taking away the pain. "You will not break me, because I know that this is not real."

"Not real?" the Maze said. "Are not your injuries real, your broken bones? Were you not defiled by Zerachiel's son?"

"No," I said, and as I said it my rib bone knit back together, my limping leg grew straight again, my cuts and burns and bruises healed. All the shattered pieces inside me were made whole.

"It didn't happen," I said. I stood before the Maze with my heart and my body in one piece. If there was a trace of darkness, a trace of fear, left inside me, the Maze would never find it. "Do your worst. You will never, never, never defeat me."

The Maze gave me a speculative look through Ramuell's eyes. "I never thought to be beaten by a creature as low as you."

"Yeah, well, I have a long history of not living up to people's expectations of me," I said.

The Maze gave a short bark of laughter. "Lucifer's will beats strongly inside you. I should have seen this."

"It's not Lucifer's will," I said. "It's mine. Now, if we're not going to dance anymore, take me to Gabriel."

Ramuell bowed to me. "As you wish, my lady."

The corridor we stood in slowly lightened. I realized the structure of the Maze was disappearing. The walls and ceiling faded away until we stood on an open, rocky clearing surrounded by the enormous trees of Amarantha's forest. In the center of the rocks was a cage, and inside the cage was Gabriel, looking at me in astonishment.

I started toward him.

"I have not enjoyed playing the game so much in many years," the Maze said behind me.

I didn't look back as I answered. "Wish I could say the same."

Ramuell's laugh echoed behind me, and then slowly disappeared. I didn't care. I only had eyes for Gabriel.

I slowed as I approached the cage. Gabriel sat in the dead center, well away from the bars. He squatted on his haunches, still dressed in the ridiculous loincloth of

Amarantha's. There were burn marks on his wrists from the cuffs she had put on him. He looked haggard and exhausted, but there was something in his eyes that I hadn't seen when he'd first entered Amarantha's throne room. Hope.

"Madeline," he said, and his voice sounded raspy and underused. "The cage is bespelled."

I nodded. "Right. On the off chance that I actually made it here Amarantha wouldn't have wanted it to be easy for me. You can't touch the bars?"

He shook his head. His dark hair, normally so impeccably groomed, hung in lank and sweaty tendrils around his cheeks.

"I saw something like this in the Forbidden Lands," I said. "The Grigori used cages that caused the nephilim unspeakable pain whenever they touched the bars."

"That is what happened to me when I touched them," he said.

I studied the bars for a minute, and then the sword wanted my attention. "Of course. Stand back as far as you can, Gabriel."

I swung the sword near the top of the cage and it cut cleanly through the bars. I slashed it at the bottom and several bars fell outward, creating a makeshift doorway. They sparked as they hit the rocks.

"Step out carefully," I said.

Gabriel folded his wings as small as he could to his back and inched through the bars. I didn't breathe until his bare feet touched the rock and he stood before me.

He put his hand on my cheek and I sank into his touch, all the horror and blood and fatigue of the last several hours coming back to me. It hadn't been real, but it had *felt* real when it was happening.

"Gabriel," I said, and there was a lifetime of longing in his name.

"You came for me," he said, wonder in his eyes, his lips a breath from mine.

"Of course I did," I said, and then he gave me what I needed.

After a long time we came apart, mouths swollen from kissing. He wiped the tears that I didn't know I cried from my cheeks.

"I believe Amarantha will be quite shocked when you return with me," Gabriel said.

"Then let's go shock her," I said. "And remind me to give that bitch a smack in the mouth just on principle."

"Well, well, isn't this a touching scene," said a sneering voice behind me.

I turned around to see Antares standing a few feet away, looking quite the worse for wear. One of his horns had been sliced in half and he was covered in whip marks. Blood streamed from a nasty-looking cut above his eye.

"Are you freaking kidding me?" I said. "What are you, part cockroach? How did you get out of the Maze?"

"The walls suddenly disappeared," Antares said. "I assumed that meant I had defeated it."

No, I thought sourly. *I defeated it, and you just got the benefits.* Apparently the Maze wasn't done having fun with me yet.

"So now that I have defeated the Maze, I will return with the thrall and claim all honors from my master Focalor," Antares said.

I was tired, I was hungry, and I really just wanted to go home. I was not in the mood to play games with Antares.

Before he could think, I summoned a ball of nightfire and then turned it into a rope. The rope lashed around him and he cried out in surprise. I pulled on the rope and swung it to one side to launch him into the cage that had so recently held Gabriel. Antares slammed into the electrified bars and howled in pain.

Somehow I knew that the sword could rebind the bars that it had so recently cut. This new knowledge was more than a little disconcerting. It was like having Evangeline inside me again. As useful as the sword had been for me, I wasn't sure I wanted another entity working through me.

I waved the sword at the fallen bars and they lifted from the ground, rejoining the rest of the cage. Before Antares had stopped screaming I had pressed the blade to the cuts in the metal and they instantly resealed. Antares was trapped.

"What was that again about claiming honors from Focalor?" I asked.

Antares glared at me. "You will pay for this, sister."

"Oh, I don't think so. You see, you are an outcast from Azazel's court. That means that Focalor is in big trouble for harboring you against the laws of Lucifer's kingdom in addition to all of his other crimes. It also means that Azazel will be very happy to know your location."

I leaned close to the cage and showed Antares my teeth. "Do you think our father will be happy with you when he finds you?"

Antares couldn't hide the fear in his eyes. "I will be long gone before Azazel arrives."

"We'll see. These cages have bound the nephilim for thousands of years."

He scuttled on his knees to the bars, but was careful not to touch. "When I am released from this cage, sister, I will . . ."

"Tear out my entrails, eat my eyeballs, cut off my tongue, blah-de-blah-blah. Get a new tagline," I said.

Then I turned my back on him, took Gabriel's hand in mine, and walked away to the sound of his furious howls.

We had walked for a while in silence when I said, "Do you have any idea where we are?"

He shook his head. "I was blindfolded and placed in the cage. The cage was then put in the heart of the Maze and my blindfold removed. I am sure that Amarantha did this deliberately to prevent my assisting you should you reach me. But, Madeline, we do have wings."

I smiled at him. "I don't know why I always forget that. It would probably be a lot easier to find Amarantha's castle from the sky."

He grinned back, and despite the obvious suffering he had endured he was still the handsomest man I had ever seen. Suddenly he went still, coughed, and blood covered his smile. It was then that I saw the arrow protruding from his chest.

"Gabriel!" I shouted, and he fell heavily to the ground on his side.

"Oh, gods above and below," I said, falling to my knees. I was sure this wound would be nothing to him if he wasn't so weak already. But he had been tortured and abused for days, and likely starved. I put my hands over the wound in his chest. "What should I do?"

"Arrow," he said, and it was a struggle for him to get out that one word.

"Right, get the arrow out," I said. Obviously I wasn't thinking clearly. The tip had sliced cleanly through his skin so I needed to break the shaft and then pull each half from his front and back.

But I didn't get a chance, because that was when the train wreck hit me. Again.

A huge and heavy body knocked into me and sent me flying. I slammed into a tree and fell to the ground, dazed.

Samiel stalked toward me, his green eyes furious and insane—Ariell's eyes. He wore a bow slung over his shoulder. I scrambled to my feet and blasted him with nightfire before he had a chance to get his paws on me. I wasn't about to let him beat the crap out of me again.

The nightfire hit him square in the chest. I could see it rend his skin, leaving a horrible burn. But he didn't make a noise, and he didn't stop. He just kept coming at me, hands curled into fists.

I gave him another blast and then dodged out of the reach of his hands. He simply turned and continued to come after me with the same bullheaded determination. Pain didn't seem to affect him.

I felt a little squiggle of panic. Then I saw the sword that I had dropped at Gabriel's side. I called it to me and it came to my hand. As Samiel approached, I swung the sword down toward his chest.

And he took it *right out of my hand*, even though the blade sliced his palm open. He flipped the sword in an instant and slashed it down toward me. I held my hand up like an idiot to block his blow, and the blade sliced off the last two fingers of my left hand.

I screamed and gave him a full blast of nightfire in the face. He couldn't ignore that, so he dropped the point of the sword to the ground and backed away for a minute, rubbing his eyes. He still had not made a single sound.

"Okay," I said, cradling my injured hand to my chest. Blood spouted from the stumps of my fingers in quick bursts. I pushed my wings out and winked out of sight.

I wasn't going to stand there and let Samiel chase me all over the clearing. My magic was ineffective against him. He had taken my sword and part of my hand. My best bet was to grab Gabriel and fly out of there before Samiel had a chance to figure out what was going on.

But as I spread my wings to fly up, Samiel grabbed my ankle. Right. He was an immortal. He could see me even though I would be invisible to a human. Stupid. My brain wasn't working right. I was too tired from my ordeal in the Maze and, hey, just a little blood loss.

I blasted his hand where it gripped my ankle but he held on tight. It was as if he'd been programmed to destroy me and he was not going to stop. Ever. He dragged me down and began to hit me in the face with the same steady determination that he had used the first time we'd met.

It is very hard to strategize when you are being pummeled to death. But I had a flash of wrapping Antares in a rope of nightfire.

I called up all my strength, all my will, all the power that had helped me survive the Maze. The clearing was suddenly lit with a blaze of sunlight, and I knew that it came from me.

A sinuous strand of nightfire curled out of my palm and wrapped around Samiel's arms. It whirled around him until he was bound completely from neck to midthigh. He fell to the ground and so did I, my eyes momentarily blinded from sweat and blood, and my head dizzy.

After a minute I was able to get up, collect the sword, and stagger over to Samiel. He sat on the ground wrapped in the nightfire rope, and his face was furious.

I knew that if I killed him, Lucifer would be pissed at me. Amarantha was right—Lucifer was fanatical about his bloodline. But if I didn't kill Samiel, he would just keep coming after me until he succeeded in pounding me to a pulp.

I raised the sword, intending to cut his head off. He watched me, not flinching, not making any attempt to save his own life. He was angry that he had lost, but there was also something resigned in his face.

That resignation made me stop, made me lower the sword to the ground.

Samiel shook his head at me, and he seemed angrier still that I had halted his execution. "Ed-by."

"Ed-by?" I said. "What is that, some kind of demon curse?"

"Ed-by!" he shouted. "Ed-by, ed-by, ed-by, ed-by!"

Something in the rhythm of his words reminded me of the vision I'd had of him and Focalor in the Forbidden Lands. Ed-by. Enemy.

"Enemy?" I repeated and as I looked at him all the pieces clicked together.

Samiel's total silence in the face of pain. The grunting and gesturing he'd used to communicate with Focalor. The strange pronunciation of "enemy."

Samiel couldn't hear.

"Ed-by!" he shouted, and his green eyes were filled with furious tears that ran down his face. "Ed-by! ED-BY!"

I backed away, shaking my head. Suddenly he didn't seem like first cousin to the Terminator. He seemed like a lost and broken child. He'd come after me because he had seen me harm his mother, and now that I wouldn't fight him he had nothing left.

I sat down on a rock and covered my face with my right hand. What the hell was I going to do with him? He was an abused kid who'd been raised by two psychopaths. I couldn't kill him, no matter what he had done to me and mine.

My hand still bled, although the flow seemed to be slowing a bit. I held Lucifer's sword to the stumps and they cauterized as my wounds had in the Maze. And yes, it hurt like hell and there was a lot of yelling involved.

I ignored Samiel for a moment and crossed the clearing to Gabriel. He still breathed, although it was so slow and shallow that I wasn't sure how long he would last. I broke the arrow in half and pulled it from his body, grateful that Gabriel was out cold. Then I used the sword to seal the wounds, and turned back to Samiel.

He was rocking in the center of the clearing, his legs straight in front of him like a child's. He kept repeating "ed-by" over and over again.

I knelt in front of him and put my hands under his chin so he would look up at me. He yanked his face away from my touch and I dropped my hands.

"I am not your enemy," I said slowly and clearly. I'd seen him communicate with Focalor in the Forbidden Lands, so I assumed that he could read lips.

"Ed-by," he repeated stubbornly.

I shook my head. "Not your enemy."

"Ed-by!" he shouted.

I held up my hand to show him my missing fingers. "I have paid a blood price for harming your mother. Our quarrel is over."

He stopped shouting at me and looked thoughtful for a moment, then shook his head. He clearly understood me if I spoke carefully.

"Dead," he said, although it was a struggle for him.

"I did not kill your mother," I said. "Ramuell killed her."

This was true. I had fought Ariell to a standstill, but Ramuell had eaten her.

His eyes filled with tears again. "Dead."

"Yes," I said. "But I am not your enemy."

He hung his head, and tears dripped off his face. I hated to keep him wrapped in the nightfire rope. It had to be causing him horrible pain even if he didn't express it.

I released the spell that held the rope together, and suddenly Samiel was free. He looked up at me in astonishment.

I stayed crouched where I was, only a few inches away. I was taking a terrible chance. If I hadn't gotten through to him, he would probably descend on me before I was able to respond.

"I am not your enemy," I repeated again.

Then I put my hand over my heart, and reached my broken hand toward his chest. He went as still as a deer that hears a wolf in the forest. I covered his heart with my hand.

"Friend," I said.

He looked down at my hand on his chest, the one that was missing two fingers, then up at me. His gaze was still suspicious.

"Friend," I said again.

He closed his hand around mine, and I was struck anew by his overwhelming strength. I think he meant to be gentle but he was crushing my remaining fingers in a death grip.

I nodded, trying not to show how much he was hurting me. If I yanked my hand away, he might change his mind and decide to attack.

He gave my fingers a final squeeze, and then let go. I exhaled the breath that I had been holding and stood up. Samiel stood up, too, looking lost.

"Do you know the way to Amarantha's castle?" I asked him.

He looked puzzled.

"Faerie castle?" I tried again. There was no reason for him to know the queen's name.

His face cleared and he nodded.

I gestured toward Gabriel. "Can you carry your brother?"

Samiel glanced at Gabriel in surprise, then back at me. I knew what he was asking.

"Same father," I said. "Ramuell."

Samiel closed his eyes, and it seemed that he was not reliving happy familial memories. I could only imagine what it must have been like for him, growing up in the Forbidden Lands with an insane angel for a mother and a murderous nephilim for a father.

Then he opened his eyes again, and gently lifted Gabriel into his arms. There was a heartbreaking tenderness on his face.

He smiled for the first time, and it was like seeing the first blossoms of spring after a long winter.

"Okay, let's get this show on the road," I said.

That was when Beezle flapped into the clearing, looking completely exhausted. Samiel tightened his grip on Gabriel and stood in front of me, as if to protect me.

I put my hand on his shoulder and made sure he was looking at my face. "It's okay. Beezle's a friend."

Samiel looked doubtful, but he stepped aside.

Beezle landed on a tree branch, looking super grouchy. "What in the four hells has been taking you so long? I've been looking for the stupid Maze for the last two days."

"Two days?" I said. I hadn't realized that much time had passed. "What were you doing looking for me, anyway? I thought you'd given me up as a lost cause."

"Don't be a dork, Maddy," Beezle scoffed, grooming one of his wings and studiously avoiding my eyes. "I've never given up on you yet."

I blinked and felt a tear rolling down my cheek. Beezle looked up and frowned.

"Well, don't get all sappy about it, all right? I'm here now, we're reunited, I knew you would succeed, yay. And who's the big fella holding on to Gabriel?"

"Samiel," I said.

He crinkled his forehead. "The son of Ramuell and Ariell?"

I nodded.

"The one who tried to kill you?"

"Twice," I said.

"Is there a reason why he's walking along next to you like he's out for a Sunday stroll?"

"He's coming home with us," I said. I wondered what Lucifer would think of that.

"What are we, some kind of halfway house for nephilim children?" Beezle said. "I hope he doesn't like popcorn, because I'm not sharing any of mine."

I smiled at Beezle as he settled on my shoulder. "Don't worry. There will be enough popcorn for everyone, especially you."

He glanced down at my left hand, the cauterized and bloody remains of my last two fingers. "I thought you told me you'd come back in one piece."

"I've still got all the pieces that matter," I said.

"Let's go shock the hell out of Amarantha," he said, shifting around to make himself more comfortable. "Wake me up when we get there."

17

TO SAY THAT WE CAUSED A STIR WHEN WE ENTERED
the throne room would be an understatement. I threw the
doors open and strode ahead of Samiel. I must have been a
sight to see—my torn clothes, my missing fingers, my face
swollen and blackened from Samiel's punches, and trailing
behind me a strange half angel carrying Gabriel.

Amarantha was perched on the edge of her throne when
we entered. Focalor sat beside her on a low stool, and he
had obviously just said something to make her laugh when
I entered. When she saw us, the smile faded from her face.
Focalor blinked at me in surprise.

I came to a stop before them, the assembled courtiers
whispering all around us. Samiel sidled up to me and
pressed his arm against mine. I could tell that the crowd
made him nervous and I gave him a reassuring little shoulder bump.

Amarantha and Focalor stared at me.

"Surprised to see me?" I asked.

"How did you survive the Maze?" Focalor asked, standing. "Where is Antares?"

"Antares is in the cage that used to hold Gabriel," I said. "And I'll be calling Azazel ASAP to pick up his wayward son, so if I were you, I would clear out of here before he arrives. You'll probably want to pick the time and place for your groveling."

Focalor came down the stairs toward me, and I actually could see steam emitting from his nostrils. I wondered vaguely if he could breathe fire. His breath stank of brimstone and I could feel heat emanating from his body. It was like standing too close to a furnace.

"I will not grovel to Azazel or anyone else. If you survived the Maze, then it was by trickery. Queen Amarantha assured me that no human could possibly withstand its powers."

I raised my eyebrow at Amarantha, who actually cringed. "Did she, now? I'd hate to think that the queen purposely sent me into the Maze with the intention of killing me by proxy."

"Of course I did not," she said regally, but there was fear in her eyes. "You agreed to the terms of the contest, just as did Antares."

"But you had no intention of actually negotiating with Lucifer even if I did win. It seems that while I was away you and Focalor have gotten quite close."

"It is my right to do as I please in my own court," she snapped.

"And it is my right as ambassador to Lucifer to call you false, to say that you have conspired against him and me from the beginning, that you have attempted to sow discord in my party using magic, that you have committed grievous offense by hosting Focalor under his own banner and accepting, even temporarily, a thrall of Azazel's as your own prize. To say nothing of your other intentions," I said, and let that hang unsaid between us for a minute. I didn't want her to think I'd forgotten about her plan to have a child of Lucifer's bloodline.

She stood from her throne, her face pinched and white. "You will not speak to me thus in my own court."

I shouldered Focalor aside and strode up to her. "I will do as I please. You have broken the laws of etiquette of your own kingdom, you have risked the safety of humanity on a war for your own pleasures, and you have deliberately tried to murder me. Lucifer is not going to buy that you were a neutral party in all of this. He's going to hold you responsible for encouraging Focalor."

"I do not fear Lucifer," she said through her teeth.

"You should," I said softly. "If you don't, then you're dumber than I thought."

"Leave this court, Ambassador. You are no longer welcome here," she said angrily.

"Gladly," I said and turned on my heel. Then I turned back. "Almost forgot."

I slapped her across the face.

"How dare you," she said, her face livid.

"I dare because your actions have betrayed you as a selfish, spoiled brat with no thought other than that of your own desires."

"We will have a score to settle, Madeline Black," Amarantha hissed.

"Bring it on, bitch. There isn't anything you have that I haven't seen before."

Then I turned away from her and strode toward the doors.

The court was deathly quiet as I walked out, Samiel still carrying Gabriel and glued to my side. As I reached the doors, I suddenly heard the sound of applause.

I turned back to see Wade grinning at me and clapping his hands. He winked when I acknowledged him, and I gave him a little bow.

Then I walked out of Amarantha's court, hopefully forever.

As soon as the doors closed behind me, I felt my body slump.

"You can't collapse yet," Beezle whispered. "Wait until you're alone."

"Right," I said, struggling to stay on my feet. "Too bad I don't know how to get back to our room."

"I can help with that," J.B. said from behind us.

It didn't hit me until I saw him how scared I had been in the Maze, or how happy I was to be alive and not insane. It didn't hit me until I saw his face, so reassuringly normal, and the relief that was evident there.

I threw my arms around him and pressed my face into his neck.

"Well, hey, there," J.B. said.

I didn't say a thing, just held on tight.

"I'm glad you're alive," he whispered.

"Me, too," I said, swallowing so that I wouldn't cry into his neck. I knew that eyes were still watching us, even if I couldn't see them. I spoke softly into his ear, so that only he could hear. "Would you just hold on to my arm for a little while? I feel dizzy all of a sudden."

"That won't be a hardship," he said, and then he looked at Samiel. "Who's the new guy?"

I sighed. "Samiel."

His eyebrows winged up. "Samiel, who tried . . ."

"To kill me, yes, but it was all a misunderstanding and it's okay now, so can you just get me somewhere I can sit down?" I said.

"I'm so glad that you're still you," J.B. said dryly, and helped me to my room.

As soon as I entered my room, the connecting door swung open. Nathaniel stood there, looking utterly amazed. Then he seemed to collect himself.

"I don't know why I am constantly surprised by you when all you ever do is exceed expectations," he said.

He seemed like he'd healed up a little more in the past two days. I was still angry with him, even though I knew that at least part of what happened had been a spell of Amarantha's. But that jealousy and anger had already been inside him, even if he would never have acted upon it.

And it was hard to look at him without thinking of what happened in the Maze. Still, I owed him a debt for giving me the sword.

"Thank you for the gift," I said sincerely. "I wouldn't have survived without it."

"I am glad that you did survive. Although I see that you left something of yourself behind," he said, indicating my hand.

"Oh, that wasn't the Maze. That was something else," I said, not wanting to get into it. Somehow I had a feeling that all the men in the room would think worse of Samiel if they knew he had chopped off two of my fingers. "Listen, are you strong enough to heal Gabriel? He's in a pretty bad way."

Nathaniel looked like the request did not thrill him, but he did as I asked. He seemed different now, somehow humbled. I wondered if it would take or if he would go back to being a pain in my butt once he returned to Azazel's court.

I desperately wanted to sit down, to rest, but I needed to get out of Amarantha's court more than I needed sleep. I asked J.B. to get us a car while I packed up.

Nathaniel managed to produce some clothing for Gabriel and Samiel to wear, since they were both clad in nothing but a strip of cloth across their privates.

Samiel seemed bewildered by the mechanics of putting a shirt on over his wings, and Nathaniel was oddly patient while he showed Samiel how to fold his wings through the openings in the back. Samiel was built on a wider, more muscular scale than Nathaniel so the clothing strained at the seams.

Fifteen minutes later all of us, including J.B., were squished in a car with Amarantha's half-troll driver. I didn't ask why J.B. was leaving with us when it was his mother's court and she could probably use his support. I understood wanting to get away from a parent. It was exactly how I felt whenever Azazel was around.

I could tell that they all wanted to ask me what had happened in the Maze. Five pairs of eyes looked at me expectantly, but now that we were finally seeing the back of Amarantha and the stupid faerie court I felt myself drifting off to sleep.

"Will someone call Azazel and tell him where to find Antares?" I mumbled, and then I went out.

The next thing I knew Gabriel lifted me from the car. The night air was cold, and I shivered as it touched my skin. I was still wearing a sleeveless shirt and cutoff pants—not exactly appropriate for winter in Chicago.

Samiel and Beezle got out with us, and I indicated to Gabriel that he should put me down. I stuck my head inside the open car door and saw J.B. and Nathaniel glaring at each other. Nathaniel's face was bruised and both eyes blackened.

"What happened?" I asked.

"Nothing for you to be concerned with," Nathaniel said curtly. "I will speak with you soon, Madeline."

"Uh, okay," I said. I looked at J.B. "See you soon?"

"Now that your little adventure in the court is over, you're back on the clock, Black," he said. "So expect to see your usual letter with your pickups tomorrow."

"All right, Cranky," I said, slamming the door. What happened to the sweetheart I'd known at the faerie court? He was back to being J. B. Bennett, world's worst boss.

The driver had dropped us in the same place he'd picked us up—the alley. The car pulled away and Samiel meekly followed Gabriel and me through the backyard and up to the porch. Nathaniel had been as good as his word. A shiny new door hung in place of the one he had torn out of its frame. It was probably a lot nicer (read: more expensive) than one I would have bought myself. This one was actually properly insulated and weather-stripped and everything. And bonus—Nathaniel had been smart enough to make the new lock fit my old key.

I glanced questioningly at Beezle as we all headed up the stairs.

"What's up with Nathaniel's face?"

"You were crying out in your sleep," Beezle said. "And all the men in the car interpreted those cries correctly. Well, Gabriel and J.B. did. I'm pretty sure Samiel thought it looked like fun to hit Nathaniel because everyone else was."

I felt my face redden in embarrassment. I had not wanted Gabriel to know about Nathaniel's attempted assault on me. He didn't say anything as we entered the apartment, and I wondered why he was being so cold all of a sudden. I realized he had barely said a word to me since Nathaniel had healed him.

I dropped my bag in the kitchen and slumped into one of the dining room chairs. "I feel like I could eat a whole pig."

"Barbecue sounds good," Beezle said hopefully.

I thought about the tiny amount of money in my checking account that was not Azazel's. We could probably order out but we wouldn't have much left over for anything else important until I got a paying job again. On the other hand, I wasn't capable of cooking anything more strenuous than toast at the moment.

"Bring me the phone," I sighed.

Beezle clapped his hands together in delight and flew to the portable phone. Gabriel and Samiel watched me in silence. It was eerie. Neither of them looked like Ramuell, thank goodness, so they didn't resemble each other as siblings. But they wore identical expressions of expectation.

"What are you going to do about Samiel?" Gabriel asked.

"He can live here," I said.

"And how are you going to explain that to Lord Lucifer and Lord Azazel?" Gabriel replied. "At the very least, he should be brought before the courts for the crime of releasing Ramuell."

I'd kind of forgotten about that. "Technically, I suppose, he was responsible. But you know that it was Ariell who was controlling him and Ramuell both."

Gabriel shook his head stubbornly. "The Grigori will not see it that way. He released Ramuell and created portals to draw the nephilim back. He was responsible for his own actions."

"Are you seriously trying to tell me that I should throw Samiel to the wolves? Don't you have any compassion at all? Azazel successfully argued to spare your life when you were a baby. Why wouldn't I be able to do the same for

Samiel?" I couldn't believe he was acting like this. Samiel was his half brother, for crying out loud.

"I was innocent when Azazel saved me. Samiel has committed a crime. That compounds the sin of his birth. He must go before the assembly of the Grigori to face judgment," Gabriel said.

Samiel watched this argument avidly. I wasn't sure how much of it he was getting but I already suspected that he was a pretty adept lip-reader. His eyes were wide as he turned his head back and forth between Gabriel and me.

"Why are you trying to pick a fight about this?" I said angrily. "You know I would never consent to such a thing. Samiel stays here with us. End of story."

"No, it is not the end of the story. I have told you time and again that you do not comprehend Lucifer's kingdom. His law and his word are absolute. There is no flexing of the rules. Samiel must pay for his crimes."

Gabriel was white as the moon as he said this, and the corners of his eyes looked tight. Something else was going on.

"This is not about Samiel," I said. "What the hell crawled up your butt and died? You'd think you'd be happy and grateful that I saved your ass from being used by Amarantha for all eternity."

"I am indeed happy and grateful, *mistress*," Gabriel said tightly.

"What's with the mistress business?" I said.

"I was Azazel's thrall until I was taken by Samiel and given to Focalor. Then I was Focalor's thrall. Then I was Amarantha's thrall. You have won me from the Maze as your prize; therefore, I am now *your* thrall," he shouted.

I looked at him in dawning comprehension. "You belong to me now."

"Yes."

I shrugged, relieved that this was all he was upset about. "So I'll free you, and that's that taken care of. No big."

Gabriel stalked forward, his eyes an exploding field of stars on a canvas of black. "You do not understand. It is like you deliberately choose not to understand. How many times must I tell you that Lucifer's law is the only law? I am a thrall in his kingdom; therefore I am always a thrall. You cannot free me. Only Lucifer can do that."

"So I'll ask him to free you," I argued.

"Which he will not do. It would set a dangerous precedent."

"Well, so the hell what?" I shouted, losing my temper. "Isn't it better to be my thrall than Azazel's or Amarantha's? You know I won't abuse you like they would. I've always treated you like my equal anyway."

"But I am not your equal," Gabriel said, and his jaw was clamped tight. "I will never be your equal. And do you think that I could stand before you as a lover, knowing that I am always below you, that I must submit to your will above my own? Could you accept me thus, never knowing if I was telling you what was in my heart or just what you wanted to hear?"

The anger ran out of me in a rush, my temper deflated. I hadn't thought about Gabriel's status in those terms, or really thought about it at all. I'd been so focused on getting him back, and yes, I'd pictured a lot of happy canoodling once we were reunited.

But I didn't think I would be his mistress. I didn't think that he would be my slave. It didn't matter if I treated him as an equal. The fact of his thralldom would always stand in our way.

"Now do you see? You may have kept me from Amarantha,

but now my status is a bigger impediment than before. At least before I felt I could speak my feelings to you freely, even if I was unable to act upon them," he said bitterly.

"You still can," I said fiercely. "Nothing is going to change between us."

"Everything already has," Gabriel said. "And I would advise you not to become too attached to Samiel, for the Grigori will come for him, sooner or later."

"They won't take him from me," I said, and I looked at Samiel as I said it. It was a promise from my heart. "They won't take you from me. You're safe here."

"Do not make promises you cannot keep," Gabriel advised, and then he walked out of the kitchen.

I rubbed my eyes with my hand. "Really, how many problems can one girl have in a day?"

"Yeah, you totally made an enemy of Focalor and Amarantha, and you broke a bunch of rules by taking in Samiel like a stray dog," Beezle said.

I turned to see him hanging in the hallway with the phone is his hand.

"Enjoy the show?" I said.

"Not particularly. Contrary to what you may think, I don't enjoy seeing you hurt," Beezle said, then he cleared his throat. "So are we having barbecue or what?"

I held my hand out for the phone.

The deliveryman had looked at me funny when he delivered the food, and I realized afterward that while I'd made sure Gabriel was healed by Nathaniel I hadn't done the same for myself. Most of my aches and pains had cleared up while I slept, but my face was still bruised and my clothes still covered in blood. And my fingers were still missing. I wondered if anything could be done about that, or if I would be a three-fingered lefty for the rest of my life.

After dinner I settled Samiel in for the night on the pull-out couch in my living room. He seemed completely over-whelmed by the trappings of civilization. The food—and its method of delivery—was amazing to him. The toilet got flushed about four hundred times in a row once he figured out what purpose the handle served.

He couldn't stop touching the lightbulbs, the face of the microwave, lifting and lowering the phone from its cradle. His immense pleasure in the sheets and blankets that made up his bed was apparent. I wondered how long he had been living in that cave in the desert.

I turned out the light, resolving to devise some better method of communication with Samiel tomorrow. He could understand pretty much anything, but he had no way of telling me what he wanted. And I wanted to know more about him, about his life before.

Beezle fluttered up next to me. "I'm going to sleep in my nest tonight."

"Okay," I said, a little surprised. I'd thought that after my near-death experience he'd want to stay close to me.

He flew out the front window without another word, and I walked slowly down the hall to my own room. I shut the door in deference to Samiel and sat on my bed.

In the past week I'd lost Gabriel, lost Beezle, survived two attacks by Samiel, discovered the bodies of three wolves, found Beezle and Gabriel, killed a giant spider and a leviathan, lost my magic several times, totally screwed up my assignment as faerie ambassador but had averted an uprising in Lucifer's kingdom, made a new enemy in Ama-rantha, been assaulted by my fiancé, lost part of my left hand, taken on the new responsibility of Samiel and defied all expectation and survived the horrors of the Maze.

I was tired.

I was also alone, and I hadn't expected to be. I curled up on my bed in my bloodied and torn clothes and waited for the tears to come. But my eyes stayed dry all night long.

18

I MUST HAVE SLEPT FOR A WHILE, BECAUSE THE NEXT thing I knew my eyes were open and my heart was beating a thousand miles a minute. The digital clock on my bedside table showed me that it was past three in the morning.

I wondered if a nightmare had woken me from my sleep. I was sure that I would be carrying the events of the Maze around with me for quite a while.

But I didn't remember a nightmare. Maybe a noise had woken me. Maybe Samiel had gotten up to use the bathroom and I'd registered the sound unconsciously. I wasn't used to another living being besides Beezle in the house.

I listened for a moment, but didn't hear anything. I tried to close my eyes again but now that I was awake my brain was whirling. I sat up and swung my legs over the edge of the bed. Lucifer's sword winked at me. It was leaning in the corner of my bedroom next to my closet. I didn't remember leaving it there, or in fact carrying it into the house at all.

A second later I saw a strange burst of green light outside. I stood up and went to the window. The light was coming from the alley behind my house. I couldn't see its source from the angle that I stood at, but it flashed once, twice, three times. And it didn't look like the kind of light that occurred naturally.

I didn't relish the prospect of yet another paranormal encounter when I'd just gotten home from my big faerie adventure, but I needed to see what was going on in the alley. A lot of normal people lived in my neighborhood and as far as I knew I was the only person equipped to deal with supernatural weirdness.

"Maybe it's just some witch's teenager playing at spellcasting," I mumbled to myself, but I didn't really believe it.

I pulled on my boots and a sweatshirt, then started for my bedroom door. The sword winked at me again, and I picked it up. As before in the Maze, the snake on the hilt writhed reassuringly under my palm.

I opened the bedroom door quietly and peeked down the hallway. Samiel was a motionless lump under the blankets in the living room. Beezle was outside. Gabriel was downstairs.

I thought briefly of waking Gabriel to come with me, but our recent conversation suddenly put any request that I might make of him in a mistress/thrall light. I didn't want him to think he had to come at my beck and call. So I left him alone, and went down the back stairs by myself, wincing every time the wood squeaked. I felt like I was a kid sneaking out of the house while my parents slept.

The new door eased open without a sound—thank you, Nathaniel—and I stepped onto the porch. The light was concentrated directly behind an eight-foot-high wooden fence that surrounds my property, and it was almost blinding now that I was right in front of it. I am constantly surprised by the fact that my neighbors never notice all the really obvious signs of magic generated around my house. It just goes to show that people are adept at seeing only what they want to see.

I swung the sword up, both hands wrapped around the hilt, and crept forward carefully through the yard. The dried and frost-tipped grass crunched under the soles of my boots. I sidled up to the fence and peeked through the slats.

There was a . . . thing in the alley. I don't know how else to describe it. It was a monster, for sure, but like no monster I'd ever seen before. Its skin was a translucent greenish blue. I could see the play of muscle and bone underneath, the pulse of blood as it rushed through its veins. Its face was turned away from me but large batlike ears protruded from the back of its bare, oblong skull.

It squatted on elongated, froglike legs that ended in slender primate feet tipped with sharp claws. The curve of its spine was long as it bent over something on the ground. Wings nestled against its ribs, and the skin stretched over the wings showed the joints of bone where they connected.

The green light was coming from the creature's body. I shifted, trying to get a better look at what the creature was doing. It was then that I saw the body the monster was eating.

All I could see was the top of a head, a yellow ponytail with streaks of gray, and the motorcycle boots that protruded from the other side. But that was enough for me to know that this was the other member of Wade's pack that had been in Amarantha's court.

And that meant that this creature was the thing that had been killing the wolves all along.

I pushed out my wings and flew over the fence, holding the sword high. I descended on the monster in a silent rush, intending to behead it before it realized I attacked.

Something betrayed me—a whisper of breath, the night air moving over my wings, or maybe just the instinct of prey and predator. An instant before I landed the monster turned, saw me, and leapt away down the alley.

I felt the toes of my boots drag across the asphalt for an instant and then I swept after it. The creature turned to face me and I was nearly blinded by green light. I covered my eyes, squinting, and the monster bounded toward me.

I swung the sword down as the monster reached me and felt its reverberation all the way up to my shoulder. The blade sliced through one of the creature's arms and it screeched a terrible noise. My eyes were practically shut, squinting in the blazing light coming from the creature's chest.

The creature lashed out with its other arm, knife-sharp claws slicing at my stomach. I sucked in my belly and danced backward, managing to get away with just a slender cut.

I tried to open my eyes a little more but it was impossible to be this close to the monster without sunglasses. I flew upward in a shot and turned back to blast the creature with nightfire. My spell bounced off the creature harmlessly.

Great. It was immune to nightfire and it was nearly impossible to fight the creature at close quarters without being dangerously blinded. What now? It wasn't as though I had a whole ton of spells in my arsenal.

The creature flapped its giant wings and followed me into the air. I zipped away toward the lake, and it gave chase. I flew as hard and fast as I could, trying to think. Maybe I could knock the thing into Lake Michigan and drown it. At the very least I needed to lead it away from populated areas to reduce the risk of collateral damage.

The monster gave another high, keening cry, almost like the scream of a raptor. I glanced behind me to see that it was terrifyingly close, and that its clawed fingers reached for my ankle. I could just barely see the glitter of the creature's teeth as it smiled.

I sped up, my breath coming hard and my heart beating a thousand miles a minute. The lights of Lake Shore Drive glimmered below us, and beyond that Lake Michigan swirled and crashed in its winter fury.

I stopped abruptly and dropped several feet, leaving the creature confused for a moment. It continued forward for a few seconds, allowing me to dip underneath it and come up behind. I slashed out with the sword and sliced one of its wings from its back.

Bluish blood spurted from the wound and the monster howled in pain. It dropped abruptly, unable to compensate for the loss of the wing. It spun down toward the beach in the darkness, the light from its chest shining like a beacon.

I flew down after it, headfirst, legs tucked in behind me like a skydiver, and using the monster's own light to follow. I was going to finish this thing off, then call Wade and tell him to come and get the monster's head.

And then the green light abruptly winked out.

I slowed my furious descent and came upright, wings flapping behind me, toes pointed toward the ground. Had I killed it, or was this some sort of trick?

I flew cautiously down to the place where I thought the creature might have landed. My boots slid in the sand and the lake rolled and crashed against the shore. In late fall, city workers had rolled in with earth movers and created a kind of breakwater out of the beach, mounding up the sand in small dunes. The dunes cast strange moving shadows in the lamplight from the lakefront bike path. There was no sign of the monster anywhere.

I fluttered up again, just a few feet above the beach, and moved north slowly, following the line of the shore. I wondered if I dared risk a light. If the monster was lying in wait for me, then it could use the light to find me. Of course, without light, I wasn't sure if I could find any evidence of it. And it really would not do if some sunrise dog walker came across the decomposing corpse of a hideous monster in a few hours.

I decided to try to make a small light and try to focus it like a slender beam of a flashlight. Like so many new spells, though, I required an extra dose of concentration to get it going.

That meant I was a little distracted when the creature came screaming out of the darkness of the dunes and crashed into me.

The sword was knocked from my hand and flew away. A hand came around my throat and squeezed. The creature stood, slowly crushing my windpipe. My legs kicked underneath me as I clawed at the fingers holding me up. Lamplight fell across the creature's face, and my hands fell away in shock.

It was Baraqiel. One wing stood white and proud in the moonlight, and the other was just a few ragged shards of feather. He smiled at me, and his mouth was covered in wolf's blood.

I felt my magic surge up in anger, and a blast of heat burst out of me. Baraqiel shouted and dropped me to the ground. I rolled over, gasping for air, and stood up, facing him.

"You?" I said in disbelief. "You?"

His silver blue eyes glittered in the light, and I realized

I had seen those eyes before. They were the eyes of Wade's most recent pack member, James.

"You're a shapeshifter," I said, astonished. I had never heard of such a thing—an angel that could shift its shape. And I had certainly never heard of a shapeshifter that had more than two shapes. Baraqiel could become James the human, James the wolf and the hideous blue monster in the alley. What other tricks did he have up his sleeve?

"Lucifer does enjoy seeing the results of his affairs," Baraqiel said. "I am unique among all of his children."

"Lucifer?" I said. I was starting to sound like an idiot.

But it made sense. When I'd felt the magical pulse of energy and found the body of the first wolf, I'd thought that it felt like Ramuell, a thing not meant to be. I'd been half right. Baraqiel wasn't a nephilim, but he was, like Ramuell, a thing not meant to be. Was there nothing Lucifer wouldn't copulate with? What was he trying to do, manufacture the perfect monster?

There were things I didn't understand, though. "Why would you kill all these wolves? Why the pointless bloodshed?"

"Pointless?" Baraqiel growled. "The wolves have thwarted and defied my father at every turn. Tyrone Wade has been a sworn enemy of Lucifer for more than thirty years."

"Yeah, well, I defy him at every turn, too," I said.

"A fact that I was attempting to remedy," Baraqiel said, and his insane grin made me shudder. "I tried to plant evidence of your involvement at the sites of the killings, but Wade seemed to believe your innocence. I thought that if a body was found right on your doorstep, the wolves would demand your head as compensation and Wade's hand would be forced."

"Does Lucifer know that you're doing this?" I asked.

"Who knows what my father does and does not know?" Baraqiel said craftily. "In any event, I do not think he would be bothered by a few dead wolves."

"But he might be bothered that you're trying to incriminate me," I said. "He kind of likes me, you know, because of Evangeline."

"Yes," Baraqiel hissed, and for a moment his form shifted back to that of the blue monster before returning to his angelic one. "That is all I hear about, all anyone hears about. Madeline Black, his beloved granddaughter, last child of Evangeline's line. No child of his own has ever been more adored than you."

Well, that came as a surprise. I knew that Lucifer was partial to me because I was the last direct descendant of Evangeline, but he wasn't exactly an affectionate relation. Most of our exchanges seemed to involve commands and threats.

"Whatever my relationship—or yours, for that matter— to Lucifer, these wolf killings end now. I'm going to make sure that you are brought to justice for this," I said. "And if Lucifer won't do it, then I'm sure the wolves will take care of you."

Baraqiel stalked toward me. "What makes you think I am going to let you take me?"

I sighed. "I didn't think you would make it easy for me."

He reached for me again, and I flew upward, dodging away. His missing wing made it impossible for him to give chase once I was above the ground. I focused my power, pushed it through my heartstone, and let loose the blast of sunlight that I had used to kill Ramuell.

A blaze lit up the beach and for a moment it looked like a midsummer's day. Then the blaze faded, and Baraqiel stood there, laughing at me, his missing wing magically regrown.

"Thank you, cousin," he said. "That was exactly what I needed."

Okay. So apparently the sun, which was fatal to Ramuell, made Baraqiel rejuvenate his powers like Superman. Wonderful. Nightfire didn't work, sunlight didn't work, and I'd lost the sword. What was I supposed to do, annoy him to death?

He launched from the beach and came after me. I feinted to one side and then flew the other, swooping low over the sand and desperately searching for the sword.

It was then that Baraqiel let loose a magical pulse. As it rippled across me, my wings disappeared, my power flickered out and I fell to the ground.

I rolled over, my mouth and eyes full of sand. I scrabbled desperately at my face, trying to clear my vision. Baraqiel fell upon me, his hands closing around my throat again.

I kicked up and into his crotch with my boot. Yup, that works on pretty much any male, no matter what their species. He yelped and loosened his grip for a moment, which allowed me to push to my feet and sprint down the beach as fast as I could.

I had no magic, but it seemed that Baraqiel didn't have much in the spell department except for the ability to shapeshift and knock out other creatures' powers. So at least we were on even footing there.

Of course, he had wings again, and I didn't, and he was about fifty times as strong as me. So big advantage to Baraqiel.

I heard his wings pulsing behind me, and I picked up speed. It wasn't easy. Sand is not the fastest surface to run on, especially when you're wearing combat boots and are totally out of shape.

I tripped over my own feet just as Baraqiel swooped in for the kill. Thank goodness I was the clumsiest thing going.

Lucifer's sword glittered in the sand right under my nose.

I grabbed it and pushed up to my knees as Baraqiel made another turn. His silver blue eyes were alight with murder and madness. I let my sword hand hang at my side and allowed him to carry me into the air, his hands closing around my neck.

I didn't struggle against him, but I lifted the sword and ran it through his chest. I felt his heartstone give under the blade, and for the second time that night there was a gigantic explosion of light.

I held tight to the sword as Baraqiel's hands went limp and he dropped me into the sand again. I was lucky I didn't land on the blade. I jumped to my feet immediately and ran back to where his body lay in the sand, bluish black blood pumping out from the hole in his chest.

He glared up at me, his face both angry and resigned. "I cannot believe that Lucifer's own sword chose you over me."

I glanced down at the sword, wondering. Had it just been a coincidence that Nathaniel had given me the sword, or had the sword planted the idea in his head? It was a little creepy to think that a piece of metal was that sentient.

"Yeah, well, I seem to defy expectations everywhere," I said. "For some reason my enemies never seem to think much of me."

I wasn't taking any chances. I'd seen enough horror movies to know that if you left the monster alone just when you thought it was dead, then it would pop back up and try to kill you one more time.

I swung the sword for the last time, and the head of Baraqiel ap Lucifer rolled away into the sand. A few moments later the head and body started to decompose rapidly until all that was left was a kind of tarlike goo.

I kicked a whole lot of sand over the goo so no one would step in it accidentally. Also, I wasn't sure that Baraqiel couldn't regenerate from the light of the sun even in this condition.

I was pretty sure I'd buried him well enough that no one would dig him up accidentally—it was winter, after all, and not many kids would be down here with their sand pails for several months. The sun was just starting to come up, which meant that I'd been out for at least three hours. Samiel had probably woken, and Beezle might be up, too. They were probably panicking.

Unfortunately, my magic was still out and my cell phone was still in my travel bag, sitting on the floor of my kitchen.

I sighed, and started to climb the dune. It was going to be a long walk home.

19

AS I'D EXPECTED, BEEZLE WAS UP AND TOTALLY freaking out when I got home. He, Samiel and Gabriel were all sitting in the dining room with their heads together, apparently devising some action plan.

"Anyone for cinnamon rolls?" I asked, leaning against the doorjamb.

They all looked up, three identical expressions of surprise on their faces. Beezle flew toward me first and put his clawed hands on my face, examining first one side and then the other.

"New bruises on the neck but nowhere else," he announced. "Where in the four hells have you been?"

So I sat down at the dining room table and told them about Baraqiel—how he was Lucifer's son and the wolf-killer, how he could shapeshift, and how he had tried to first frame me and then kill me. Gabriel looked graver than usual when I finished my story.

"You have killed another of Lord Lucifer's progeny," Gabriel said. "He will not be pleased with you."

"Believe me, I've thought of that already," I said, waving my right hand. "I try not to contemplate Lucifer's feelings too closely. It makes me queasy."

Samiel grabbed my hand out of the air and turned it over, looking at it. Then he looked up at me, questioning.

I stared. There was a mark there that I hadn't noticed before. It looked almost like a henna tattoo, and it was the exact shape of the snake that adorned the hilt of Lucifer's sword. The snake seemed to wink at me as I looked at it.

"It couldn't be," I said. I crossed the room to the place where I had left the sword leaning against the wall. The blade was still covered in blue-black ichor from Baraqiel's body.

I picked up the sword and examined it. The snake had disappeared from the hilt. I looked down at my hand again.

"You've got to be kidding," I said. "I think the sword branded me."

"Perhaps that will save your life when Lord Lucifer discovers you have killed Baraqiel," Gabriel said. "In all the years that Zerachiel and Nathaniel carried the sword it never marked either of them."

"Did you know? About Baraqiel?" I asked Gabriel.

He shook his head. "The fallen have always known Baraqiel only as Lord Lucifer's messenger. I do not know how he managed to hide the evidence of his paternity, but one should never question the Morningstar's ability to deceive others. As I have told you time and again, he is a law unto himself."

"Right," I said, and sighed. "Well, I should call Wade and

tell him I've solved his pack problem. And that he should come and pick up the body in the alley."

"Speaking of alleys," Beezle said thoughtfully. "We never did find out who put that portal in the alley where we found the second body, the one that led to Amarantha's kingdom."

I shrugged. "Maybe it was Baraqiel. Maybe he wanted a fast way to get in and out of the kingdom."

Beezle shook his head. "It doesn't make sense. That location is far from anywhere useful in her kingdom."

"I don't think I'm up to solving any more mysteries this week," I said. "We'll just have to die not knowing."

"Ignoring this problem means it will come back to bite you in the ass," Beezle warned.

He was probably right. He usually was. But I really wasn't up to any more investigating. The mystery of the portal would just have to be.

A couple of hours later Wade and Jude arrived to pick up the body of their pack mate. We had moved it out of the alley and into my garden shed, which looked totally suspicious but again, none of my neighbors seemed to notice. Gabriel had magically wiped the alley clean of any blood and gore.

Wade and Jude loaded the body in the back of their pickup truck. Baraqiel hadn't had a chance to tear the body to pieces like the others, so at least they would be able to bury this one.

Wade shook his head as my entourage and his stood awkwardly behind the truck bed. "I cannot believe that we were all so deceived by James. How could we not know that was not his true form?"

"He was a spawn of Lucifer," Jude growled, and he directed his glare at me. "They are most adept at deceit."

"Don't look at me," I said. "I'm the spawn of Azazel."

"And Madeline Black was the one who stopped Baraqiel for us, so we owe her our gratitude," Wade said, his voice mildly reproving.

Jude shut up, but I didn't think he'd be thanking me anytime soon. He turned without another word and climbed into the driver's seat of the truck.

"You must not mind Jude," Wade said. "He has a . . . history with Lucifer."

"Whatever." I shrugged. "I'm getting used to people not liking me."

"Whatever Jude may feel, our pack owes you a debt of gratitude. You may call on us whenever you feel the need, Madeline Black, and we will be there to assist you." He placed his hand over his heart and bowed his head. "You are a friend to our pack."

"Thanks," I said. It was nice to be welcomed by someone for a change instead of being threatened. "Back at you."

Wade smiled. "Until we meet again. *En Taro Adun!*"

"Uh, Wade?" I said, and he stopped and turned back to me. "What exactly does that mean?"

"'*En Taro Adun*'?" Wade said. "It's from StarCraft."

"StarCraft?" I said blankly.

"It's my favorite computer game," he replied.

"So, you're like the world's biggest dork?" Beezle asked.

"How do you think I won leadership of my pack?" Wade said. "I am the reigning StarCraft champion."

He got in the truck as we all stared after him, wondering whether or not he was joking.

Jude glanced back before he pulled away. The snake on my palm shifted restlessly, like it recognized his stare, and then they drove down the alley and out of sight.

*   *   *

Azazel called a couple of hours later, demanding the whole story. It seemed that the tale of my slapping Amarantha had already carried back to his court and he was royally pissed at me. Somehow the tale-carrier had neglected a few details, so I told him everything that had happened from the time Gabriel had been taken up to and including my killing of Baraqiel. I left out Nathaniel's assault. That was between me and Nathaniel.

Azazel was silent after my recitation. "Well, I cannot say that Lord Lucifer will be pleased to hear of Baraqiel's death, but it does seem that you have averted a war between Focalor's court and my own."

"You're welcome," I said. "Did you pick up Antares?"

"When we arrived, the cage was open and Antares was gone," Azazel said.

I shook my head even though I knew Azazel could not see me. "I swear, when the apocalypse comes and all living things in the world are wiped out, Antares will be the last man standing."

"And you should have told me of Gabriel's disappearance," he rebuked.

"You would have killed him, and that is not acceptable to me," I said.

"Do not begin to start getting ideas above your station, daughter. You are still below me in rank," Azazel said angrily. "It is my word that is final, not yours."

I looked at the palm of my hand and the squiggling serpent there. "I'm not so sure that you still outrank me, Father. And since I have more than proven my worth by averting a demon uprising and by being the only person to ever survive the Maze, I think you should start giving me a little more respect. I'm not a child to be pushed and manipulated by you. Don't expect me to behave that way anymore."

Azazel sputtered into the phone.

"Oh, and I'm not marrying Nathaniel, either," I said, and hung up.

Okay, so there would be some fallout from that conversation, but I'd really had enough of Azazel. Sometimes I couldn't believe that I'd ever wanted a father when I was a child.

I turned to see Gabriel staring at me moodily. "You should not speak to Azazel thus. He is still your father."

"And I'm still his daughter," I retorted. "I'm not his slave."

Slave was probably the wrong word to use. It hung awkwardly in the air between us.

"What are you going to do with Samiel?" Gabriel asked.

He glanced into the living room, where Beezle was gleefully beating the half nephilim at checkers. Beezle is a sore winner, but I had a feeling that Samiel would be kicking his little gargoyle butt on a regular basis once Ariell's son figured out the rules.

"Like I said, he's staying," I said firmly.

Gabriel stared moodily at Samiel. "It is strange to find that I have a brother."

"But kind of nice, too, isn't it? To have family?"

"I do not know," Gabriel said. "My family members have always wanted to kill me."

There wasn't a real easy segue from that. I looked down at my left hand and wiggled my three remaining fingers.

"I can try to heal you," Gabriel said, and took my injured hand.

It was the first time he'd touched me since I'd released him from the cage in Amarantha's forest. My breath sucked in sharply and he dropped my hand. There was a meteor shooting across the black expanse of his eyes.

"I do not know how we will resolve this, Madeline," Gabriel said. "We cannot be."

I shook my head at him. "You always say that. Anything can change."

"I do not think what you want will happen just because you want it," he said.

I thought of what happened in the Maze, how I had survived by my strength of will. "Just wait and see."

A few days later we had fallen into a pretty regular routine. Beezle was asking for doughnuts every three seconds and trying to justify his piggy behavior by saying they were for Samiel. Samiel did seem to have an unnatural love of sweets matched only by Beezle's.

Gabriel and I were teaching Samiel sign language. Well, Gabriel was teaching me and Samiel, I guess. Samiel was learning way faster than I was, but at least we could exchange some basic information.

I was back to work and collecting souls as usual. J.B. had gotten over his recent bout of adorableness and gone back to being a crab every time I talked to him. He had tersely informed me not to put any stock in anything he had said to me while at his mother's castle. Amarantha, he asserted, had cast a spell on him so that he would be drawn to me. Actually, she'd cast a spell on our whole party—it just didn't take with me for some reason. She'd figured if Nathaniel attacked me, then I would turn to J.B., and then she'd have a different kind of family tie to Lucifer.

"So you didn't mean any of it?" I said. I wondered why it hurt so much. J.B. was just a friend.

"My mother was hedging her bets," he said.

"That's not an answer."

"That's all the answer you're going to get," he said, and walked away from me. This was becoming a theme with the men in my life.

It was almost comforting to have an argument with him every time we saw each other. It made it easier to forget the look of need on his face when he thought I was going to die in the Maze, and it kept me from wondering whether or not that feeling was real, false or just amplified by Amarantha's spell.

Gabriel avoided me unless we were working with Samiel. I refused to ask him to be my bodyguard again. In fact, I refused to make any requests of him at all. I was determined to show him that things could be different between us. He didn't seem to be buying it yet, but I could work on him. I'd learned how to wear someone down from the best teacher ever—my annoying gargoyle.

Nathaniel had sent me eight dozen roses in various colors the day after my fight with Baraqiel. I didn't have the heart to throw out so many beautiful flowers, but I crushed all the notes into the garbage unopened. It probably goes without saying that my feelings were confused where he was concerned.

Four days after the dawn had broken over the gooey remains of Baraqiel on the beach the day was unseasonably warm and sunny. Beezle and Samiel fell asleep in a sunbeam on the sofa in the front room. Beezle seemed to have adopted our stray.

Feeling oddly restless, like I was waiting for something to happen, I decided to step outside for a breath of fresh air and went out to the front porch. It felt like sixty degrees outside, and I pulled off my sweater and sat in my shirt-sleeves in the sunshine. I closed my eyes for a moment, enjoying the warmth.

When I opened them again, Lucifer stood in front of me, looking terribly ordinary. He'd hidden his wings underneath a long black overcoat, and underneath he wore blue jeans and a black sweater a lot like mine. His hands were tucked into his pockets and his expression seemed deliberately neutral.

"I've been expecting you," I said, and when I said it I knew it was true. I'd felt him coming all day.

"Sometimes I see Evangeline in your face," he said. "Just now, when you turned your face to the sun. She used to look at me like that, like I was her sun."

I didn't really know what to say to that, so I just watched him sit down on the porch next to me and stretch his legs out in front of him.

"You seem to be making a habit of killing my children," Lucifer said.

"But I'm preserving your grandchildren against all odds, so that should count for something."

"I'm not sure the Grigori would agree with you. They were most disturbed to hear of the existence of another of Ramuell's spawn."

I didn't want Lucifer to dwell too long on this subject, especially since I wasn't ready to have to fight for Samiel yet. I'd hoped to have time to devise a strategy before they took him away.

"Anyway," I said. "How was I to know Baraqiel was one of your children? It's not as though you advertised the fact."

"Would knowledge of his paternity have stopped you from acting?" Lucifer asked shrewdly.

"Well, no," I admitted. "He was trying to kill *me* at the time."

We sat in silence for a while, then Lucifer spoke again.

"Your hand. I do not know if your father told you. Your fingers will grow back, in time."

I looked at the cauterized stumps. "Cool. I'm like a starfish now."

"I have been very impressed with your actions, Madeline. When I asked you to be my ambassador, I did not expect such an outcome. You have averted a great crisis with Focalor as well as revealed Amarantha's hidden intentions of making a child of my bloodline. They will both pay dearly for crossing me."

"Did you ever really want to renegotiate a treaty with Amarantha?" I asked curiously. "Because it did occur to me that if that was what you wanted, you might have sent a more skilled negotiator."

Lucifer smiled enigmatically. "Perhaps subtlety is not always wanted. And perhaps I wanted to see how you would handle yourself."

"So it was a test?" I asked in disbelief. "I almost died in that Maze, you know."

He had the gall to chuck me under the chin. "No, you did not. Your will is stronger than even you know. I need an heir for my kingdom, you know. An heir that has demonstrated the kind of strength of will that you showed in the Maze."

"Oh, no," I said, alarmed. "Don't even think about it. Why not make one of your sons heir? You seem to have them popping out of the woodwork all over the place. And really, what benefit would it be for an immortal who has survived eons to make a mortal half human your heir?"

"One never knows what might happen. And my heir must be a creature of immense power so that the courts will continue to respect my rule."

"So you're basically trying to collect me and put me in your trophy case to show to the other fallen?" I asked. "And you think I'm a 'creature of immense power'? Aren't you supposed to be all-knowing and all-seeing?"

"You're thinking of the other guy," he said.

He leaned in close to me, and I could see the light of the sun sparkling in his eyes.

"In my kingdom, my word is law. When my heir becomes ruler, that individual would be able to make her own laws."

I understood exactly what he was saying. If I ruled Lucifer's kingdom, I could free Gabriel. I looked at him sourly.

"I don't know if you've checked lately, but my name isn't Eve."

He opened the palm of my right hand and touched the place where his sword had marked me with his symbol. He winked at me, and an apple appeared there. I closed my hand around the shiny red fruit as he stood from the stair and stretched like a cat.

"Don't think you'll maneuver me into place," I warned. "I know how to play chess, too, you know."

He smiled at me, and it was the smile of the serpent in Eden.

"Then let the game begin."